BLACK WINGS BEATING

BLACK WINGS BEATING

ALEX LONDON

THE SKYBOUND SAGA **BOOK I**

FARRAR STRAUS GIROUX NEW YORK

Farrar Straus Giroux Books for Young Readers
An imprint of Macmillan Publishing Group, LLC
175 Fifth Avenue, New York, NY 10010

Printed in the United States of America
Designed by Elizabeth H. Clark
First edition, 2018
4 6 8 10 9 7 5 3

fiercereads.com

Library of Congress Cataloging-in-Publication Data

Names: London, Alex, author.
Title: Black wings beating / Alex London.
Description: First edition. | New York : Farrar Straus Giroux, 2018. | Series:
    Skybound saga ; book 1 | Summary: Twins Kylee and Brysen must fight for
    survival in a remote valley called Six Villages as war approaches, she by
    rejecting her ancient gifts for falconry and Brysen by striving to find greatness.
Identifiers: LCCN 2018001439 | ISBN 9780374306823 (hardcover)
Subjects: | CYAC: Falconry—Fiction. | Brothers and sisters—Fiction. |
    Twins—Fiction. | Fantasy.
Classification: LCC PZ7.L84188 Bl 2018 | DDC [Fic]—dc23
LC record available at https://lccn.loc.gov/2018001439

Our books may be purchased for promotional, educational, or business use. Please contact
your local bookseller or the Macmillan Corporate and Premium Sales Department at
(800) 221-7945 ext. 5442 or by e-mail at MacmillanSpecialMarkets@macmillan.com.

For Tim, to whom I'll always fly,
and for my parents, who taught me how.

—A. L.

LOWER JAW

SKY CASTLE

RISHL BRONZE PITS

PARSH DESERT

TALON FORTRESS

You but half civilize,
Taming me in this way.
Through having only eyes
For you I fear to lose,
I lose to keep, and choose
Tamer as prey.

—THOM GUNN,
"TAMER AND HAWK"

. . . forgetting his own thoughts he had known at
last only what the falcon knows: hunger,
the wind, the way he flies.

—URSULA K. LE GUIN,
A WIZARD OF EARTHSEA

AN IMPOSSIBLE BIRD

ALL BIRDS OF PREY MOCK HUMAN GLORY BUT NONE SO CRUELLY AS THE ghost eagle. It looks down upon the world from its mountain eyrie and sees only scuttling rats. And yet mankind, the clever rodent, has found some ways to trick the eagle, to blind its all-seeing eyes and bend the bird to its will.

But first it has to get into the scuzzy trap.

"Come on, you stupid bird," Yzzat grumbled, wrapping a boar pelt around himself. Frost clumped in his blond beard, and he shivered against the whipping mountain wind, but he kept his ice-melt eyes fixed on the sky above. Ghost eagles built their nests inside dark caves as high as possible, shielded from wind and light and prying eyes like Yzzat's. The altitude alone made less hardy trappers ill.

Yzzat knew, from thirty years of tracking and *almost* finding, of too long waiting and too late arriving, that the eagle's lair would be littered with the bones of hawks and buzzards. There would be goat skulls and the rib cages of wolves. There would be the bones of male ghost eagles, because the females killed their mates when they were through with them. There would be one or two skeletons of the distinctly human variety.

The ghost eagle was an opportunistic hunter, and people presented plenty of opportunities. It had a wingspan wider than a mule and flew faster than ground lightning, with feathers so black, they could blot out the night itself.

Yzzat knew the giant bird was near. He'd climbed from the dusty lowlands of the Six Villages, through the blood-birch forest where the Owl Mothers reigned, and into the high crags of the Nameless Gap in its pursuit. From his turf to the eagle's, like countless failed trappers before him. Like the rare few who had succeeded.

The eagle knew the territory better than Yzzat ever could, saw to the horizon in all directions, and had surely been watching his approach for days. But Yzzat had patience, patience to match its own, and he was determined to wait this bird out.

When he did, he'd become a powerful man.

No more haggling at the market for second-rate sparrow hawks and counterfeit breeds of falcon; no more standing at the scuzzy battle pits, ending a night of gambling covered in bird droppings and pigeon guts. He'd have a valet with an umbrella to keep the filth from falling on his head. And he'd eat lamb. Fresh lamb. No more chickpeas and onions for dinner. His children would learn to respect him, and he, in turn, would share his new fortune.

Yzzat knew his children were terrified of him, but he also knew he could be kindly. He *would* be kindly, just as soon as the world showed some kindness to him. Until then, he would do the twins no favors by treating them like high and mighty kyrgs in the castle, when their lives were as cursed as his own. He only beat them down to keep them grounded. When he took flight, so would they.

This was the night. He was perched on the edge of happiness. All of them were.

He tugged the thin silk string, small and strong as a spider's web, that led from his fingertips to the tail feathers of a hobbled corral hawk. The shimmering pink raptor was enraged at the insult of being tethered. Proud birds, these hawks were. Not used to being bait. This one flapped and shrieked, rising from the ground as far as the string would let him. Yzzat yanked him down again, simulating the motions of a bird that had been injured.

Ghost eagles would only eat live prey, so Yzzat had captured this fine hawk first. Normally, the sale of a corral hawk at the market would be enough to keep him in drink and gambling at the Broken Jess for a full moon or two, with enough left over for his wife to stop nagging him about clothes for the twins or alms for her Crawling Priest, but this hawk would hardly be worth the weight of its beak by the time it had served its purpose tonight. The loss of the hawk would be repaid with the reward of the eagle.

> *It watches high upon the eyrie,*
> *Thus only fools approach unwary,*
> *Yet for the faithful, it reveals*
> *The dreams they're seeking*
> *Or it kills.*

He whispered the old Uztari poem to himself while he waited. The trap was his own design, a delicate operation that relied on perfect timing and absolute attention. Only one falconer in a thousand could capture a ghost eagle, and only one in ten thousand could hope to keep it once caught. It could not be tamed but might be controlled.

Might be.

He had a buyer ready, a great kyrg of the Sky Castle, one of the Council of Forty, who already had an impressive cast of raptors in his mews. There were perfect gyrfalcons and peregrine falcons and kestrels in every color imaginable. But the kyrg wanted a ghost eagle more than anything. A man who'd mastered a ghost eagle would be revered. He could command armies and decide the fate of dynasties. He could crush a rebellion or ignite one. A man who mastered a ghost eagle might rule.

Whether or not *this* man could master a ghost eagle was not Yzzat's problem. He'd been willing to pay any price Yzzat could name just for the chance to try. Prices Yzzat hadn't even the imagination yet to name.

All he had to do was get this one into his net.

Mountain, field, and forest alike were littered with the bones of those who'd tried and failed before him. The ghost eagle loves a worthy fight but kills all who disappoint it. It has long found humans the greatest disappointment.

Yzzat, however, had made a lifetime study of disappointment. His wife was disappointing with her fits of pious melancholy, guilty tithing, and awful cooking. The twins were the disappointing offspring she'd given him.

The girl had a gift for falconry, a once-in-a-generation gift, but was reluctant to outshine her brother.

What had Yzzat done to deserve a timid daughter?

And to think of her brother . . . Yzzat felt the blood rise behind his eyes. Her brother was a waste of a boy if there ever was one.

He was timid like his sister and pretty like her, too. He was slim and slight for a boy who should've been molting into manhood. In appearance, he was as far from Yzzat as a fish was to a falcon, but he looked back at his father with the same mountain-blue eyes that Yzzat saw in his own reflection.

His son had no special talents, no great intelligence or strength. He took up space and ate the mediocre food from Yzzat's table and outgrew clothes beyond his mother's mediocre mending, and his every sigh and sniffle reminded Yzzat that this was the boy who would replace him one day. All sons destroy their father's legacy—that was the widening gyre of generations—but this one might do it while his father still lived.

No amount of beating seemed to motivate the boy. He bled and bruised and burned, but he never learned. When men looked at his son, they saw Yzzat's own failings. If the fruit was rotten, so was the tree from which it grew, no?

Yzzat shuddered. These thoughts weren't his. The bird must've been readying to attack.

They said a ghost eagle could not only see the hot breath in your lungs and the warm blood in your veins but could also see the weakness in your heart and show it back to you. This was a bird that drove its prey to madness before it devoured them. Brave men soiled themselves when it was near, and pack animals hurled themselves from cliffsides as it circled above.

Yzzat cleared his head and focused his thoughts on the one thing that mattered now: his purpose. He was in position. He was ready to pull an impossible bird from the sky.

Then he heard a stir from the slope above him and glanced up toward the lip of a ridge near the top of the Nameless Gap. There was a person skulking in the shadow of a shrub. He'd been followed!

Was it some poacher thinking to take his score once he'd done all the dangerous work? Or perhaps one of his buyer's enemies on the Council of Forty, another kyrg, or a kyrg's assassin? A religious fanatic who thought the trapping of a ghost eagle was blasphemy, or one who believed the ghost eagle would bless them if they could take it? The great bird gave wing to unlimited wants.

He drew his knife. The curved, black-talon blade slid silently from its dog-leather sheath. He gripped the handle in a fighting stance, let the cold metal rest against his forearm, the razor edge facing out so he could slide it straight across the throat of his night stalker with a backhand swipe.

He took a breath in, held it, listened and looked into the dark, trying to relocate his prey with the same intensity as a hawk on the wing.

There!

He saw the shrub shudder, and through the leaves, a glimmer of starlight reflected off an eyeball. He sprang toward it.

But his feet never hit the ground.

Gigantic talons came from the dark behind him, snatched him by the shoulders, and pinioned him. He dropped his knife as he felt himself being hoisted into the air.

The tethered corral hawk shrieked, unscathed. The trap remained unsprung. The eagle had him, not he the eagle.

"REEEE!" it called so loud his ears rang.

He was airborne, as every falconer dreamed of being, but there was no joy in this flight. He knew the bones in his arms were broken. He knew one lung was pierced.

He also knew, as certain as the eagle's beak would tear out his throat, that he would not be missed below. He watched as the human shape that had distracted him cut the corral hawk free with Yzzat's own knife. He screamed.

The person below watched, unmoving, as Yzzat was carried away into the starlight, and Yzzat allowed himself to cry with the shame of it all. His tears fell like paltry rain, and they were the last piece of him that ever touched the earth. Everyone in the Six Villages heard his screams on the wind as he was carried away, aloft and alone.

He did not go quietly.

KYLEE

TETHERS

1

IT WAS THE DAY BEFORE THE HAWKERS' MARKET, AND KYLEE FOUND her twin brother exactly where she had hoped not to find him: at the battle pits.

Brysen stood in a throng of the usual battle boys, his sleeve-less vest buttoned to the neck, his long goatskin jacket on the ground at his feet. There was a coil of battle rope around his shoulder, and he had on his elbow-length leather glove. His hawk, Shara, stood perched and hooded on his fist, tethered by short leather jesses to the forearm loops on the glove.

Brysen was easy to spot in the crowd. His storm-cloud-gray hair spiked out in all directions like a hatchling's fuzz, and his lower lip bulged with a wad of hunter's leaf. When he turned to spit, he saw Kylee at the gate, met her eyes between the jostling shoulders of gamblers and spectators.

But for his hair, Kylee and Brysen were the mirror image of each other. Hers was still black, like his had once been, but they had the same elk-brown skin as their mother, the same ice-blue eyes as their father, bright as cloudless mornings. They were the kind of eyes that held windstorms. You'd be blown away if you looked too long.

Folks in the Villages thought Brysen's prematurely gray hair made him look wild and dangerous, like a haggard falcon, and he did his best to encourage those ideas, used them as a shield against other people's pity. Kylee couldn't have cared a puke what other people thought of her.

She opened her palms toward him, questioning what he thought he was doing there when she needed him working. This was the most important market of their lives, and he knew it. Brysen turned his attention back to the battle pits.

"Dirt-biting scuzz-muncher!" Kylee cursed.

After her morning climb up the knife-edge ridges, she'd come home to find his bed empty and had made her way down the rocky slope from their house, over the rickety bridge that crossed the meltwater river—the Necklace, as they called it—and into the Six Villages. Just a few weeks earlier the Necklace had been solid, shining ice. The Six Villages were strung like beads along its bank, more one town than six separate townships.

There was no formal date in the Uztari calendar for the Hawkers' Market, but the thawing of the Necklace told the time. When the Necklace flowed knee-deep, the tents began to rise along the road. When it rolled waist-deep, the market opened.

There was no announcement, either. Spies simply watched the river and sent pigeons back to tell their masters, who were traveling along the haulers' routes from the Sky Castle in the north to the Talon Fortress in the south.

Everyone knew who the spies were, of course, and for whom they spied. Spying was a Six Villages tradition, passed through families for generations. The more prestigious the noble family, the more prestigious the village family who spied for them. There were no secrets in the Six Villages, after all. With the surety that ice turns to water and back again, when the river ran, the customers would come and the spies would buy the first round at the Broken Jess.

Her brother couldn't resist. Kylee watched, seething, as Brysen laughed with the other battle boys. The current fight drew to a close, and two of the youngest boys swept up the footprints, blood, and scattered feathers from the pit.

Running off to the battle pits the day before the Hawkers' Market was the kind of recklessness for which their father would have beaten Brysen breathless. Then again, their father had never needed an excuse. He seemed to enjoy the sport of hurting her brother the way a hawk enjoys stunning a mouse.

Good thing Da's dead, Kylee thought, and spat once on the ground, then stomped the spit into the dirt to keep him that way. *Mud below and mud between. The dead can't rise to a sky unseen.* It was a superstition but a satisfying one. Some men didn't deserve sky burial.

Travel across the plateau was becoming dangerous, and prices for Six Villages birds were soaring. From one end of the steppe to the other, everyone knew the Six Villages offered the best birds of prey—for hunting, racing, fighting, or companionship—and the market was the only time the best buyers would risk traveling all the way there. Word was that this would be the last good market for a while. Word was that war was on the wing.

What "word was" didn't concern Kylee, but she knew that if they could sell off all the birds Brysen had trapped and trained this year, they could finally pay off their inheritance: gambling debts their father had racked up at the Broken Jess. After three seasons of desperate scraping for every last bronze they could get, Kylee and her brother could break even and close the business; they could be free of falconry.

Not that Brysen wanted to be free of the profession. But Kylee did. *She* could finally be free.

Already the roads and inns sparkled with throngs of eager village visitors. Even Altari holy men crawled in, the backs of their sunburned necks shining angrily up from knee height. One of them bumped his head against Kylee's leg as he approached her on all fours at the gate of the Broken Jess.

"Alms for your skyward sins," he groaned through the din of the growing crowd, lifting one dirty hand at her without looking up. The Crawling Priests had bloody knees and hoarse voices from shouting doom upon the falconers' craft, but they kept their eyes fixed firmly on the dirt. They believed the Uztari training of birds was blasphemy and that only the ancient Altari cult of reverence for the wild and untamed sky was the true faith. They saved their harshest words for Altari who left the religion and became Uztari, with a bird on the fist.

They were, however, happy to beg for Uztari bronze.

"Go away," Kylee grumbled.

"It is not too late for you to repent," the man cried, gripping her by the shin so hard that his knuckles went white. "Repent the wicked wind you worship and accept the true faith of our land. Repent and be saved from the coming destruction and—*ooof!*"

His face bit the dirt when a foot swept his other arm out from under him.

"Suck a vulture's toe," Vyvian Sacher laughed at the Crawling Priest as he pushed himself back up on all fours. "Get out of here!"

"Your kind brings the curse of the Kartami upon us," he growled at her, and lifted his head to look Kylee and Vyvian in the eyes. "None shall be spared."

Vyvian raised her rolled-up umbrella and the Crawling Priest winced, then looked down and crawled away, leaving the rough crowd of the Broken Jess behind.

"You believe that cockatoo?" Vyvian scoffed. "Threatening us in our yard."

"It's the usual nonsense." Kylee shrugged. "Not even half as bad as the stuff my ma says."

"Yeah, well, your mom's a fanatic," Vyvian said, running a hand through her long, dark hair and tying it back into a knot. She wore black-and-brown leather pants and a long feathered robe, and the way she stretched looked more like preening than working out a kink in her neck. Vyvian wanted to be seen, which was why she carried an umbrella to protect against bird droppings but never opened it. Only the truly wealthy actually opened their umbrellas, caring more for their fabrics than the view other people had of them. Vyvian aspired to riches but had a long way yet to go. She did love market days, though.

When they were little, before she'd taken up the family business, she and Kylee would play bone dice underneath the market stalls. These days, both of them were too busy when the market came around; Kylee hustling bronze and Vyvian hustling secrets. Her family spied for one of the kyrgs at the Talon Fortress, so she usually knew what was happening on the rest of the plateau before most Six Villagers. "Your mom has the sense to do her ranting in private. This priest doesn't have the right to spread panic at the Broken Jess. People are nervous enough about the Kartami already."

"Do you think it's true?" Kylee asked. "Are they coming?"

The Kartami—also called the shards—were a roving band of religious fanatics who lived in the farthest reaches of the Parsh Desert. Even the Crawling Priests were too moderate for them. While the Altari believed that humans taming birds of prey was a sin, the Kartami believed that the birds themselves carried the sin. The Altari looked away from the sky in awe; the Kartami looked directly at it with disgust for what it had become. Where one group prayed to repent, the other prayed for annihilation.

In the Six Villages, the Altari were moralistic scolds, while the Kartami were merely a distant threat that parents used to scare their children: *Eat your greens, or the Kartami will steal your songbirds while you sleep. Clean the mews, or the Kartami will steal all the birds from the sky.* But the Kartami had been growing bolder, attacking closer, cutting roads between settlements, and cutting the fists from every falconer they found. Minor Altari nobles—those who had been pledged to Uztar—had begun to surrender, committing their souls to the Kartami faith, their bodies to the Kartami cause, and their resources to the Kartami war machine. The Council of Forty urged calm throughout Uztar as towns and villages begged for the Sky Castle's protection.

Now that the thaws of the ice-melt season had come, rumors of Kartami advances flew as fast as sparrow hawks.

Vyvian shrugged at Kylee's worried question. "You know my family doesn't give out information for free. What kind of spies would we be if I didn't make you pay for it?"

"An old friend?" Vyvian frowned, and Kylee rolled her eyes. "I don't spend bronze on rumors."

"Who said anything about bronze?" Her friend turned back to the battle pits, raised an eyebrow at Brysen on the edge. He was talking to his trainer, Dymian. They were leaning in close. "I can take *all kinds* of payment."

Kylee groaned. "Even if I were the kind of sister who'd sell you her brother, you are singing to the wrong bird." Brysen had his fingers laced between Dymian's, his lips whispering against the older boy's ear.

"It's a tragedy," Vyvian sighed. "The things I could teach your brother about a body . . ."

"Gross."

"I'm just saying, if he ever stops preening for Master Bird-nester over there, send him my way."

The trainer, Dymian, had taken his own falcon from a nest he'd found when she was still a baby eyas. Someone who took eyasses from their nests was called a birdnester, but Kylee was pretty sure that wasn't what Vyvian meant by it. Dymian was a few seasons older than Brysen.

"You can't see it because he looks like you, but with that hair and those eyes . . . your brother's keener than a prize peregrine. And you're not such a plain pigeon yourself."

If Kylee could've rolled her eyes straight out of her head, she would've.

"I'll take a fight!" Brysen shouted over the crowd, and the rough boys around him cheered and patted him on the shoulders, ruffled his thunder-struck hair. Dymian squeezed their interlaced fingers.

The Broken Jess had been a temple in ancient times, of

what kind no one knew. Like most sacred things in Uztar, it had been put to more human uses than its founders could have imagined. All that remained of its sacred past now was a big stone sanctuary that housed the pub, piles of random stones scattered about its yard, and a great rock painting of two falcons in combat that decorated the cliff face behind it.

Below the sheer cliff face and the hawk mural were the battle pits. There were three pits around the edge of the property and one large "show pit" in the center. Brysen was at the smallest pit.

The pits were about as deep as a sinner's grave but wide enough for two people to circle each other. The sides sloped up, wider at the top than at the bottom, and spectators sat and stood around the rim, crowding, shouting, and cheering the fighters they'd bet on. Brysen had begun his climb into the pit when a man slid down the edge opposite him.

What was Brysen doing? They did not have time for this!

His opponent wore the pale tunic and loose pants of a longhauler. Not master of a convoy, but someone higher up than a driver. His red beard was thick and full, bejeweled with colorful desert glass, and his copper hair was hidden under a flat white hat that was also dotted with more desert glass.

He removed his tunic to show a pale, muscled chest

covered in long-hauler's ink. He had markings along his collarbone for every journey he'd made across the Parsh Desert,
ornamented text of a hauler's prayer to the flocks scrawled up
his side, and, across the rippling expanse of his back, a colorful scene from the *Epic of the Forty Birds*. The tattoo was filled
with symbols whose meanings were known only to long-
haulers, but he showed it off now to make one thing clear: His
back had never met the whip.

Had Brysen ever taken his shirt off in public, his back would
tell a very different story.

The long-hauler's companions whispered to one another,
laughing beneath their colorful round umbrellas, which cast
their faces in shadow. The man in the pit had a female kestrel,
square-tailed and brown-striped, that sat steady on his glove.
He removed her ornamented leather hood, and the teardrop
eyes in her white face fixed on Brysen and his hawk.

Brysen swiped Shara's plain hood off, revealing her bloodred
eyes. The pupils were so wide that the red barely ringed them,
two blazing eclipses held afire inside a bird's skull. When she
saw where she was, she shrieked and spread her wings, clutched
her talons around Brysen's wrist, footing him hard. He whispered something to her. The bird calmed.

Shara was a goshawk—far bigger than the kestrel but far

moodier, too. She had a crooked wing and a nervous temper, was prone to fits of brutal violence and days of sullen pouting. The two of them weren't so different, Brysen and Shara.

She shifted her weight nervously on his fist. His thumb rubbed one of her talons.

"Here's some news for free," Vyvian whispered in Kylee's ear. "That long-hauler's nickname is the Orphan Maker."

"Don't do this!" Kylee called to Brysen, shoving her way through the crowd to the edge of the battle pit. Brysen's ambition in the pits was not always matched by his talent. He always tried to take on the biggest opponent with the longest odds. When he won, he won big, but when he lost, there were scars.

"The challenge is accepted, Ky!" Nyck, one of the battle boys, called across to her. "He can't back out now."

"Don't worry about it," Brysen shouted up. "When I win, I'll buy us all lamb leg for dinner."

He smiled but not at her, then unhooked the short string that tethered Shara to his glove, unwound the battle rope from his shoulder, and, with one hand, tied the split end to the jesses around her ankles. The rope had a clasp on a swivel below the bird's ankles, giving Shara a free range of movement while keeping her attached to the glove. They were bound to each other in the battle, tethered from wrist to ankle, from earth to air.

Mud below and mud between.

"Wish me luck," Brysen said.

"When have you ever had luck?" Kylee asked.

Brysen scowled, then drew his black-talon blade.

2

HER BROTHER TURNED TO FACE THE ORPHAN MAKER AND GRIPPED HIS
knife in the fighter's stance. The curved black blade mirrored
the brutal beak of a hawk, and Shara's eyes glanced at it
unsteadily.

The knife was old, but how old they didn't know. It'd been
inscribed with symbols their father had always said were in "the
Hollow Tongue," the ancient language of the birds. But their
father was also easily deceived and might've just convinced himself that was true to avoid facing the fact that he'd been ripped
off for a fake antique. No one could actually read the Hollow
Tongue or even knew for sure what it would look like in writing.

Regardless, it was the only thing they had left of the man, and Brysen had wanted to keep it. He had scars on all his fingers from where their father missed whenever he played a drunken game of pinfinger using Brysen's spread hand pressed against the table. Why Brysen clung to it puzzled Kylee. Strange magic bound a blade to the wounds it made.

Brysen crouched, arm across his chest, resting the base of the knife handle on the middle of his gloved forearm and forming a T with the blade as its base.

He waited.

The Orphan Maker assumed the same position, and Brysen's eyes fixed on him.

Shara saw the other blade and the other falconer and the other bird. It was a familiar sight, surely, but not a comfortable one. She shrank back into herself; this was a bad time to show fear.

A frightened goshawk perched with its talons tucked under its tail feathers and its head pulled back is a ridiculous sight. They're big birds but stubby, shaped like a thumb drawn by a child, with the beak an angry V in the center of the face. And Shara, who perched with a slight tilt to the side, looked more ridiculous than most.

Her chest was striped gray and white in a herringbone pattern, and her red eyes were hooded with black. The rest of her feathers were a mixture of grays, which helped camouflage her against the rocky terrain of the foothills but stood out brightly against the lush green grasses down in the Six Villages as the melt came on.

Nyck whistled, and the opponents circled each other. The birds sat on their gloves with a stillness known only to a predator and its prey. Kylee could feel the stillness in herself.

Anyone who grows up in a home where they are prey to a parent's rage learns to sip silence the way the rich sip wine. Silence has infinite flavors, with endless shades and notes. The sharpest of all the silences, and the most necessary to know, is the silence before an attack. Kylee took half a breath in and held it just as the other falconer thrust his arm up, launching his bird.

"Utch!" Brysen shouted, and thrust his own hawk arm up. For a heartbeat, Kylee feared Shara wouldn't let go, would foot her brother so hard that not even the glove would protect him. But just as his arm reached the apex of its rise, offering her to the air, the air accepted. Her wings stretched, her head pulled out of her shoulders, and she took flight. His arm jolted.

The bright white underside of Shara's wings glowed like snow on mountain peaks. Her tail feathers opened, her flight feathers spread, and her talons tucked up beneath her. She flapped furiously in the opposite direction of the brown kestrel and screeched. Brass bells tied to her anklet, meant to keep track of her during a hunt, jingled as she flew, and the battle rope unfurled behind her.

When she reached the rope's full extension, Brysen planted his feet and turned his torso, steering her back toward the other hawk, which had caught an air current and spread her wings to glide, swooping beneath.

Shara looked down, her eyes following the line back to him. His muscles strained against her power and the wind's pull. He circled to keep his distance from the other man and whistled, more a warning than a command. Shara tucked her wings against her body and dove.

She was a sleek streak of gray across the sky. Head forward, eyes fixed, tail feathers wavering to steer her straight for the brown kestrel. The air rushing through Shara's anklet bells shrieked. Brysen's hawk, so gawky and afraid on the fist, had become grace and perfect form, never more beautiful than when doing what she was born to do: kill.

Shara's strafing dive was aimed at the smaller bird. The kestrel saw her coming and reacted instantly, turning her body so their talons clashed and tangled in a midair collision that sent them rolling, tumbling in imitation of the cliffside mural behind them. Just as quickly, they parted and swooped away from each other in opposite directions.

A few feathers whorled to the dirt.

On the ground, Brysen and his opponent tried to control their hawks with their gloved hands while closing the distance between themselves.

Brysen shuffled his feet around the perimeter of the pit toward the long-hauler. The long-hauler's arms were thicker than Brysen's thighs and his bird smaller than Brysen's, so he moved with far more ease, cutting the distance between them straight across instead of along the edge. His blade came up, and he swiped it fast, straight for the rope that connected Shara to Brysen's glove.

If the tether between hawk and human was severed, the match was lost. The match was also lost if bird or man or both were killed. Every fight in the pits could be a fight to the death.

Brysen twisted away from the Orphan Maker's blade, using Shara's tether and his light weight to swing sideways. As he moved, he slashed with his own knife, blocking the attack. There was a clang of metal on metal. Kylee winced as the power of the blow shook her brother's hand. His opponent was far too strong for him, but he was faster.

The second and third knife attacks went wide while Brysen dodged the blade with a dancer's grace. Even his slight weight pulled Shara low as he regained his footing, but he timed the last pull so that her drop put her just below the circling kestrel.

When he released the line again, Shara was able to shoot straight up, her wings beating mightily, and she slammed into the underside of the other bird, slashing at its belly.

There was a tangle of talons in the sky, a drizzle of blood. The two fighters on the ground were pulled toward each other by their entwined battle lines.

The birds broke apart, circled, and clashed again, shrieking, talons tearing for each other but unable to hold on. With every turn and attack, the battle lines below became more twisted and Brysen was drawn closer to the Orphan Maker.

"I'd rather cut your pretty face than your rope, little bird," he taunted, and slashed his blade at Brysen with blinding speed.

Brysen's parry connected and he protected his face, but the force of the attack was so strong, it snatched the curved blade from his hand, sent it scuttling away in the dirt. He moved for it, but the long-hauler tugged the tangled lines and pulled Brysen back. He could've cut Brysen's battle rope right then, but instead he yanked Brysen closer, spun him like a dried-grass doll, and gripped him from behind with his gloved forearm. The battle lines whipped and twirled while the falcons fought, but the long-hauler's thick arm locked Brysen in place against his chest.

The air turned to stone in Kylee's lungs when the Orphan Maker put his knife to Brysen's throat.

3

IT WAS CONSIDERED BAD FORM TO KILL YOUR OPPONENT WHEN YOU had the option of cutting the line, but it wasn't against the rules. It wasn't murder if it happened in the pit. The rules did, however, say you had to offer a chance to yield three times.

"Do you yield?" the long-hauler hissed into Brysen's ear, so loud that everyone could hear.

Brysen struggled to break free.

"Yield, little bird, or I'll give you your first shave with this blade."

Brysen struggled. His eyes scanned for Shara in the sky.

Five melting seasons ago, their eleventh, he'd rescued Shara from the battle pits after she'd lost their father a full moon's fortune. She was wounded, and Brysen hand-fed her for weeks, snuggling her to his chest at night to keep her warm and training her in the few hours he could snatch in the meadow whenever their father was away.

"Shara's got potential," he always said. "She'll show she's a great hawk when she's given the chance."

The hawk had yet to show greatness, but Brysen still had the scars from protecting her from their father's rage.

"Hawks aren't your pets!" their father had grunted as he whipped Brysen with a dog-leather leash the night Brysen brought Shara back home. He'd cradled her under himself to protect her. *Crack!* The leather had struck his skin. *Crack!* "I'll teach you what loving one will cost you!"

Crack! Crack!

Later, Kylee had helped Brysen scrub his own blood from the floor, but he cleaned it from the bird's feathers himself one by one in a cold bucket. The bird had let him do it and never made so much as a chirp. They'd been a pair ever since.

Brysen returned to the battle pits with Shara, match after match, chasing a victory so high and wild, it would blow away the past. He hadn't found one yet, and he lost far more matches than he won. There was no convincing him that only a fool chased the approval of a dead man.

"Yield!" Kylee shouted. She looked for his friends, the rag-tag gang of battle boys, and saw Dymian. He was maybe the only person whose advice Brysen would heed. *Maybe.* "Dymian, tell him to yield!"

Dymian locked eyes with Kylee, frowned, and opened his palms up to the sky. He couldn't make Brysen yield any more than she could. Her stupid brother would rather die than fail. He slammed his lips shut and clenched his jaw.

The long-hauler grinned. "Last chance, little chick. Do you yield?"

Their hawks screeched above. Shara had bitten the other bird's wing and forced them apart. The creak of the clasps straining against the leather gloves sounded like a body being stretched on a torturer's slab.

Kylee's heart screamed for her brother. In his face, she saw their father's brutal stubbornness. She hated to see it in Brysen, hated the part of her brother that hated himself so much.

As her heart screamed, she felt it reach out to him, like an invisible tether that looped between her chest and his, an endless figure eight. Her pulse quickened, and a strange wind rushed through her, like the sky bursting from her lungs. She felt she would explode if she didn't exhale. It hurt to hold it in.

In her mind, she saw her father towering over Brysen, his

thin back a loose nest of bright red lines cut by the whip. She saw herself cowering with her mother, no one coming to save Brysen, no one offering to protect him. She'd felt that burning breath then, too, but had fought it back, had been afraid to let it out. Had sworn she would never let it out. Even now, she was still afraid of it. But she could not hold it in.

"*Shyehnaah,*" she exhaled, and the strange word burned her mouth as she spoke it.

Shara shrieked.

The goshawk broke from the battle above and dove, furious, at the Orphan Maker's face. She hit him with enough force to break his nose. Kylee felt the impact in her own bones. He yelled and lost his grip on Brysen, who wasted no time spinning away and diving for his knife. Shara dug a talon into the long-hauler's cheek and the other into his scalp.

"Argh!" the man screamed as the blood from his forehead blinded him. Brysen used the moment to lunge forward, blade up. Shara took off from the man's face as Brysen sliced the big man's leather leash clean through.

Above, the Orphan Master's kestrel flew free, flapping away toward the horizon.

"Match!" the battle boys around the pit called out. "That's the match! Brysen wins!"

Brysen looked up at the cheering throng, breathless and grinning. Shara swooped down to land on his extended fist and he gave her a morsel from his vest pocket, praising her, although it was the meat she liked, not the praise.

He met Kylee's eyes and winked, as if she'd had nothing to worry about, as if he'd been in control during the whole match, when, of course, it'd been *her* who'd saved *him*. Maybe he didn't know. Maybe he chose not to know. It had been such a long time, maybe he'd forgotten.

Next to Kylee, Vyvian stood, not watching Brysen celebrate but watching her.

"What?" Kylee asked, her cheeks feeling hot. "What are you looking at?"

Vyvian cocked her head. "Nothing," she said, curiosity tugging the corners of her mouth. "Wild fight. Surprising end."

"Yeah," Kylee told her. "Good thing Shara's so loyal to my brother."

"Good thing," Vyvian replied, the weight of what neither of them was saying perched between them. Kylee looked back at her brother.

He'd turned to find Dymian, and his face had sunk. She followed her brother's gaze to the trainer. He wasn't cheering like the rest of the battle boys, and he wasn't running into the pit to embrace Brysen—which was what Brysen really wanted.

Instead, Dymian had sidled up to Nyck, counting out bronze to pay for his . . . *loss?*

Of all the grub-sucking finch-faced mud-eaters! He'd bet *against* her brother. He'd bet Brysen would lose.

And Brysen saw. Brysen knew. All the joy of the victory drained away from her brother's body, and his shoulders slumped. Even the gray of his hair seemed to grow more ashen. Leave it to Brysen to win a miraculous match and break his own heart at the same time.

Her brother was so fixated on Dymian in the crowd, and Kylee was so fixated on him, and Vyvian so fixated on her that none of them saw the bloodied Orphan Maker step behind Brysen until it was too late.

In the long-hauler's shadow, Brysen turned just in time to get a fist in the face that knocked him straight back into the dirt. Shara launched herself as he fell, but the long-hauler slapped the bird down midflap, knocking her back into Brysen. Then he grabbed up his knife and cut the slack battle line attaching Brysen to Shara. He squinted through his blood-streaked eyes.

"I'm gonna slice the skin off your skull, boy!" he roared as he came at Brysen, knife up. Shara, startled, used Brysen's chest to launch herself away, untethered.

"Shara!" Brysen groaned.

"Stop!" Nyck shouted, his voice breaking. "The match is called!"

But the long-hauler didn't heed that rule. Wounded and enraged, he kicked Brysen in the side and slashed at him.

Then the battle boys rushed the pit.

4

THERE WERE EIGHT BATTLE BOYS IN ALL WITH NYCK IN THE LEAD, EACH
of them dressed in colorful vests and brightly striped pants,
trying to outdo each other with the lavishness of their outfits.
Last ice-wind, when Nyck got a tattoo of a peacock's regalia
around his neck, the others rushed to get their own ink—
scenes from the *Epic of the Forty Birds*, pictures of lithe men
and women in various stages of undress, snippets of poetry in
the most vibrant colored inks the village tattoo artists could
create. They had feathers in their ears and bracelets made of
hollow bones. Even the handles of their knives were decorated

in garish colors. Rushing for the pit with blades drawn, they looked like a flock of bloodthirsty parrots.

The other long-haulers jumped in to take the Orphan Maker's side, but they were outnumbered. The battle boys flanked them.

"Back off, or we'll slice you from crotch to crest," Nyck warned, revealing a bone-handled hunter's blade. Nyck was smaller than the other battle boys but spoke big enough for all of them. "This isn't one of your route houses on the plains. We've got rules."

It dawned on the long-haulers that they were indeed strangers here, and to break a rule at the Broken Jess was to incur the wrath of the Tamir family. The Tamir family did not abide cheating at their establishment—unless they were the ones doing it—and they encouraged the battle boys to be their enforcers in exchange for unlimited milk stout and hunter's leaf. If the haulers hoped to get out of the Six Villages with their goods and all of their limbs, they'd do well to back down. The Tamir family was as close to nobility as the Six Villages had, and the taxes they paid to the Sky Castle ensured that they could do whatever they wanted in their small domain. A dead long-hauler or three would be politely ignored by the kyrgs. The same, however, was true for Brysen. If his throat was slit today, business at the Broken Jess wouldn't even slow.

"It's not worth the blood," Nyall warned the long-haulers.

Nyall was a tall, broad-shouldered battle boy with skin nearly as black as raven feathers and grass-green eyes that matched the bright feather in his ear. Of all the battle boys, Nyall was the only one Kylee would call a friend. He'd once stood down the rocky slope from her house and whistled birdsong toward her door. Her father had chased him off, thinking he'd been whistling for Brysen, and then he gave her brother a black eye for "dabbling in romance like some seed-eating dove." Nyall had felt terrible about the misunderstanding and made himself their friend from that day on.

He didn't make his bronze betting, thieving, or working for the Tamirs like the other battle boys but instead had a decent job at Dupuy's Equipery selling hawk furniture. He'd make a respectable Six Villager one day, but that didn't mean he wouldn't fight. That meant that when he chose to fight, he meant to win.

The bloodied Orphan Maker looked like he might charge again, but the hardness in Nyall's eyes and the eagerness in Nyck's blade made him hesitate.

The long-hauler lowered his weapon and let his friends mop the blood from his brow. Almost as one, the crowd exhaled—half-relieved, half-disappointed—and the business of the battle pits resumed. Bronze chips and rounds passed between dirty fingers with clinks and clanks.

"Good choice!" Nyck grinned as the long-haulers left the pit. "Now, who had 'win by line'?" he called out, scrambling back up the pit's side and reaching for the money pouches he wore on his belt. He ran the small pits for the Tamir family, and collecting the winnings was as important as enforcing the rules—probably more important. The rules existed to bring in bronze, not the other way around. "That's two rounds and a half to you, and one round to you, and one quarter—*pfft, some bet*—to you. You had Shara dead, Rolly, don't go skulking away. That's three rounds and a chip to me . . . you can't *kill* that bird."

"Is your brother okay?" Vyvian rested her hand on Kylee's shoulder.

In all the action, Brysen hadn't moved. He just lay there in the dirt looking at the giant mural behind him and the pale afternoon sky overhead. Shara circled high, calling "Ki! Ki!" shrill and sharp. The severed battle line trailed behind her like a sad banner in a lonely parade. Brysen stared at her and the blue-gray void beyond her.

The hawk flapped three times, then settled herself down on the top of the painted cliff, and fluffed and preened her gray feathers. She tucked her talons beneath her and turned her head to rest it in the feathers on her back.

Kylee left Vyvian and slid down to Brysen in the pit. She

picked up his black-talon knife from the dirt and gave it back
to him.

"Did you prove what you needed to?" she asked.

"I won," Brysen grunted, pushing himself up and dusting
off as he took the blade back. He had a small dot of blood on
his neck and a trickle from his nose. His eyes searched the
crowd above, and his sneer faltered. He bit his lip.

"He's not worth it," she told her brother without having to
say Dymian's name. He was always perched on the invisible
edge of Brysen's mind. "Anyone who'd bet against you isn't
worth a spit."

He fixed his eyes back on her. "You've never shown him *any*
respect."

"The scuzzard's never earned any."

"Don't call him that."

Dymian was a real hawk master, trained and sealed at the
Sky Castle, the second child of some Uztari noble, but he
was a gambler and a liar, and his family had cast him out at
the end of his apprenticeship and forced him to make his own
way in the world. He'd made his own way to the Six Villages,
and Brysen followed him around like he was tethered to his
glove.

His disgrace and his youth meant he was cheap and available as a trainer, and Brysen had to become a decent falconer

because Kylee had no desire to be. She'd care for the birds of prey because that was the business they were in—at least until they paid off what their father died owing the Tamirs—but she didn't want anything to do with actually flying the birds. So she found money they didn't have so they could pay for the cut-rate hawk master she didn't like who was supposed to teach Brysen all the things he didn't know.

He'd managed to learn a lot about birds, far less about people. His was a soaring soul, longing to fly higher than his wings could carry him, higher than the winds of his world allowed, but he never let a little thing like real life get in the way of his longing.

"Well done!" Dymian appeared at Brysen's side and wrapped him in his arms, pressing the slighter boy into his chest before handing him his jacket back. "I'm proud of you."

Brysen looked away as he put the jacket back on and pulled a few green hunter's leaves from its pocket. He shoved them into his mouth. "I almost lost."

"But you didn't!" Dymian smiled. He planted a kiss on the top of Brysen's head. "You showed heart; you showed patience. *That* is what great falconry's all about."

"In that case," Kylee interrupted. "You've taught him all you can? No need for more lessons?"

Dymian laughed and ran a hand through his chestnut hair,

smiled at her. "He's got a few skills left to master." Never one to talk himself out of a payday. "*You* should train with us."

"I'm sure you'd love to get paid double," Kylee replied. This was an old conversation, one Dymian wouldn't drop.

"Ah, you'd get the family discount. We'd love to have you join the great and noble tradition of falconry. A falconer never goes hungry, after all."

"That's not true," Kylee replied. "The hawks eat better than we do."

"Train with me. I know talent when I see it."

"Don't *bet* on it," she snapped at him, wishing words could pierce flesh as deeply as a talon.

Dymian's sharp jaw clenched and his eyes darted to Brysen, who kept his face blank. "I win some; I lose some," he said quietly.

Brysen looked down at the ground. "Why'd you—?" he began, but was cut off when Nyck appeared between them, grinning wide and clapping Brysen on the back so hard, Kylee winced.

"Well won, Bry! You showed that dirt hauler how we fight here in the Six!" He dropped some bronze into Brysen's pocket. Brysen shrugged but tapped the bronze to feel their weight. He wanted to pay off their debts just as much as Kylee did, but he'd rather earn the bronze at the pits than at the market. There

were no cheering crowds at market tents. Glory was the coin
he truly craved, and actual coins were just the most ready measure for it.

"And, Dymian!" Nyck guffawed. "Another loss on the books,
huh? You can't even win when your boy here does it for you!"
His teeth were stained leaf-green, and his eyes darted, prey-
like. If he'd been clearheaded, he'd have kept his mouth
shut.

The money pouches strung around his belt jangled. He
was probably the only person at the Broken Jess who could
show off the coins he carried without getting robbed, because
none of them were his. Just to remind any would-be cutpurses
whose bronze he carried, each pouch was held on his belt with
a counterweight carved in the Tamir emblem: a rosewood eagle clutching bone-white doves in its talons, a single watchful
ruby for an eye. Each purse's counterweight was worth more
than what the pouches contained, and Nyck wore five of them.

"What kind of fool bets against his boyfriend?" Nyck
laughed, not bothering to read the frowns on all their faces.
"Gonna lose his shirt one day."

Dymian looked like he was about to punch Nyck, and Kylee
wanted to punch both of them. The trainer tried to break the
tension with an insouciant smile aimed straight for Brysen.
"Would losing my shirt be such a bad thing?"

Brysen's smooth cheeks colored, even though he stayed focused on his feet. He spat a green glob into the dirt.

Among hawks, males—called tiercels—are about a third the size of females. The injustice of humanity was that most of the battle boys at the Broken Jess were bigger than Kylee. If she punched one of them in the teeth, the rest of their flock would be on her faster than a hummingbird's heartbeat. Battle-boy loyalty was charming . . . until it was painful.

She jabbed Dymian in the chest. "You bet against my brother again, your shirt will be the only part of you they find."

Nyck, who Kylee had known since before he was a battle boy and before he was called Nyck, knew when to run into a fight and when to back away from one. He chose, wisely, to back away now. "Uh . . . I'll see you later. I gotta get some . . . uh . . . cheese . . . for my . . . uh . . . mice . . . and some . . . er . . . mice for the . . . birds . . . uh . . . yeah . . ." He left so fast, his shadow had to stretch to catch up.

Dymian stepped back from Kylee's finger and held open his palms in surrender. "Some mood you're in. All I said was that you should train with us."

"She doesn't even *like* birds," Brysen interrupted. "And we don't need her around clipping our wings."

"Fair enough." Dymian nodded, knowing better than to push it.

"Why don't you help us get Shara down?" Kylee suggested, pointing up to the bird on the boulder. "Show us how it's done?"

"I don't need any help getting her down," Brysen grunted.

He put the fingers of his right hand to his lips and whistled three times—three shrill bursts. Then he held his gloved fist out to show Shara where to land.

She didn't come down.

Dymian glanced to the hawk on the top of the cliff, then to Brysen. "If you take a piece of—" he began.

"I know what to do—don't worry about it." Brysen stopped him.

Subtle as Brysen thought he was, he was obviously embarrassed and clearly wanted Dymian to go. He also very clearly wanted Dymian to stay. The hawk master looked to Kylee for guidance.

Her stare was as impassive as a hawk's. No one toyed with her brother's emotions and then got an assist from her.

"I'd love to help you, Bry," Dymian said at last. "But I've got a meeting with some . . . clients. Can't be late." He locked his thumbs together and crossed his hands, holding his fingers out like the wings of a bird, then pressed them against his chest.

"Sure, Dymian," Brysen said. He returned the gesture.

Dymian gave the same salute to Kylee, but she did not

return it. He shook his head and left them, disappearing through the kitchen and into the dim interior of the Broken Jess.

"Thanks a lot," Brysen grumbled at his sister. "I won today. Why'd you have to ruin it with one of your *moods*?"

"I'm not in a *mood*." Kylee hated the assumption that boys always made when she got mad, like her emotions weren't a part of her thinking mind like theirs but were rather tied to the moons and the winds like an animal's. Surely her own brother knew better.

Brysen whistled for Shara again. Three more staccato bursts, which caused the goshawk to look down at him but not to move. Hawks didn't respond to calls unless they decided it was in their interest to do so. They weren't dancing rats or juggling bears. They were even less like dogs, who wanted nothing more than to please their masters. Hawks stayed with people because it was convenient for them to do so. They flew to the fist because it meant food and shelter and comfort, but they had the run of the skies. They could fly anywhere they chose.

A falconer's thrill came, in part, by being chosen. A falconer's heartache could come just as easily.

In these foothills, the first Uztari who crossed the mountains were also the first to train birds of prey to hunt and to fight. They fought off and exiled the Altari, whose bird worship forbid falconry, and built a new civilization in their place. From the ancient sky cults of the nomads to today's kyrgs at the Sky Castle, the nation of Uztar was held together by the lore of the falcon, by the love of beak and talon, and by faith in the ancient flocks who had led them to the valley—a faith that was not always rewarded.

Shara wouldn't come down until she was good and ready, and all the whistles and pleas from Brysen wouldn't change her mind.

"Can I help?" Kylee offered as gently as she could.

Brysen glared at her. "I thought you were only good at chasing things away."

"I wasn't trying to chase anyone—"

"I *don't* need your help," he grunted. "You just make things worse."

"*I* make things worse?" Kylee couldn't believe it. She'd saved his life *and* gotten him a win. Every bronze in *his* pocket belonged to *her*. And she'd done it for him. She'd done it because she cared about him!

"Why don't you just join the Crawling Priests or something," he grunted. "And stay out of my business."

She knew it was just embarrassment and hunter's leaf making him act like a scuzzard, but still, it pushed her over the edge. Seething, she bent down and grabbed an old stone from her feet, palm-size. It was one of the bits of ancient rubble that littered the ground. She tossed it once in her hand to get a sense of the weight, then flung it at a scrubby bush by the gate leading to the road.

A big jackrabbit bolted from cover, and at the same time, Kylee whistled for Shara.

The raptor's head snapped around, instantly catching the rabbit's mad flight for new shelter. The hawk wasn't in so much shock that she'd let such a tasty morsel get away. She launched herself from the cliff, then tucked her wings to dive, coming down hard on the rabbit's back. She pinned it to the ground, crushing it in her talons as it struggled. Other birds in the yard shrieked, but the hunt had already ended. Shara stood on top of the rabbit, hunched her shoulders, and mantled her wings over its corpse, guarding it from the greedy eyes of other hunters as she broke into its flesh with her beak.

Then Kylee whistled again. The hawk raised her head, turned, and looked back at her. Kylee held out her fist.

"No," said Brysen. "Don't."

But the wind burned in Kylee's lungs again, the pressure built. She saw the pain on Brysen's face, the hurt and fear, and even as she knew she'd gone too far, even as she knew she should stop herself, she couldn't. She *wanted* to be nice. She *wanted* to focus on setting up for the market and getting the birds ready, freeing Brysen and herself of their final obligation to their dead father, but Kylee *never* got what she wanted. Chasing after Brysen, making sure their mother didn't fast herself to death, keeping the business running so they could pay their tax to the Sky Castle and their debt to the Tamirs—everything she did was for someone else.

Now that she was close to the one thing she wanted for herself, her brother was being reckless. Well, she could be reckless, too. Frustration parted her lips, and the burning breath inside rushed from her in one searing word, as angry now as it had been desperate before.

"*Shyehnaah,*" she said, and in an instant, Shara unmantled her wings, scooped up the dead rabbit, and flew straight to Kylee. As she swooped to Kylee's fist, she dropped her kill at Kylee's feet and opened her wings to slow her landing. Her bright white under-feathers practically blinded the twins. The bird hooked her bloodied talons around Kylee's bare knuckles and then stood, proud, eyes fixed on the rabbit she had killed and, for reasons she probably didn't understand herself, dropped at the feet of her master's sister.

The pain of the talons gripping Kylee's skin was like nails being driven into her hand, but she clenched her teeth and didn't let it show. The red trickle down her knuckles wasn't all from the dead rabbit.

Brysen stared at her, mouth agape. Hawks didn't bring their

catches back to their falconers. It wasn't natural. Kylee had shown off, in public, with everyone watching.

She regretted it instantly.

There were no secrets in the Six Villages. The Otak brothers had seen, and they were spies, both of them. And Vyvian, who was already making her way toward Kylee through the crowd.

All it took was one angry moment, one flash of self-pity and rage, and the power she'd silenced since she was a child was being whispered from spy to spy and would soon wing its way across the plateau. Why now, after all this time? Why today? For a searing instant she wanted nothing more than to take it back, but words weren't trained falcons. Once released to hunt, they could never be called back.

Brysen glared at his sister and his hawk. "I'm glad you two are so happy together," he grunted, not having noticed the murmurs in the crowd. He made the hooked-thumb salute across his chest, but he clenched both fists instead of stretching them into wings. The broken-wing salute. Then he stormed past Kylee, leaving the yard of the Broken Jess.

She wanted to go right after him, but Vyvian stood in her way before she could follow.

"Ky," she said, "was that . . . did you just——?"

"I don't want to talk about it," she said.

"This is huge, Ky," Vyvian told her. She glanced over at the

Otak brothers—men her father's age—who were whispering excitedly to each other. "When word gets out that you can—"

"That I can WHAT?" Kylee yelled at her. "You don't know what you heard. And if you're my friend, *that's* what you'll tell whoever pays you for your secrets, okay? My family's been through enough. Don't pick us over like a buzzard, Vyvian. Not you."

"Calm down," she said. "No one's trying to pick you over. It's just that it's a dangerous time and everyone's looking for an advantage."

"Well, I'm not your *advantage*, Vyvian," she said. She saw Nyall watching them from across the yard, his head cocked with concern. "Or yours!" she yelled. "Or yours!" she added at Dymian, who was leaning in the doorway of the Broken Jess. She was causing a scene now, she knew, but she couldn't stop herself. Like a hunter's leaf addict, she was binging on her own shame, and now the only thing left to do was storm away. Just like her brother.

Everyone watched her leave the yard, and she could only imagine how fast the rumors of her whispered word would spread from one end of the plateau to the other.

Maybe Brysen was right; maybe she should forswear all birds of prey and pledge herself to the Crawling Priests. It might be the first thing she'd ever done that would make her mother proud.

She grunted to herself. That alone was reason enough *not* to do it.

After this market, she'd leave the falconry business for good. Let Brysen carry on if he wanted, but she would be finished with birds of prey and the strange violence they drove her to. Shara's talons cut into the bare skin of her hand, but she knew she had to carry her brother's hawk back to him. She owed him that much.

She owed him much more than that, really.

She always would.

5

THEIR HOUSE STOOD IN A CLEARING IN THE FOOTHILLS ON A LONELY
stretch of rocky ground above the Villages. Their father said he
valued the quiet that living over the Six Villages on the high
side of the Necklace gave them, but they knew, even as little
kids, that it was the only patch of land he could afford. The
slopes were so bare that anyone who chose to could look up
from the villages and see them in their yard, or as they trudged
to the outhouse, or as their father staggered home. Privacy was
a luxury their landscape did not offer.

Nor was prosperity.

The soil barely sustained a vegetable garden, the path to the

Six was steep and dangerously slick in the rain, and the retaining wall against the side of the mountain had to be patched constantly to protect them from rockslides.

Still, it was home.

The front fence was made from long slats of petrified wood left from the Altari who had lived in the foothills long, long ago. Thorny briars grew through the fence, engulfing it and forming a natural barrier. Inside the property, the hawk mews were cobbled together from mismatched boards. They kept the rain out and the birds in, but when the hawks started screeching, it could be unbearably loud.

The house itself was a simple stone dwelling built in the old style, three rooms curved around a circular central room for the hearth and chimney. The main door was built into the back of the center room, and a three-pronged stone path led from the door to the gate, the mews, and the outhouse against the cliffside. The stones were uneven in the dirt, so they clicked when trod upon.

That was one of Kylee and Brysen's early innovations. When their father was still alive, they'd been able to hear him coming home by the click of the stones.

Click click. Click click. Click click.

It didn't always keep them safe, but it gave Brysen time to gnaw some hunter's leaf, which distracted him from the sting of the whip. That was why he'd started chewing it so young. He hadn't even liked the taste back then.

Kylee clicked down the path to the mews now, and put Shara inside on her perch and hooded her in one practiced motion. Sightless and soundless, Shara could finally rest. Hawks could see more and process it faster than humans could imagine. Their eyes together weighed the same as their brains, and their reactions to what they saw were instant. It made them fierce hunters, but it also made them extremely sensitive. The only relief they ever had from the onslaught of the world was beneath their finely wrought leather hoods.

There were times Kylee wished that she, too, could drop on a heavy leather hood and find peace for a few hours. Her ma had, in a way. She was constantly in prayer or meditation, clutching handfuls of dirt, insensate. When she wasn't in one of her trances, she was lecturing Kylee and Brysen on the evils of falconry and the virtues of the birdless. Still, she ate the meals the sales of the birds provided.

Kylee made a round of the remaining hawks in the mews, the ones she hoped to sell tomorrow.

There was a finch finder—a breed of hawk popular with beginners—that Brysen had caught last week. It hadn't been manned yet—trained to be comfortable around people—but it wouldn't take long. Finch finders were easy birds. Some buyers wanted the chance for their children to man one themselves.

The snow-white dovehawk had just molted and wouldn't be worth much. There were two blue-winged kestrels—a small breed of falcon. They'd sell as a pair to some collector who wanted company rather than a hunting bird. They were as friendly and affectionate as birds of prey could be.

The finest bird, the peregrine, shifted from foot to foot on its perch, no doubt eager to fly. It was a racer and a hunter, a true long-winged falcon, and more valuable than any other bird in the mews. If Brysen showed it well tomorrow, Kylee might be able to get an auction going. She wondered when the last time was that Brysen took it out to fly.

She went to the logs and looked them over, her jaw clenching tighter with each page.

They hadn't been updated in days.

The log—which Brysen was meant to keep—tracked each bird's weight, how much it was fed, when it was heavy, when it was low, and when, precisely, it was at flying weight. Without the logs, they'd have no way to be certain—or to show buyers—that their birds were in good form and keen.

"You had *one job*, Bry," she muttered, and set the log back down.

She locked the mews, triple-checking the chains on the

door, and inspected the traps around the perimeter—little dart snares and loud, rattling trip wires.

Normally, she wouldn't bother—no one in the Villages would steal from them—but around market days, with all the strangers in town, robberies and vandalism were not unheard-of. Nor was outright aviacide. A Kartami sympathizer wouldn't just kill a bird or two; if they could, they'd poison the feed of every last bird in the market. They'd empty the skies and burn the Six Villages to the ground. Although the Tamirs and the distant Uztari kyrgs swore they were safe in these foothills, Kylee gave the chains a final, extra check. If all went well at the market, she wouldn't have to worry about flying weights and logbooks ever again.

With their future as secure as chains could make it, she trudged across the yard to the house.

Click click. Click click. Click click.

Brysen was home, studying his hair in the glass on the wall, singing quietly to himself. "*Never old and never new, lay la li, lay la lu . . .*" He stopped when she came in. "You brought Shara back?"

Kylee nodded. "Brysen, I'm sorry I—"

"It's fine," he said abruptly. Silence settled between them.

They used to talk about everything. They'd had a game they'd play in whispers, where they'd pretend to be a falcon—the two of them as one bird. One would describe their house from above, then the other would take the falcon higher and describe what they could see, and then back and forth, higher and higher, describing the world as they imagined it from above—what their neighbors in the Six Villages were doing, what the convoys crossing the Parsh Desert were like, or the kyrgs in the Sky Castle and the Talon Fortress, and beyond, to places they invented—lost Altari kingdoms, bustling ports on the edges of a saltwater bay—seeing who could imagine a bigger world in more detail. A falcon could mount to the stars and still count the hairs on a goat's head. So could a good imagination.

But when their father died three ice-winds ago, they'd stopped their game. After disappearing for an entire turn of the moon, Brysen began hanging out with the battle boys, started spending time alone with Dymian, said less and less at home, shared less and less of himself with her. Life had gotten lonely.

"You hungry?" she asked, grappling for something to perch a conversation on. "I can cook something up."

Brysen shrugged.

She kept her voice level. "Where's Ma?"

"In her room." Brysen pointed his chin toward the closed door.

If she found out what happened at the battle pits, what Kylee had done, there'd be a long night of chanting and repenting ahead. Damning your daughter to a skyless hell took a lot of energy, and she'd forget to eat if Kylee didn't put the food right in front of her.

"I'm making dinner!" Kylee shouted toward the door, and grabbed a heavy iron pan from the hook on the wall. "We've got some grains I can toast and the last of the smoked rabbit sausage," she told Brysen, talking just to fill the air. "I figure we can eat it today, because we'll have enough bronze to buy fresh tomorrow."

"Uh-huh," Brysen grunted, and pulled down the wooden box of candied ginger they kept on the high shelf. He popped a piece into his mouth and put the box back. Whatever he was thinking about their future after they paid off the Tamirs, he was keeping to himself.

"I think we'll get a good price on the peregrine," Kylee continued. *If she's ready to fly*, she thought. *If you didn't overfeed her.* She dropped a handful of grain into the hot skillet. It was time to make amends. Brysen would be able to run the business however he wanted soon, and until then, they might as well not argue about it. "The dovehawk probably won't fly; she just finished her molt. Looks like she plucked out one of her blood feathers this morning?"

"Someone'll buy her," Brysen said, chewing.

"I thought you and Dymian could show the birds together tomorrow, while I negotiate the prices?" At that, finally, Brysen perked up.

"That'd be good." He actually smiled. "People like to see a real hawk master in a tent. Gives us credibility, raises the price. Good thinking."

A compliment! She resisted nagging him about the logbook.

"I think I'll keep the peregrine on my fist," he continued, warming to the subject of the market, "to show how agreeable she is. We'll keep the others tethered to the perch until people ask about them. Maybe I'll see if Nyall will loan us some of the nicer bird boxes from Dupuy's shop. Unless *you'd* rather ask him . . ."

Kylee could feel her brother's grin without looking at him. She stirred the warming grains in the pan over the fire, dropped in a spoonful of goose fat to melt and soften. "Whatever," she said.

"Ha!" Brysen laughed and stepped up next to her, leaning against the wooden table along the wall. "Your ears twitched. You *like* him."

"Oh, come on," Kylee replied. "We've known each other since you two used to have peeing contests off the cliffs. I do not *like* him."

"Well, you know he likes you," Brysen replied.

"Yes, well, everybody likes one another here. We're all one big, happy valley." Kylee was the one getting snappy now—her brother's main source of amusement when he did seem willing to speak was in making her uncomfortable. She had no interest in romance, but its shades and shapes were his favorite subject. If he ever bothered to read anything, she was certain it would be the filthy love stories old people sold for a chip of bronze alongside jugs of rose-petal wine.

"You keep brushing him off like that, you're gonna lose him," Brysen told her. "He's got lads and ladies alike throwing themselves at him every day. He is, objectively, gorgeous. You do see that, right?"

"You like him so much, why don't you go after him?" she told her brother, dropping a sausage into the pan and watching it sizzle. She laughed to herself at the symbolism.

"I'm taken, Ky. You know that," Brysen said, and Kylee had to bite her tongue. She worried that she'd said the wrong thing. Brysen's good moods were like hummingbirds. Fleeting and fast. One wrong gesture and they'd dart away. "Anyway, you can't be attracted to someone you peed off a cliff with when you were little," he joked. "It's a law of nature. Nyall would tell you the same. Maybe that's why he likes you so much. Never saw you pee."

"You've got an odd view of courtship, Bry."

He smiled a boyish grin that reminded Kylee her brother was still in there. "I'm a romantic; what can I say? Talk to him. Give him a chance."

"We'll see how the market goes," she said, as if that had anything to do with Nyall's chances. "Tell him *that* when you negotiate for the boxes."

"Sis, you are devious with your feminine wiles!" her brother laughed.

She poked at him playfully with her spoon, but he dodged, taking up a chipped plate like a shield. She thrust and he parried, spinning away. She jabbed again and missed.

"Come on, great huntress!" he goaded her. "Get me!"

She jabbed again and he blocked. Once more, and he knocked the spoon out of her hand. It hit the floor and he dove after it, scooping it up to aim at her. The bits of grain at the tip had picked up some dust and maybe a mouse dropping or two.

"Yum! Eat up!" He charged spoon-first.

"Ah!" She ducked, but he followed. "Gross!"

She faked left, went right, but he dropped the plate and grabbed her arm, pulled her to him, a move just like the longhauler's that had nearly killed him. She was trapped in his grip. He raised the spoon high, aiming it toward her face. "Market day's tomorrow! You'll need your energy. Yum yum yum!"

"Ew!" She squirmed and pushed, laughing. His smile was wide, and she even dared a glance back at his eyes, which were lit with a kind of giddiness.

"Bry, stop!" she yelled, but he didn't stop. He was still grinning. "Stop it!" She pushed again, harder, and his shirt popped open.

He leaped back from her as if he'd been stabbed, the smile vanishing from his face. She saw the tangle of smooth scarring on his skin, a tight weave of burns that stretched from the waistband of his pants, up his entire left side, and across his chest to just below his collarbone.

He dropped the spoon and buttoned his shirt nimbly.

"Why'd you——? I wasn't really gonna . . ." His voice choked off, and the joy in his eyes disappeared.

"I didn't mean to. I'm sorry," she apologized, reaching out to take his hand, to touch him kindly and show him she hadn't meant any harm. He pulled away from her.

"I gotta go," he snapped. His voice was cold. His eyes were once more like a wind off the high steppes. "I'll ask Nyall about the boxes."

"Should I keep some food warm for you?"

He turned his back on her and left without an answer. Beside her, the sausage cooked in the pan, and the sound of meat sizzling made her shudder.

Click click. Click click. Click click.

He was gone.

Her mother's door creaked open. "You made a lot of noise," she said.

"Sorry, Ma," Kylee answered without looking back. "We were just playing around."

"I don't mean now," her mother said, hoarse. "I mean today. You, Kylee, made a lot of noise. Too much."

Kylee turned, but her mother had shut the door to her room again, and Kylee was alone. Her mother wouldn't come out for hours, and she wouldn't see her brother again until morning.

At least, she hoped she would see him in the morning. A hawk you'd had for a dozen seasons could fly away from you at any moment. When you released the tether and let fly, you trusted the hawk to the world and hoped that the world would return it unharmed. People weren't so different. Sometimes they left and never came back.

GLASS GRINDERS

THE SUN HAD JUST PEEKED OVER THE HORIZON ON THE PARSH DESERT
when the dancing started.

The dancers were a mirage, an illusion of hot air rising off
the sand—one of the many curses of the desert. Altari folktales
told of men and women who longed for these morning dancers with such passion that they left their camps and watering
holes and raced toward the horizon after them. The stories all
ended the same way: dry bones in the desert and the dead's
desires unfulfilled.

Anon would not have his followers chase morning dancers.
He had promised them things with as much substance as a

mirage—justice and vengeance and righteousness—but he would make those things real. He would deliver.

Beside him, a half-starved hawk master shivered in the morning cold.

"Stay focused, Aylex. When this is done, you'll get a blanket, some ale, breakfast."

The skin-and-bones bird man stood up straighter, eager to please. Or at least eager to be warmed and fed. The chains around his ankles had rubbed him red and raw, and the bronze collar around his neck had been even less gentle. His bare chest was burned an angry red and still bled where they had scraped the offensive falconry tattoos from his skin.

Anon would have words with the hawk master's guards. Though he was their prisoner, he should not be abused. Were they not all prisoners of the earth, and would they not be confined again to dirt one day?

The Altari faith was the oldest on the plateau; the Altari people had been in the mountains before the Uztari had come and expelled them past the plains, into the wind-blasted desert. Generations of Altari had crawled so long through the sand that they ground it to glass beneath them. That was the slur the Uztari used against them: glass grinders.

Over time, many Altari had abandoned their faith, joined the Uztari bird cults, pledged themselves to the Sky Castle.

They took falcons on their fists and hauled goods and equipment across the plains for the Uztari kyrgs in exchange for the briefest of earthly powers. They trapped hawks and traded in eagles. Even the Crawling Priests, who claimed to follow the old ways and cursed Uztari falconry, gladly lived beneath the protection of Uztar. They let the blasphemers feed them like baby birds in the nest. They were all complicit.

But there were other ways. Purer ways. Anon would *not* be a glass grinder. Anon would be the sharpened shard of glass that sliced the sin from the world. He was Kartami, the shard, who cut down the self-proclaimed rulers of the sky. Kartami faith was unshakable and Kartami power was unstoppable. They would roll like a sandstorm straight to the heart of Uztar and they would seize the skies. They would be purified, emptied, and sinless. When the sky was empty, they would be saved. They were almost ready.

But for now, victory demanded sin. Until their victory, Anon needed this hawk master at his side.

"Will it fly to you?" he demanded of his captive.

The man nodded. He raised his leather-cuffed arm, and though it shook, he held it out to the morning.

They'd raided a merchant convoy during the rising-wind season and had captured this master, Aylex. They'd slaughtered everyone but him. Even the ones who pleaded that they, too, were of his people—Anon cut out their lying tongues first. They thought that to be an Altari was a birthright, a bloodline, because they knew no history. Altari and Uztari were identities as changing as the winds, and to serve Uztar, to live like an Uztari on stolen land with eyes bent up into the blue, was to *be* Uztari.

Besides, if he wanted the defended towns and cities to fall, he needed fear to fly ahead of him. Word of his brutality might lead later foes to surrender without a fight. When facing a much larger army, terrorizing them in advance was his best hope of beating them.

After the executions, they took the silks for their kites and the wood and metal for their war barrows, anything precious they could find, but they left all the hawking furniture—the bird boxes, perches, leashes, bells, and jesses. The finely wrought hoods and anklets. The birds themselves, all save one, they ransomed back to the kyrgs or gave the mercy of death, one clean cut across the throat. The ransom was needed to fund the conquest, but the bloodshed was a holy act. Sacred carnage.

The hawk master didn't speak for a week after the slaughter. He sunburned the way Anon used to as a boy, until his skin had hardened against the desert sun. It had taken some time to make the hawk master useful again, to accustom him to desert life, for which he was ill-suited. Had not so many Altari exiles been ill-suited to it as well? They had adapted. So would he. The Kartami spared this man's personal hawk and let him care for it until it was sent to the Six Villages.

And this morning, it returned.

The bird flew away from the rising red sun, passing through the mirage of dancers like an arrow through smoke, and time seemed to slow as it bent back its wings, stretched out its talons, and caught its master by the fist. The small leash from the glove was quickly attached to the hawk's anklet, so that master and bird were tied together again.

A tear trickled down the hawk master's cheek.

"You are happy your bird is returned to you?"

Aylex nodded. "Yes. I am."

Anon took a deep breath. He was offended by the sight of the hawk on the man's arm. He hated the man for taming the bird, and he hated the bird for allowing itself to be tamed. "Give me the message."

Aylex untied the small box from the bird's anklet and handed it to Anon, who used the ring on his index finger as the key to open it. He unrolled the parchment inside and read the words his spy reported, his lips half-parted and his heart pounding in his chest.

"Visek! Launa!" he shouted, which made the hawk and hawk

master jump where they stood. Two of Anon's squad leaders came running from their tents to stand before him.

Visek and Launa were echoes of each other in appearance, the younger man with skin as dark as the older woman's, like the black soil of the mountains to which all Altari longed to return. They had been with Anon since the start of his campaign, when he rose up against an elevated Altari ruler of a grassland village, his false title given to him by the occupiers of the Sky Castle. He was a traitor and a fool and he'd disgraced the community by holding pigeon games, a stupid sport where gamblers tried to lure each other's flocks. A local novice, a boy studying to be a Crawling Priest, had arrived to denounce the sport and had, in his zeal, poisoned some of the bird feed. When caught, he was to be whipped.

Anon, who did not call himself Anon at the time, intervened. He took the whip from that foolish ruler's hand and choked him to death with it. Then he declared that all who would restore the greatness of their people and free the skies of sin should rise up with him as the last shards of the true Altari civilization. That was the moment the Kartami were born. Only the novice boy and his young mother followed. They were Visek and Launa.

Kartami numbers grew as they attacked Altari collaborators and slaughtered traveling Uztari. Anon saw the power of the pair of fighters who loved each other as mother and son. So he devised that all his warriors would be paired by bonds of love. Parents, lovers, siblings. To be a warrior of the Kartami was to love so greatly that you would tie your life to another in battle, and the life of your pair to the fate of your faith. The brave went into battle for their own beliefs, but the victorious went into battle for their beloved's belief in them. Only Anon fought alone. His love was for all of them.

His warrior pairs had never lost a battle.

"Tell the commanders," he ordered them. "We will break camp and ride ready. Four lines, eight squads across, eight barrows per squad."

They each looked to the earth once sharply, then turned to inform the commanders. It would not take long. Anon had devised a system of command that could mobilize all 512 of his warriors as suddenly as a storm, and he could command them with flags and calls while they rolled across the desert without slowing.

"May I have that blanket now?" the hawk master pleaded, his eyes cast down at his blackened feet.

"First we must send our reply," said Anon.

The hawk master let a whine escape his mouth with a quick glance at his hawk. "You'll send Titi away again so soon?"

Anon slapped the master across the face with the back of

his hand, the heavy ring he wore cutting the skinny man's cheek. "Your bird has no name!" he shouted. "If I ever hear you name it again, I will feed it your organs while you still live, understood?"

Aylex nodded, chastened. *If only all Uztari were as easy to break as this one.*

Behind him, pairs of Kartami rolled their war barrows into line, tents and blankets tightly packed inside, battle kites mounted to the fronts. The flyers strapped themselves into the kites while the drivers checked their spears and bows.

Anon had no doubt that his Kartami would soon rule the skies alone, and from their vast emptiness, a new civilization could be born. Then they would break their kites and leave the sky pure and unsullied. But before that time could come, he had more compromises to make with the falconers and a deal to strike with the worst of them. He studied the parchment once again, composing his message.

"Tell them that if their report is true, I will not miss this chance," he said to the hawk master. "Tell them to do what they must to make the girl comply, but tell them that I *will* have this ghost eagle."

BRYSEN

THE WIDENING GYRE

6

KYLEE HAD BEEN ACTING STRANGE ALL MORNING. BRYSEN HAD BEEN pretty sure she'd yell at him the moment he staggered into their market tent after she'd set the whole thing up by herself. Instead, she'd hugged him.

"You okay?" she asked.

"Uh, yeah," he said, although her face told him pretty clearly how very not okay he looked.

"Great," she said, with a cheerfulness that made him nervous. "I've got the birds down here in the cart, and if you got the boxes from Nyall . . . ?"

She raised her voice at the end of the sentence like she was apologizing for even bringing it up. Why was she treating him so gently?

"Sorry," he said. "I had a long night at the Broken Jess." Her face tightened, like she was about to scold him, but then she relaxed again.

"It's fine," she said. "I'll go do it now. We've got some time before anybody gets here. Why don't you . . . uh . . . clean up a little?"

He nodded, and she slipped through the front tent flaps, letting in a brief streak of piercing, early morning light. It cut into his headache sharper than a hawk's screech. He braced himself. There'd be a lot more screeches and a lot more light when the market began.

Aside from the Six Villages merchants, there'd be tentless hawkers in the road with perch carts and a falcon or two on the fist, and there'd be pigeon peddlers and bait dealers, minor sellers of pet birds and songbirds and show birds, and more equipment makers than there could possibly be buyers for. Then the customers would arrive, kyrgs and peasants and hawk masters and long-haulers and spies and gawkers and Crawling Priests underfoot shouting up curses at all of it, and the haggling would be louder than the shouting and the squawking, and the screeching would pierce it all with bloodcurdling regularity.

Brysen's head ached just thinking about it.

Alone in the tent, he sniffed at his armpit, and it was like punching himself in the face. How had his sister survived hugging him?

He changed into the clothes Kylee had brought: red leather pants, a bright blue tunic—his nicest one, reserved for market days, festivals, and funerals—and his long striped robe. She'd known he wouldn't be home before morning, and she'd known he'd need to change.

He didn't deserve a sister like Kylee. He wanted to be kinder, though. He really did. At least, after these next few days, she wouldn't have to work in this business she hated anymore. They'd have enough money to pay off the Tamirs. She could be free.

Kylee hadn't said so, but he knew that was what she wanted. He knew her so much better than she thought he did. He wasn't going to object. He didn't care about the business anyway. He had his own plans for what he'd do when this market was done and all their debts were paid.

He was going to leave the Six Villages.

He knew how everyone saw him here: the pitiable son of a pitiful dead man. The battle pits couldn't erase that idea of him, and neither could their business. But on the road, seeing the world the way he and Kylee used to dream about, he could be anyone he wanted. He and Dymian could reinvent themselves at every oasis; neither the scorn of nobles nor the pity of neighbors could touch them. They'd be wild hunters, untethered and untamed, having adventures hand in hand. He wondered how Kylee would take the news that he planned to leave. Would she try to stop him? Would she be relieved?

He had, however, done one nice thing for her this morning, even though she wouldn't see it that way.

He'd decided not to ask Nyall about the bird boxes last night so that Kylee would have a reason to talk to him this morning. His sister might not think it, but she deserved a little happiness, and Nyall was dying to provide her with some. If only she'd give him a chance. It was like she had no romantic feeling in her at all. If they didn't look so much alike, Brysen would swear sometimes that they weren't related.

"How can you love someone who so obviously doesn't love you back?" Brysen had asked his friend last night. Nyall had given him a bemused look, like he thought Brysen was joking, but then he got serious when he saw Brysen wasn't joking at all.

"It's like this," Nyall said. "You love the moon—"

"I do?" Brysen wondered.

"People do," Nyall said. "People love the moon. But the moon doesn't love them back. It just is. Our love for it doesn't require it to love us in return. I'd rather live in a world where

I get to love the moon than in one where I don't, even if the moon won't return the feeling."

"You want the moon? I'll give it to ya!" Nyck shouted at them, then jumped up and dropped the back of his pants, waved his pale cheeks right in their faces.

"To the moon in all its shapes, smooth and hairy alike!" Brysen toasted.

"Your sister's got a hairy moon?" Nyall looked worried.

"What's in a person's pants is no one's business but the sky's," Nyck scolded, hitching up the back of his own again.

"But still I'd love her with a hairy moon!" Nyall cried out. "There's always a *waxing* moon, after all!" He raised his glass, laughing, and they all toasted to love and to the phases of the moon.

That was the last clear memory Brysen had. He'd woken up alone on a bench in the Broken Jess. There'd been a string of falcon droppings dangling from a perch just over his head, an effective alarm. He'd bolted up before it fell into his eye.

Now he took a stroll around their tent, making sure the hawks were in good form. They all sat calmly on the perch in the back, tethered in place. They had iron bands wrapped around their ankles just below the leather anklets that held their bells and jesses. The iron bands said SKYBREAKER FALCONRY— the name their father had given the business. Kylee had wanted to change it when they took over, but Brysen said they should keep it.

"With every sale we make that he wouldn't have, we pile earth on Da's memory," he told her. "We take the name he made and make it ours."

She didn't argue with him. She never argued with Brysen when it came to their father. Sometimes he wished she would. That was when he'd known she had no plan to stay in the business after their debts were paid. And that was when he knew he had no future in the Villages. He couldn't run things alone. Rather, he didn't want to do it without Kylee.

He picked up the logbook, a quill, and a pot of pokeberry ink and quickly jotted in some missing weights and feeding data for each of the birds. He made up what he couldn't remember. It was a fraud, sure, but harmless. No falconer who was serious would take a logbook at face value, and a falconer who wasn't serious wouldn't know if the logs were a little off anyway.

He blotted the ink and put the book back. His glove and a few spares hung on pegs beside the birds. The extra gloves were in case potential clients with more bronze than sense showed up without gloves of their own. If they had a noble buyer, Brysen would take the bird outside and let it fly, using one of the lures to get it to dive, to demonstrate its speed and accuracy.

He'd tried to train each hawk and falcon to wait on, which meant circling overhead until given the signal to hunt, but he'd never been much good at it. Even with Dymian's help.

"I guess you'll have to stick around to teach me the right way," Brysen always said.

"I think you're not learning on purpose just to keep me around," Dymian always replied, teasing him. Sometimes their training for the day ended then and there. Those were Brysen's favorite days.

Brysen wished it were true that he was pretending to be bad at it, though. The sad fact was he really did *want* to get better. He just couldn't focus on the finer details. He got impatient easily, and distracted. How could the techniques come so naturally to his sister, who hated everything about falconry except getting paid, when he wanted so badly to be great at it and always fell just short? Weren't they twins? Weren't they supposed to share everything? And what kind of a scuzzard did it make him to resent her talents instead of focusing on his own? Self-loathing wasn't a solitary hunter. It formed a flock with every unkind thought it could find, and then, like crows, they mobbed.

Brysen stepped out of the dim tent to clear his head in the morning air. He glanced down the avenue to his left. Nothing but hawkers' tents. To his right, the same. Straight across from them was Dupuy's Equipery, selling lures and perches, boxes and ropes, gloves and hoods. He hadn't realized they were so close. That couldn't have been an accident.

Behind his wooden table, Nyall was in gleeful negotiation with Kylee for the high-end boxes they sold to carry birds in. He was smiling and gesturing, no doubt trying to turn Kylee's desperate attempts to pay him in bronze into the promise of a walk along the Necklace instead. Male hawks pursuing females with shrill cries and tail-waggle twirls were more dignified.

"Ymal the Cask-Breaker's *Guide to the Sighting and Capture of the Ghost Eagle*?" A pinch-faced scholar in a ragged cloak and vest shoved himself directly in front of Brysen. "I've three *au-then-ti-ca-ted* fragments here, straight from the latest *ar-chae-ol-og-i-cal* dig on the southern slopes beside the Sky Castle. *Leg-i-ble* and *le-git-i-mate*, sky's honor."

The man had the accent of a North Uztari, overpronouncing words he could've said simply. He flashed three weather-worn and moth-eaten scraps of parchment from under his robes.

"Ymal tells in his own hand of two unknown eyries where the ghost eagle makes its home and six sure tricks for catching one."

"Six?" Brysen stared at the man. "Who'd need more than one?"

"One to catch the beast"—the man leaned in conspiratorially and smirked—"and five to survive the *en-count-er.*"

The market was lousy with parchment dealers like this. They sold counterfeit scraps of paper claiming to be the original, firsthand knowledge of the great trappers of the past. At best, any fool who bought one would find himself on some cold cliffside no closer to wealth and glory than if he'd stayed home sipping dandelion wine in the nude. At worst, he'd end up with a lonely sky burial. The trade in false trapper's manuscripts was expressly forbidden and was, therefore, thriving.

"Your moth holes are too even," Brysen told him, pointing to the shabby papers. The man's brow furrowed. "Moths don't nibble perfect rounds." Brysen knew a lot about moth holes. "Looks like you made them with . . . what? A leather awl?"

The man pulled his hand back from Brysen's shoulder as if he'd been burned. "How dare you accuse me of—"

Brysen shrugged. "My head hurts too much to accuse you of anything," he said. "But peddle your bird droppings someplace else, or you'll find out where else a man can stick a leather awl."

The scholar's whole body became a frown, and he huffed away into the crowd. He'd surely find a buyer by the end of the day but not a Six Villager. They knew the only true tales of ghost eagles were told over cups of milk stout and vats of hunter's leaf. The truth never allowed itself the insult of being written down where any old moth could eat it.

At that moment, an Uztari kyrg on horseback clomped down the road with his retinue of servants behind him. He wore the purple and green of his clan. His robe, intricately embroidered with gold stitching, glimmered against his amber skin. He needn't have dressed so finely. On his arm perched a massive gilded eagle, unhooded but perfectly serene.

Only nobles could afford a bird like that. One so calm had clearly been trained well. A gilded eagle could take down a deer on the open plain or knock a mountain goat to its death. They posed a danger even to men, and to march one unhooded through the shrieking crowd on market day was the towering height of arrogance.

A little boy, one of the village urchins who cleaned droppings for a bronze chip a day, was playing with a finch on a string, swinging it high to catch bugs. He wasn't paying attention and he wandered right out into the middle of the road, the small bird flying into the horse's face.

The horse reared. The eagle on the kyrg's arm shrieked and bated, diving away, but he was tethered by strong leather jesses, so he flipped upside down, pulling the kyrg with such force that he almost fell out of his saddle.

"You vermin!" the kyrg yelled, regaining control of his eagle and his horse. "I should have you flayed!"

The boy squatted, covering his head and cowering while his finch flew off. "I'm . . . I'm . . . I'm . . ."

He couldn't even get an apology out before one of the kyrg's servants was off his own horse, grabbing the boy by the shirt and lifting him one-handed. From his other hand he unfurled a six-talon whip, a wooden handle with six leather strands off the end, each tipped with a small curved talon. Another innovation the Six Villages had given Uztari civilization. The talons on this whip were from a merlin, one of the littlest falcons. If the six-talon whip had been tipped with eagle talons, the boy would've been torn to shreds. As it was, he'd be scarred. Brysen shuddered.

"Hey! Symon!" he shouted, inventing a name for the boy as he made his way over. He grabbed one of the pigeon crates from his tent as he walked. Hopefully, the boy was smart enough to play along. "Why are you bothering these fine gentlemen?"

"I . . . I'm not Sy—" the boy spluttered, terror-stricken eyes fixed on the talon tips of the whip.

"Sorry, sers," Brysen said to the servant and his master. "My little brother is a fool, and, I'll tell you, Mother will flay him mercilessly when she gets back from her master's hunt."

"Your mother is on a hunt?" the servant asked with some skepticism. He had a wide face with thin lips bent into a sneer and wore his long hair pulled back tight. "During the market?"

"Yes, ser. She's the bait keeper for Yaga Verosan of the river-bend pasture. She's been on the hunt for a month but returns today. I will tell her of my little brother's stupidity and, wow, will this baby scuzzard suffer!"

The boy hung from the servant's grip like meat on a hook.

"You don't look like brothers," the servant said. The boy's ruddy complexion gave away the lie pretty plainly.

Brysen dropped his head to his feet with a feigned look of shame while he hunted a better lie. "My mother has a fondness for her Altari master . . . ," he said. "My little brother is her only legitimate heir. I'm—"

"The Altari's village bastard," the kyrg laughed.

Brysen had made up Yaga Verosan's name, of course, but the Uztari kyrgs were bound by noble duty to show grudging respect to the elevated rulers of the grassland plains, where Altari were allowed to rule as long as they tithed doubly to the Sky Castle. This kyrg would have no interest in following up on some village bait keeper and her affair with a minor land-keeping noble. It was a gamble on Brysen's part.

"Why don't I give you a nice snack for your fine eagle, there?" Brysen held up the pigeon box. "My gift and apology. Of course, if you'd rather have him whipped, I understand completely. I sometimes whip him myself just for fun. He's so used to it, he doesn't even cry anymore, although I bet you could bring out a tear or two if you tried hard enough."

The boy whimpered at the thought.

"Pffft," the kyrg muttered. The servant set the boy down and took the pigeon. "Hardly worth our time." He gave Brysen a withering up-and-down glance. "It is too bad his father had no sons," he said, and the kyrg's retinue rode on.

"My name's Rhyme," the little boy said through a quivering lip.

"Like a poem?" Brysen smiled and squatted down in front of him. The boy nodded. "And I'm Brysen," he said. "Listen, you've got to watch where you're going on a day like today. That kyrg could've killed you if he'd wanted to."

"I didn't mean to scare his eagle," Rhyme sniffled.

"I know." Brysen cleared his throat. He took a piece of candied ginger from his pocket. He'd hoped to use it to settle his stomach later, when last night's mistakes came back to haunt him, but he pressed the candy into the boy's hand instead. "You have a home?"

Rhyme nodded.

"Is it safe? You stay there?"

The boy nodded again.

"Okay, run off home then," Brysen said. "And don't come back to the market. Stay out of sight and you'll be fine. He'll forget about you as soon as his bird takes a crap on his shoe."

Rhyme smiled. Brysen ruffled his hair and sent him running.

As he turned back toward the tent, his sister's friend Vyvian nodded at him from the corner of another tent. She had a pigeon in her hand, a message tied to its ankle, and she let it fly. Then she shook her head at him sadly.

"What?" he called over to her.

"You know who that was?"

"The kid?"

"The kyrg."

"I'll leave politics to you, Vy," he said. "I'm a lover, not a schemer."

"Be careful, Brysen," she told him. "The former doesn't protect you from the latter. Clouds are rolling in."

7

BRYSEN PULLED THE FLAPS OPEN FOR THE MORNING'S BUSINESS TO
begin and pushed Vyvian's ominous warning out of his head.

"That was twice as stupid as it was brave, and it was incred-
ibly brave." Dymian's voice startled Brysen from the back of
the tent.

"I'm not much for math." Brysen turned to him. "How'd
you get in here without me seeing you?"

"I slipped in from behind," Dymian said.

Brysen was about to make a joke, but Dymian didn't look
in the mood. His cheeks were shadowed with light-brown

stubble, and there were dark circles around his eyes. There was a bruise on his forehead only partly covered by his hair.

"That kyrg with the eagle was Kyrg Yval Birgund," Dymian told him. "Defense counselor at the Sky Castle."

"Well, he was also an arrogant dirt biter who hurts little kids," Brysen told him. "I should've turned the whip on *him*."

"You'd have been dead before your body hit the ground, but still . . ." Dymian smiled. "I admire your pluck."

"My *pluck?*" He raised an eyebrow.

"A killer in the pit, a hero in the streets," Dymian cooed. "A little of both in between the sheets . . ."

Brysen's chest tightened, and he felt the blood rush to his head. The blood rushed everywhere. "Wasn't sure if you'd show up today," he told his trainer casually, fearing his heartbeat might start an avalanche.

"I need to talk to you." Dymian glanced at the tent opening. "Privately?"

"On market day?" Brysen shook his head. "Everybody's watching everybody. Vyvian Sacher just sent a pigeon about me, I think." Dymian bit his lower lip, frowned. Brysen didn't like this timid version of his trainer. "Hold on."

He closed the tent flaps, giving his sister a gesture across the way that it'd only be for a moment. Kylee held her hands up at him and shook her head, her jaw hanging open.

Once the tent flaps fell shut, he turned around in the dim light filtering through the canvas. Dymian crossed the space and stood before him, so close that Brysen had to look up for their eyes to meet. The hawk master put his hands on Brysen's shoulders.

"I want to apologize for yesterday," he said. "I know you saw that I bet against you."

Brysen swallowed.

In stories, people said they were dumbstruck by love, but those storytellers knew nothing. Love didn't make you dumb; it made you too smart, too quickly. In the span of a breath, a person in love could imagine everything they should say and its opposite, every tone of voice they could use and why each one was a mistake. They could weigh every word and analyze every gesture. He was not great at math, but Brysen could calculate the emotional trajectory of an eyebrow and the infinite combinations of two lips touching, and the knowledge stuck his tongue. A person in love was paralyzed by the brilliance of their own longing.

"Whatever," his voice cracked out.

Yeah, the instant genius of the lovestruck sounded a lot like stupidity.

He tried to add a shrug, but Dymian took the gesture wrong and pulled him against his warm chest, gripping him tightly.

Brysen was glad the hawks were hooded on their perches. They'd sense the riot beneath his skin and start shrieking.

"I know it bothered you," he whispered into Brysen's hair. "It's what's so great about you. 'Your heart's a wing, a feather-fragile thing.'"

Brysen laughed. "You're a poet now?"

"It's from the *Epic of the Forty Birds*," Dymian told him.

"Never read it."

"It's amazing. I'll read it to you one day. The first hawk knows there is more to the world than she has seen but can't discover it all alone. She has to unite all the birds, one by one, hearing each of their stories before they can fly off together in search of the truth of the world. How have you not read our *founding* epic?"

Sometimes being with Dymian made Brysen forget he was just some Six Villages hawker's kid. And other times, it reminded him. "I didn't have tutors or schooling like you did," he said. "I learned what I learned when I learned it."

"Of course," Dymian said sweetly, and brushed a lock of Brysen's gray hair from his forehead. When Dymian touched his head, it didn't feel ash-heap gray. It felt like pure silver. "And you always amaze me by how much you do know. More than you give yourself credit for."

Brysen smiled. It was a lie, obviously, but still, it was a kind lie, and he loved that someone like Dymian would make the effort to lie a smile onto his lips. The truth was rarely kind, so why not let a lovely lie linger?

"Anyway, I'm sorry about yesterday," Dymian repeated. "I had no choice. I needed some money, fast, and . . . well, I thought you were outmatched by that long-hauler. I should've told you to let Shara loose and take a loss safely."

"*Told me to?*" Brysen pulled away. How was it that the person who could launch you to the clouds was the same one who could snare you to the ground? "I make my own choices, D. I'm not some harem boy you can boss around. You don't *tell* me what to do."

"I know. I know. I'm sorry."

Dymian should have been snapping back at him, or making a crude joke about harems, or knocking him down into the dirt right there in the center of the tent, pinning Brysen beneath him, telling him a thing or two that might be fun . . . but instead, he just said, again, "I'm sorry."

"What's going on?" Brysen demanded. "You're worrying me here."

"It's nothing, Bry. Really. I just owe the Tamirs some money."

"Everyone owes the Tamirs some money," Brysen grunted.

"More money than I have right now . . ."

"Oh . . . well . . . do you need an advance on your pay?"

Brysen suggested. "With my winnings yesterday and the market on, we're about to pay off everything we owe them anyway. Kylee won't be happy about it, but I'm sure we could throw in some extra for you."

"Kylee hates me," Dymian said.

"She hates that I like you," Brysen corrected him. "But she likes me. She'll do it if I ask her to. I am, technically, her *older* brother."

"By about half a chime of the bell on a falcon's ankle," Dymian laughed. "And I've got a few seasons on both of you. I shouldn't be asking you for money."

"I respect my elders." Brysen grinned. "Let me help you. When we're on the road together, we'll be splitting costs evenly anyway . . ."

Dymian laughed and pulled him by the belt until there was no air between them. "It's just—" He lowered his eyes to the floor. "It's not only bronze. Last night, I promised Goryn Tamir that I'd—"

"Oh, how sweet!" The tent flaps opened with a slash of light. "A tender moment between a fledgling and his mama bird. You gonna feed a worm into his mouth now?"

Brysen's head snapped around to see five big silhouettes in the opening. The central figure carried a hawk on his arm while the other four held sturdy leather clubs. They lumbered inside and let the flaps fall behind them. The perched hawks sensed the change in energy, perhaps sensed the arrival of the new bird on the glove, and shifted on their feet.

"Ser Goryn, I was going to find you later," Dymian said.

The man in the middle of the group laughed and pulled a small piece of bloody meat from his pocket. He held it up to his bird's beak, then pulled it away, leaving his gyrfalcon hungry and keen for a kill. Her feathers were white and silver, her beak a razor-sharp, pearl-white hook. She was bred for snowy mountain hunting, not foothill and brush like the short-tailed hawks most folks in the Villages had. Goryn liked her because blood from a kill would glisten bright red against her perfect, pearlescent feathers. She was an expensive predator bred for luxurious violence.

His goons spread out, flanking Brysen and Dymian.

"My mother trusted me with great responsibility over the finances of her business," Goryn Tamir said. The dirty fingers of his free hand rubbed the thick black stubble on his chin and brushed the silk collar of his long jacket. No matter how finely the Tamir children dressed, their fingers always stayed dirty. It was a sign of pride. The Tamirs did their own work.

"When I study the ledgers," Goryn continued, "as I do regularly, I see a very large outstanding payment due . . . a payment from you, Dymian, that's preventing me from balancing the books. This bothers me. I like my numbers balanced. An unbalanced ledger is like an itch I can't scratch right at that spot on the small of my back. You know that spot, Dymian? That spot where, right now, you've got a trickle of ice-cold sweat?"

Suddenly and without the slightest signal, one of the men behind Dymian lashed out, striking him in the lower back with a club.

"Ahh!" Dymian cried, and dropped to his knees, gasping.

Brysen rushed for him but found himself tripped with a blow across the shins from another goon's baton. He fell forward but had spent enough time in the pits to turn the fall into a roll. The hit was hard enough to make him limp later, but for now he didn't feel a thing. Even his headache had vanished. Nothing like sudden brutality to sharpen your senses first thing in the morning.

He sprang back to his feet just in front of the bait boxes. He snapped one open and a pigeon burst out, racing for freedom, which caused the unhooded gyrfalcon on Goryn's glove to rouse and launch herself, still tethered.

The noise was enough to make the five hooded hawks on their perches bate, leaping to the end of their own tethers before being yanked back, scrambling, screeching, and blind.

In the chaos of shouts and feathers, Brysen delivered a high kick into the chest of the man who'd tripped him, grabbed the baton, and smacked it across his head. At the same moment, he drew his black-talon fighting blade and whirled around, a weapon in each hand.

He needn't have bothered.

The other two had Dymian held up, his arms pinned behind his back, and the stiletto point of an assassin's dagger against the soft underside of his throat, already drawing a bead of blood.

"You've got heart, little bird," Goryn said to Brysen, smoothing his hawk's feathers as if he were petting some domesticated chicken. "More than your old man did, anyway. But you've got your mother's glass-grinder blood in you, and you're letting it get the best of your brains. What did you plan to do? Beat me and my men into submission and then . . . what? Ransom me back to my mother one finger at a time?"

Goryn looked giddy at the thought. Brysen kept his weapons up. He had simply wanted to keep them from beating Dymian. He turned as the man he'd knocked down stood up.

Goryn clucked. "You know we would make meat of you and your sister out there and then we'd send some of our friends to visit your mother. I'd burn your home to ash and bury your picked-over bones beneath it."

Brysen's eyes darted around the dim tent, plotting his next attack.

"Put your weapons away, kid," Goryn sighed. "Our problem's not with you. You've got your blood up, and I can forgive that at your age. Put your weapons away, and you and your family get to live. We won't even take Dymian's private parts off as punishment."

Dymian whimpered.

"But make me wait another breath," Goryn hissed, "and you'll suffer beyond the limits of imagining."

There was no suffering Brysen couldn't imagine, but Goryn didn't make idle threats, and he didn't want Kylee punished for his fights. He dropped the club and sheathed his knife.

Goryn nodded, and the goons let go of Dymian, shoving him hard to the ground.

"You made a deal with me, Dymian," Goryn told him. "Honor that deal, or you die."

"I'm going to kick your teeth out one day," Dymian threatened, and Goryn closed his eyes and smiled. Then he crossed over to Dymian, raised his foot over the back of Dymian's shin, and stomped.

"Ahh!" Dymian yelled, his lower leg cracking. "*Ahh!*"

"I've never understood why you make life so hard for yourself, Dymian," Goryn said, then looked right at Brysen. "Some people just don't know their limits."

He smiled, then left the tent with his men as suddenly as

he had arrived. The settling tent flap narrowed the streak of light across the ground to the size of a blade, then a needle. It yawned wide and bright again when Kylee and Nyall burst in. Nyall was hauling five large bird boxes.

"That was Goryn Tamir himself!" he exclaimed.

"What in the flaming sky was *that* about?" Kylee demanded.

Brysen rushed to his trainer, who was writhing on the ground. When Dymian finally looked up at him, his eyes were damp and darting. "I'm in trouble," he said, half-breathless, clutching his broken leg. "Sky-high trouble."

Brysen felt an odd sensation course through him right then. It wasn't pity or love or fright.

It was pride.

A strange and miserable time for it, he knew, but he couldn't help standing a little straighter. Dymian was asking *him* for help. *Anything for you*, he wanted to say, but instead his sister spoke.

"Tell me what you did to bring Goryn Tamir into our tent, or I swear he won't even be able to find your corpse to spit it into mud."

"I made him a promise," Dymian groaned. "I promised him a ghost eagle."

8

THE AIR FELT HEAVY AS STONE, AND BRYSEN THOUGHT THE GROUND might give out from under him. Outside, the market bustled, indifferent. Homing pigeons with bamboo whistles attached to their tail feathers circled above, creating a mournful orchestra in the sky.

"Seeds and nuts! Get your seeds and nuts here!" a barrel pusher called, rolling past the tent where Brysen, Nyall, and Kylee were staring down at Dymian. His shadow swelled to devour the entire canvas, then shrank again as he disappeared along the road.

"Seeds and nuts, seeds and nuts!" his parrot echoed.

Behind the shifting shadows, Kylee closed in on Dymian, who was still on the ground, grimacing and trying not to look at his leg.

"You did *what?*" she scolded, as if Dymian were her servant and not a respected young hawk master who'd fallen on hard times.

Okay, Brysen thought, *maybe* respected *is an exaggeration* . . . But still, she didn't need to treat him like a slug on a fruit tree. The man had always been good to them. Better than good. He made Brysen happy. Why couldn't Kylee at least be grateful for that?

"It's okay," Brysen reassured him, taking on the new role of apprentice consoler. He gave Dymian some hunter's leaf to ease the pain. He'd cried on Dymian's shoulder enough times. He let Dymian lie to him about his scars being "beautiful." Now it was his turn to lie to Dymian, to comfort him even if the comfort was false. "It'll be okay."

A ghost eagle. What kind of fool promises a ghost eagle? No one had caught a ghost eagle in generations. There were ancient tales, like Ymal the Cask-Breaker, who got the eagle drunk on wine mixed with his own blood; Valyry the Glove-less; and the Stych sisters, who took no epithet. But no one in living memory had done it. Their father had died trying, and Dymian knew that. What was he thinking?

"What were you *thinking*?" Kylee demanded.

"Nyall!" Old Dupuy shouted from across the way. His voice turned up at the end like a screech. "Nyall! Get over here! I've got fifty jesses that need rubbing with oil, and we're short five hawk boxes. They better not be where I think they are! Someone's paying for them, and you know it won't be those two! *Nyall!*"

"I . . . uh . . . I have to go . . . ," Nyall apologized. "Don't worry, Ky. I've got you covered on the boxes."

"We'll pay for them," she said.

"Sure. Sure," Nyall said, giving Dymian a pitying look before he ducked outside. "Just not today."

He pressed his hands as wings against his chest. This time, Kylee returned the gesture, and Nyall smiled. At least someone was having a good day.

Brysen knelt down next to Dymian and helped him up, guided him to the only chair they had in the tent. Dymian winced with every step and leaned all his weight on Brysen as he lowered him.

"I can't put this burden on you, Bry," he said. "On either of you."

"You won't," Kylee said. "Because this is *not* our problem. Our debts are nearly paid."

Brysen shot her a look, but she shot one right back, invisible arrows that both met their marks. They looked away from each other again.

"I was in deep with Goryn," Dymian explained, his voice weak. He shoved another wad of hunter's leaf into his mouth. "You know how it is with me . . . Once I get betting, I know a good run is just over the next hill. So I bet I could bag ten jackrabbits with any hawk of his choosing. He gave me a little sharp-shinned dwarf hawk. A tiny male. It was an insult! Goryn's idea of humor. But a bet's a bet . . . I bagged six jack-rabbits. *Six*, can you believe it? Even one would've been a miracle with a bug-eating bird like that. But I still had to pay. I couldn't. So we went double or nothing on a day at the pits. I was doing well early—"

"We know how well you did," Kylee grunted.

Dymian looked at his feet. "I didn't *want* to bet against you, Bry, but that long-hauler was huge. I couldn't imagine you'd pull off a win. I'm so sorry . . ." Dymian's lip quivered. A stream of tears fell down his cheeks. Brysen wiped them with his thumb, held Dymian's hand. "When you won, I was happy for you, really . . . but I have to pay my rent. Months back, plus food, and a drink every now and then. Chicks for my little Sabi, and you know the Tamirs bought out all my debt from the feed dealers. They called it all due. *All of it*, can you believe that? Stupid Goryn's trying to prove he's a businessman so his mother will let him rule over his sisters. I couldn't pay. It was a fortune. They were gonna sell me to a slaver's caravan."

"You should've let them," Kylee muttered. "Least you'd be alive."

"I'd die in a cage," Dymian objected. "I had to find another way."

"So . . . was it your idea?" Brysen asked, terrified that this had been going on so long and he hadn't noticed, hadn't even sensed any trouble. Did Dymian really keep so much from Brysen when Brysen's soul was wide open to him? He tried not to make Dymian's pain all about himself, but it stung anyway.

Dymian took a deep breath. "It was Goryn's," he said. "Last night, he made an offer. Told me that all would be forgiven if I trapped him a ghost eagle." Dymian looked at his leg. "Some good I'll be at that now."

Brysen felt his own knees wobble. They didn't speak of that bird. Whenever its shriek echoed down from the mountains, they acted as if they couldn't hear it.

No one spoke of the ghost eagle around them, either. That was Six Villages custom. When a trapper was lost to the ghost eagle, you didn't mention it in front of the family. It was a tradition of silence honored for generations, and in a breath, Dymian had broken it. Twice.

It took just as little time for Brysen to say the next words, words he'd never have said if he took any longer to think about them: "I'll get it for you."

"Brysen, no," his sister gasped, or maybe she'd just thought so loud that he heard her voice in his own head.

But he knew this was what he was meant to do. This was what his father never could. He'd gone into the mountain filled with rage, and it had been his death. Brysen would go as an act of love, and he'd survive.

He grabbed Dymian's face in his hands, lifted it to meet his eyes. "I will do this for you. I swear it, Dymian. I *will* save you. I will pull down the sky itself to save you."

And he would have to do just that.

9

HE WAS ON HIS FEET AND OUT OF THE TENT BEFORE HIS SISTER COULD stop him, but she was on his tail faster than a grouse flushed from the brush.

"You can't do this," she called after him. "You *know* you can't."

"Who's looking after the tent?" he asked her without glancing back, weaving his way through the crowded market.

"Dymian can handle it."

"Dymian's leg is broken."

"Right, so shouldn't you be with him?"

"Don't do that," Brysen warned her. "Don't try to play me."

She knew him well enough not to reply.

"Peregrine eggs!" a birdnester shouted as they passed him. "Buy as they are. Some may hatch, some may not. Try your luck and get the deal of the season. Three bronze for one, eight for three!"

"Go back, Kylee. You won't talk me out of this," Brysen warned her.

"You're leaving?" Kylee had to jog to catch up to him. "Just like that. You're running off to play trapper in the mountains?"

"What?" Brysen stopped and turned on her. How dumb did his sister think he was? "Of course I'm not running off to the mountains *right now*! I have to get supplies, pack, and prepare. Right now I'm going to see Goryn to tell him to leave Dymian alone until I get back."

"He could kill you as easily as a . . . as a . . . a . . . ghost eagle could." She stumbled on the words. They sounded unnatural coming out of her mouth. Still, Brysen couldn't bring himself to say them at all.

"I'm not afraid of danger," he said instead, which sounded childish, but his sister *was* treating him like a child. "You won't stop me this time."

"This time? What do you mean by—?" But then recognition spread across her face. "Oh," she said.

"Yeah," he said back, squaring his shoulders and pretending

to be unmoved by the memory he'd just conjured for both of them. He marched through the gate and up the path to the front door of the Broken Jess, Kylee just behind him.

The air inside was thick with the smoke of dozens of scented water pipes. The long tables were packed. People of all colors, shapes, and sizes were squeezed side by side on the knobby benches, puffing away at the hoses on the end of the central pipes and exhaling the sickly sweet stench. Behind them were their hawks and falcons, all hooded and tethered to their perches. The variety of birds matched the variety of people. Brysen couldn't tell which had the brighter plumage. Everyone wore their finest for market day, and they all glanced up at him when he walked in. Then they glanced away.

Up above, in one of the private areas, the three long-haulers from the day before looked down at him with the scowls of men who weren't used to losing. The Orphan Maker had a scabby crimson crag running from his hairline to his beard. Shara's parting gift. Brysen gave the men a winged salute across his chest and a sarcastic smile.

"I hope it gets infected," he mumbled through his smile as the long-haulers turned away. He shoved a fresh wad of hunter's leaf into his mouth. The leaf tasted bitter on his tongue, and Kylee's judgmental glare was hardly sweet, either.

"For my nerves," he told her as they strolled through the pub. Bits of conversation at the tables chirped around them.

". . . went up into the mountains with a fake parchment and twenty guides and trappers. Not one came down again."

"Ghost eagle got 'em?"

"Eagle or Kartami."

"There's no Kartami this far in."

"They hit the bronze pits at Rishl last week."

"That was bandits."

"I know what I know. Kartami are marching. The kyrg herself couldn't pay enough for me to work out beyond the . . ."

Brysen lost the rest of the conversation through the noise. At the base of the stairs, a woman with long, braided black hair and bread-kneading knuckles blocked his way. Those hands could crush the eyes right out of his sockets if she wanted them to, but he was more worried about the six-talon whip she wore on the belt that cinched her cloak closed. He spat into the big brass spittoon next to her.

"I need to see Goryn, Mem Yasha," he said, hooking his thumbs and giving her the winged salute.

"He's busy," Yasha grunted. Her lower lip came over her

upper lip, which gave her face the look of a wild boar. "The market's on."

"Is it?" Brysen mocked. "I hadn't noticed."

She grunted, and Kylee elbowed him in the side.

"Look, Yasha, he'll want to see me," Brysen explained. "Tell him it's Brysen from Skybreaker Falconry. Dymian's . . . friend."

"I know who you are, Brysen. Since you were born." She jerked her chin at Kylee. "And I know she's no friend of Dymian's."

"I'm coming with him," Kylee said firmly. "We're seeing Goryn together."

"You're seeing Goryn if I say you're seeing Goryn." Yasha looked up the steps to a pair of narrow double doors. The stairs were original stonework from the temple that had stood in this spot before the pub's existence. One of Goryn's attendants—the Tamirs would never call them *bodyguards*— looked down at Brysen. It was the same one he'd kicked in the chest not a hare's nap ago.

Brysen felt suddenly how a rabbit must feel, shuddering in the brush when a hawk is overhead. He couldn't stay still, but if he ran, he'd run right into danger.

The man nodded, and Yasha stepped aside to let them pass.

"What do you think you can do by coming here with me?" he whispered to Kylee as they climbed the steps.

"Keep you from getting killed, maybe," she whispered back.

"I've kept myself alive so far," he replied.

"Barely."

"You can still go home," the guard at the top of the stairs told them. "Nothing's done that can't be undone."

"Thanks for the tip," Brysen replied, puzzled that the attendant would care enough to warn them off. It was another reminder that in the Six Villages, you'd always be what you always were, and Brysen would always be Yzzat's unfortunate son.

Until he changed things. Until he captured a ghost eagle. Then they'd tell different stories about him. Ymal the Cask-Breaker, Valyry the Gloveless, and Brysen.

As he and his sister stepped through the doors into the darkness, he thought how he'd need a good epithet. Something fitting for the legendary hero he was about to become. Brysen the Heartstrong. Brysen the Limitless. Brysen the Boy Who Didn't Die in Goryn Tamir's Office.

He'd have been happy with any of those for the moment, especially the last one.

10

THE DOORS SLAMMED SHUT, AND KYLEE AND BRYSEN STOOD IN A
pitch-black chamber. Brysen felt Kylee's hand brush against his,
and, out of habit, he took it.

The room shuddered and began to sink. Gears clanked and
cables strained. The chamber was a cage in the walls of the
Broken Jess attached to a pulley system that could raise and
lower it into the crypt below. The only way in or out of Goryn
Tamir's private office was by this moving cage, the only one
like it outside of the Sky Castle. Everyone knew about it, but
Brysen had never expected to ride in it. It was quieter than
he'd imagined and smelled like oiled ropes.

As the chamber sank, they passed the turning gear wheel in a torch-lit wall niche. It was lit purely for the benefit of the passengers. The unfortunate souls operating the gear couldn't see a thing by the firelight around them. They were hooded and hobbled.

There were five of them, a mix of men and women, all stripped down to tatters of cloth and all with heavy leather hoods over their heads—human-size replicas of falcon hoods. The hoods were bolted at the back so they couldn't be removed. Only the prisoner's lower jaws were visible, and they breathed, panting, through their mouths.

They were chained to each other by the ankles, again with heavy leather anklets and thick corded jesses, imitating a falconer's equipment, but custom-made in human size. *Someone made these hoods*, Brysen thought. Someone in the Villages had done sketches and estimated a price to make them. Some artisan was complicit in the Tamirs' cruelty. Then again, everyone who paid any piece of bronze their way was complicit. Including Brysen.

The prisoners' arms were pinioned behind their backs, elbows out and hands tied at their waists, so the bent elbows resembled wings. In the bend of the elbows, the long wooden spindle of the gear shaft had been thrust and secured with a cross bar. They trudged sadly forward in a slow circle, turning the gear that lowered and raised the small chamber.

The turn of the shaft and the circling of the sorry souls was a pale imitation of a falcon's circumscribed flight, and the alcove in which they circled had been painted—again, for the visitors' benefit only—in a sky-blue color with puffy white clouds. This was Goryn's sense of humor and his gift for cruelty, which in some men were exactly the same thing.

Brysen let go of his sister's hand. She didn't need to know his palms were sweaty.

The chamber sank below the circling slaves, its roof cutting off the sight of their heads, then necks, then chests, like the dark devouring them from above. Kylee breathed beside Brysen and their breaths fell into a quiet rhythm until the cage clanged to a stop, shuddered, and settled. After an interminable wait in the pitch black, the doors squealed open and the chamber flooded with light and noise and music.

Goryn's office was neither the bleak dungeon his prisoners at the wheel suggested nor the stodgy counting house his official title—Master of Ledgers—implied.

It was an underground party. The walls were painted dark red, and large glass chandeliers hung from the ceiling. The colorful glass was shaped like curled ribbons of fabric, styled like a market tent. Piles of thick carpets were stacked around the floors, and Tamir's attendants, friends, hangers-on, and business associates sat on top of them. Servants in white aprons came and went through indigo-blue doors at the far end, bearing silver trays of food and pungent water pipes.

There wasn't a ledger book in sight.

"He works here?" Brysen marveled.

"He wouldn't keep the family's accounts where his sisters could look for them," Kylee said. He had a stone fortress of a house on the bluffs overlooking the village, and it was surely there where he did his work. His aviary was up there, too, a wood-and-glass building with a forest growing inside. It was rumored he had over a hundred kinds of hawks and falcons. A few eagles, too.

Down here, there wasn't so much as a peacock feather. Brysen noticed that none of the men and women at the tables had birds with them. There were no perches, no cages or boxes. It was a rare sight, especially at this time of year, and an unsettling one. Maybe just taking away something familiar was enough to cloud a person's judgment.

Had Brysen's judgment been clouded by the thought of Dymian being taken away?

It had, but he didn't care. A hawk wasn't rational. No guilt, no memory, and no reasoning. It just felt, instantly and purely, everything it could feel, and it acted just as fast. People put too much faith in thinking when the heart's commands deserved at least as much respect as the mind's.

Is that why my heart's beating so loudly now?

At the far end of the room was a pile of carpets higher than any other, and it was on this that Goryn Tamir sat, alone, reclining against lush blue cushions along the wall. A squat candelabra burned bright in front of him, and light from oil lamps on the wall above flickered off the ribbons of glass to cast colorful patchwork patterns across his face. The colors danced, but Goryn sat still as a predator, heavy-lidded eyes half-closed. His carpet pile looked oddly lumpy, and it was only then that Brysen saw the legs sticking out from under it, tied in place to the floor. Goryn Tamir was suffocating someone beneath his seat.

Brysen wished he hadn't let go of Kylee's hand.

A servant led them to Goryn—one of his hands was missing a finger, Brysen noticed—and conversation hushed as they passed. Brysen's eyes found, sticking out from underneath the piles of carpets, a hand here and a sandaled foot there. Every pile had one of Goryn's enemies underneath it, or an unruly servant, or anyone who displeased him, suffocating. One wrong move, Brysen feared, and he and his sister would be lucky to end up tied to the gear wheel in the wall niche.

"Did I not just leave you cowering over that clip-winged hawk master?" Goryn asked when they stood in front of him. Brysen did his best to keep his eyes up and not glance at the barely squirming legs crushed beneath the heap of rugs. "Why would you bother me again before I've even had a bite of lunch? Did you know I get very moody when I'm hungry? My mother says I was always this way. Terrible biter. Once I couldn't get a snack, and I bit the finger off one of my house-boys. Mother gave me quite a beating for that, but she laughed the entire time. You should have seen the boy's face when I gave the finger to my little climber's falcon. He never forgot my snack again, did he?"

Goryn winked at the nine-fingered servant behind them. "No, ser," he said. Goryn waved him away.

Brysen bit down to squeeze more juice from the hunter's leaf in his cheek. No going back now. "I want to keep Dymi-an's promise to you," he announced.

Now Goryn frowned. "No time for small talk, eh? Rude." He gestured for Brysen to sit. Brysen looked again at the legs sticking out of the carpet pile. Goryn saw him look. "Sit down," he repeated.

Brysen heard himself whimper, but he crossed his legs and sat, glad for the first time for his small size. Maybe he didn't weigh enough to make a difference? Maybe the person below was already beyond suffering?

"My brother doesn't know what he's saying, Ser Goryn," Kylee cut in. She had not yet sat; she hadn't been invited to.

"We'll be paying off our debt when the market ends, and perhaps Dymian could have more time to pay off his, too, as a show of good faith?"

Goryn rested his palms on his knees and stretched his fingers.

"It sounds to me," he said, "like *you* don't know what your brother is saying. Is it time you're asking for, Brysen? You've come to plead for . . . what? Days? Weeks? A whole season? Are we to haggle for your man over a number of sunrises?"

"No." Brysen glared at Kylee. "I'm not here for time. I'm here to say that I'll do it. I'll get you . . ." He looked over his shoulder, glanced around the room. Everyone was listening. Talk too loud of a bird like the one he was after could get your throat slit, either by a poacher or by some fanatic of the old faith who thought chasing the great winged killer was the worst kind of blasphemy. He dropped his voice to a whisper. "I'll trap the ghost eagle for you."

Brysen was amazed at how easily it came out. How could he have been so afraid of mere words for so long? They were just a collection of sounds, air pushed through the throat, over the tongue, past the teeth. What made some words scarier than others, some sounds too dangerous to be said?

Memory.

It wasn't the words themselves that had power but the memories that stuck to words like ticks on deer, draining and infecting them. If you shut down your memory and ignored the knowing-self inside you, you could say anything.

"I will capture a ghost eagle," Brysen repeated, just because he could. Then, feeling the buzz of confidence, or perhaps the hunter's leaf, he picked up a copper mug from the tray in front of Goryn and spat into it.

Goryn ran his tongue over his teeth.

"You've seen your brother training?" he spoke at last. Brysen shot Kylee a sideways glance.

"Yeah, I've seen him training," she said.

"And what sort of falconer is he?" Goryn asked. "Can he do this thing? I'd hate to leave my books unbalanced just to have another member of your family die on a mountain. You haven't got that many left to spare."

"He's a good trapper," Kylee said at last.

"Good enough for this?"

"Is anyone?" Kylee replied, which brought a smile to Goryn's face.

"You're a good talker, Kylee, but it's very obvious that you're avoiding my question. There are others on the mountain as we speak, looking for the very same bird. They are better trained, better funded."

"They aren't from here," Brysen interjected. "Spoiled nobles and fools with guidebooks . . . I'm from these mountains. I have a trapper's blood."

"You also have the blood of an Altari, if I'm not mistaken?" Goryn cleared his throat. "I assume your mother would not approve of this expedition?"

"She doesn't matter," Brysen snapped. Goryn raised an eyebrow at him but returned his attention to Kylee, which made him want to throw his spit cup in the scuzzard's face.

"I'm told that you have certain talents that might be of use," Goryn said to Kylee. "Will you help your brother capture what I want?"

"I don't need her help." Brysen didn't give his sister a chance to answer. *He* would be the one to save Dymian. He *had* to be the one. "She's not a falconer."

"That's not what I hear."

"Your spies should use their eyes instead of their ears," Brysen told him. "They can't believe every crazy thing they hear. They see me flying raptors every day. She plans to leave the business the moment our debts are paid."

In his peripheral vision, he saw Kylee tense. She didn't think he knew her plan, but they were twins. How could he not know?

"This true?" Goryn pursed his lips. "Retiring so young?"

Kylee shook her head. "I don't have to. We can add Dymian's debt to ours." Her voice broke, but she pushed through it. "What's another few seasons of business? We've made it this long."

"Kylee, no," Brysen said. For himself, he didn't care if he stayed trapped in the Villages if it meant saving Dymian's life, but he couldn't bear to keep Kylee caged, too. He wouldn't let her sacrifice her happiness that way—not because of him. "You stay and work our tent. I'm doing this alone."

"Business is going to get worse in the times ahead," Goryn said. "Haven't you heard about the Kartami raids? Who knows if there will even be a market next season?"

"We'll find a way," she said. "We always have. Even if it means I have to start training with—" Goryn held up his powerful hand to silence her. He studied Brysen and Kylee with the distant focus of a cropped-up falcon, a bird that wasn't at all hungry but was still curious about the prey in front of it.

"So you're keen to go all on your own, young Brysen?"

"I am," Brysen repeated. He looked straight at Kylee. "I have to."

"Then you'll go," Goryn declared with a clap. "Maybe your sister will come to her senses and help you, but regardless, you will get me what I want. Do you understand that you are making this promise to me? You know who I am. You know how I treat those who break their promises. Fail me and you should hope the eagle has taken you, because death will be a lot quicker in its talons than in mine." Then he rested his eyes on Kylee. "And your sister will inherit your debt to me. Doubled."

A small noise escaped Kylee's lips, and Brysen wanted to turn to her, to comfort her, to tell her it would be okay, he had a plan, he could do this, they'd all be okay, but in truth, he wasn't so sure. He knew, however, that it was now too late. He could show no weakness and no doubt.

"I understand," he said. Threats didn't scare him. He'd lived through enough pain to know that real danger didn't threaten; it simply struck, like a falcon's dive.

Scuzz it, he thought. He'd been the scuttling prey for too long. It was time to be the talon that crushed the rabbit. He'd catch his prey and save Dymian, his sister, and himself, all in one fell swoop.

"Dymian stays here, though," Goryn added. "If he tries to leave town, our deal is off."

"I understand," Brysen repeated. "He's in no shape to help, anyway. You broke his leg."

"Oops." There was a giddy twinkle in Goryn's eye. "So you'll go alone, like the great trappers of old?"

Brysen nodded.

"Bry, no," Kylee pleaded, her voice no louder than a breath.

"We're done here." Goryn waved a servant to show them out. Brysen stood carefully, trying to keep his weight even until he was off the rug pile. It was the least he could do for the poor soul beneath.

"You have until the last of the convoys leave the market," Goryn explained. "Come a moment later and our deal's off." His eyes shot down to the copper cup Brysen had used as a spittoon. "And keep the mug. Hunter's leaf is a disgusting habit."

Brysen spat again. He wasn't about to take health and etiquette lessons from Goryn Tamir.

"I just hope you know what to do with the eagle once you get it," Brysen said. "It'd be a shame to see it disembowel you after I've gone through all this trouble." He set the copper mug back down on the tray, letting his bright green spit slosh over the sides as he left it behind and strode back to the pulley chamber, treating Kylee like she was invisible.

He knew that if he looked at his sister, reality would come back to him. He knew that if he looked at her, he'd realize what he'd just agreed to do and how ill-prepared he was to do it. He'd be tempted to beg for her help, but he'd already sworn to himself never to do that.

Not from her.

Not again.

ALL THINGS TRUE

IN THE SKY CASTLE, KYRG BARDU UNWOUND THE MESSAGE FROM THE
pigeon's ankle and gently placed the bird back into the pigeon
loft. "Goryn Tamir has made a deal with some Six Villages
kids"—she shut her eyes, reflected on the absurdity of her next
statement—"to capture a ghost eagle."

"Kids?" Her hawk master frowned. Beneath its ornate hood,
the falcon on his fist looked like it was frowning, too.

"Apparently, one of these young eyasses showed a remark-
able talent at the battle pits yesterday." Kyrg Bardu's mouth
twisted around the words *battle pits*. She found the whole prac-
tice vulgar. She was an avid pigeon racer, and given her

position as proctor of the Council of Forty at the Sky Castle, she was able to maintain the finest flock of homers, racers, tumblers, and divers from one end of the plateau to the other. She kept falcons and eagles, too, of course, as she must, but merely for appearances. Raptors did not terribly interest her.

The pigeons, on the other hand, were a sign of her power. She could fly a flock, confident that any falconer who mistakenly took one of her little pigeons with their bird of prey would pay for it fivefold. Such was the royal prerogative, and its enforcement on behalf of the most common members of the avian family reminded everyone of their position relative to hers. Power, like a hawk, needed careful tending and frequent flight if it was to stay keen to its purpose.

She was content to let Lywen, her very well paid hawk master, manage the care and training of her raptors. He enjoyed the status it gave him; it didn't hurt that he was her nephew.

"We have our own expeditions in the mountains, as you know," Lywen said. "They are after gyrfalcons and various eagles, but they are always looking for signs of more precious sport."

Kyrg Bardu snorted. She had no faith in the loyalty of trappers, who'd sell their catch to the highest bidder. For now that bidder was the Council of Forty, but as the Kartami grew they might have the metal to begin buying for themselves. They'd been more aggressive of late, raiding camps and convoys in the grasslands on the edge of the desert, moving toward the foothills. She had reports that they'd entered the trade of stolen raptors, using smugglers and sympathetic Altari in good standing to sell the most valuable birds they captured, in some cases ransoming them back to the very Uztari they'd stolen from. None would publicly admit that they'd paid a ransom to the Kartami, but many had.

Kyrg Bardu wanted to make paying a raptor's ransom a crime, but she had no support among the lesser kyrgs. Perhaps as these hordes of kite warriors got closer to the foothills, support for her idea would grow. In government, fear was a much more effective tool than reason. Only when their own safety was threatened would the rest of the Forty do as she demanded. Until then, she would manage the threat with the tools she had.

"If Goryn Tamir has tethered his hopes to these nestlings in the mountains, then he has reason to believe they'll succeed." She wrote some instructions for Lywen to distribute, sealed with her signet: a dove clutching a falcon in its talons. She'd designed it herself upon her ascension to proctorship of the Council of Forty. The design had been quite a scandal at the time, but all scandals lose their sting with the balm of familiarity. The other thirty-nine kyrgs of the Council would tolerate her eccentricities as long as they prospered, and for now, they prospered. As long as their prosperity continued, so would her power. "If my spies are to be believed, the girl has a gift from which we might benefit."

"As I understand, only the boy is going on this expedition," the hawk master said. "Something to do with the estranged Avestri boy . . . their youngest, Dymian."

"The boy?" Kyrg Bardu looked back down at the parchment she'd received from the Six Villages. "My note doesn't say anything about the boy."

"Perhaps your spy is mistaken?"

The kyrg shook her head. "The girl is the key. We must make sure she takes this journey."

"The Tamirs won't like us meddling in their business."

"The Tamirs have no title. They can choose not to like whatever they wish. If young Goryn Tamir wants to complain, he can come see me and explain himself. I should like to hear his explanation, in fact. I wonder if his sisters or mother approve of this little expedition?"

"You know he won't come to you." Lywen stroked the bottom feathers of the falcon's tail.

"If I end up with the eagle he's after, he'll have no choice, will he? Now, I don't want to discuss this anymore."

"It's not merely an *eagle*—"

"I said *no more*," Kyrg Bardu cut him off. She'd had enough talk of the Tamirs and their schemes for the morning. "Send a message to Yval Birgund. I'd like to speak with him about the Kartami's movements. I want to know where they're going before the shadows of their kites fall on the castle itself."

"Yval is in the Six Villages," Lywen said. "For the market. Purchasing birds for the eastern battalion. As you commanded."

"He went himself?"

"You did tell him to make the new battalion a priority. He takes your instruction to heart. He's a keen and loyal counselor."

Kyrg Bardu pinched the bridge of her nose. "*Loyal counselor?* That's an oxymoron. Does anyone else know what his business at the market is?"

"He has kept it a secret, although I do fear that, like all things in the Villages, it is an *open* secret."

"Another one. You're fond of them today."

"When a hawk master studies to earn his seal, he learns that all things are bound to and by their opposites," Lywen replied. "Truth and falsehood, predator and prey, hunter and hunted, light and shadow, good and evil."

"And power?" Kyrg Bardu asked.

"Especially power," said Lywen. "Power is, and will forever be, tethered to its own weakness."

Kyrg Bardu looked at the falcon on her hawk master's fist.

It was a great killing bird. The power of its speed in flight required bones so light that she could snap its neck with one hand. It would be a crime, of course, and a cruel sin, too, but there was in her always that temptation to push the limits of her own power and therefore find those limits in others.

She wondered about the ghost eagle, if it was, like they said, a creature of power without weakness, untethered to its own destruction, the exception that proved the rule. What could someone like Goryn Tamir do with one? What could she herself do?

And why should two country nestlings be trusted to capture it?

She began to write another letter. Perhaps it was good that her defense counselor had gone off to the Six Villages after all. If those children failed, it hardly mattered, but he would be perfectly positioned to take action on the chance they succeeded. If the accounts of the girl's gifts were true, she could prove as valuable to the defense of Uztar as a hundred falconers in the field.

And surely the kyrg's enemies knew it, too. Kyrg Bardu had many more pigeons to dispatch before the day was done.

KYLEE

FISTBOUND

11

BRYSEN PACKED LIKE A LITTLE BOY: ALL SNARES AND ROPES AND treats. Packets of candied ginger and hunter's leaf, but no bandages or herbal medicines or hard sausage. Not even a change of underclothes.

"I'll be on the mountain alone," he said. "So what if I stink?"

"You'll need layers," Kylee suggested, pulling down their heaviest cloak, a full boar pelt. "It gets cold in the Gap, even in full sunlight."

"I know it gets cold in the Gap," Brysen snapped at her, pushing the cloak away. He'd rather freeze than admit he was wrong. "Stop staring at me. You're making that face of yours."

"It's my normal face."

"You ever think maybe that's a problem?"

Kylee sat down on the edge of his feather mattress. It was lumpy from his tossing and turning. The mattress had been a lavish purchase after the first market they'd run together without their father. She and Brysen had never had beds or mattresses before, always sleeping on the floor under moth-eaten blankets. The mattresses cost most of what they'd earned from selling the poorly bred and barely manned hawks left over from their father's last real trapping expedition. It wasn't enough for the ice-wind season, and their mother had never been able to save so much as a bronze chip from their father's appetites. They would've starved without their father that first season if the town hadn't been so charitable. Meat, vegetables, beans, grains . . . they showed up in baskets every week, brought up the hill by flocks of crows with finely carved whistles on their tails. The small wood instruments trilled and moaned as they approached. The tail whistles on mourners' crows were all the same, so no one would know who had sent the charity and there would be no reason to refuse it.

Not that they would have refused it.

Only Yves Tamir—Goryn's oldest sister—came in person to deliver her charity, and only once. She dropped eighteen bronze into Kylee's open palms, as heavy as a human head, and held her finger to her lips. "Tell no one," she said, so Kylee told her brother the moment she'd left.

The mourners' crows and their lonely songs came until the Necklace flowed again and then the charity stopped. By then, Goryn Tamir had begun to demand repayment of their father's debts, and they were forced to use the rest of his sister's gift to hire Dymian.

What a mistake that had been! *If only life could be lived backward, we'd know the mistakes not to make*, Kylee thought, *and instead of losing all we knew peck by merciless peck, time would return things to us every day, bringing back everything we didn't yet know we'd lost.*

"You're taking Shara with you?" Kylee asked, noticing as her brother packed his hawk furniture—extra jesses and leashes and swivels and the tools to repair them. A hood, a small folding perch.

"She'll hunt for me in the mountains," he explained. "That way I don't have to pack any of that *delicious* sausage you're so excited about. I'll eat fresh game. Maybe jackrabbit. She's a natural at catching it. Hardly needs coaxing at all."

The jackrabbit bit was definitely a snap at Kylee. She hadn't meant to embarrass him yesterday. When the wind came up in her, she felt as if all the air in her body and all the blood in her veins were calling out. It wasn't *her* speaking . . . not on purpose.

Since she was small, she'd run from the burning words inside her. They divided her from her brother, who could not speak them and who wanted to be great so badly that to fling this talent in his face, this talent he lacked, was too cruel to imagine. She didn't want to be different from him. She didn't want either of them to be different.

The words drove her father to jealousy. He couldn't master them himself, and he couldn't get his daughter to use them. The more she resisted the burning words, the angrier her father grew at Brysen for being the one who made her hold back. He didn't take his rage out on Kylee, because he hoped she might one day be great and, in her greatness, shine glory onto him.

But Brysen, he could blame. Brysen he could beat. It was Kylee's fault; she knew it, had always known it. These burning words were the weapon with which she caused her brother so much pain. It was a stupid mistake yesterday to let them out in public, a stupid mistake she feared that she had not yet begun to pay for. Everyone had seen, and Vyvian had even *heard*.

You can be careful your whole life, Kylee thought, *but mess up just once and you threaten it all.*

But now she was only trying to help. She wasn't the one who'd made bad bets with the Tamir family. She wasn't the one who'd made an impossible promise to Goryn, and she wasn't the one running off in the middle of the market. Brysen had no right to be mad at her. With one impulsive gesture, he'd thrown their entire future into doubt, all their plans, all their hopes. She wondered, unkindly, if he'd done it on purpose. Knowing she wanted to leave falconry behind, he was tethering her to it.

Of course, that wasn't his way. He'd never deliberately try to hurt her. He just didn't think that far ahead, for himself or anyone else. He was a dreamer, not a schemer.

He shoved the last of his supplies into the bag, hung his falconer's glove from his belt, checked the black-talon blade and resheathed it, then threw on his long goatskin jacket. He walked from his room, past the central hearth, and didn't even look at the chair where their mother sat watching the fire, mouthing a prayer for forgiveness. Or destruction. It was hard to tell the difference with her.

He headed for the mews to grab Shara, and Kylee followed him. She felt stupid chasing her brother around like a duckling, but what choice did she have?

Their feet clicked on the stones.

The mews were quiet, reminding her that she'd left Dymian with five raptors, a shattered leg, and a head dulled by hunter's leaf down in the market, looking after their future while Brysen tried to save his life. Maybe he'd have the good sense to open for business. Maybe he wouldn't steal the money he got if he did. Wishful thinking.

"Don't take Shara," she warned Brysen. "You know a bird on the fist will only enrage the ghost eagle. Either she flies away before you get close, or she snatches Shara before you even hear her coming."

She loathes companionship in herself and others and will tear the head from any raptor that dares to find its solace on the fist, wrote Ymal in his ancient *Guide to the Sighting and Capture of the Ghost Eagle.* Only fragments of the book survived, and some were contradictory, but they were invaluable for any who would dare approach the eagle on its mountain. Another fragment warned, *Take care of your own birds, for the ghost eagle sees the respect you show all her avian sisters and counts offenses against them double.*

Kylee was certain Brysen hadn't read the book. He wasn't really a reader.

"I can protect Shara," he told her, unhooding his hawk and unhooking her leash from the perch to attach it to a longer cord on his belt. "I always have."

He rested his finger on a spot at his wrist and Shara playfully nipped at it, then followed it with her head as he moved it around, curious eyes eager, her little tongue nearly hanging out like a dog's. The moment his finger stopped she nipped again, not enough to hurt him, just enough to show she knew where she stopped and he began. It was a little game they played. Kylee wondered why he'd teach her to play a game that could so easily end with him bleeding, but the boy and the bird both seemed to enjoy it. Maybe he liked that she could hurt him and chose not to. Almost everyone else in his life made a different choice when they had the chance.

Brysen touched Shara on the back of her leg, and she stepped onto his fist. With another nudge and short whistle, she flew to his shoulder. His jacket was made for a traveling falconer, with thick padding on the arms, a special bar under the cloth on the left side, and loops below it to tie the leash to, so the bird could be perched while he walked and he wouldn't have to rely on her to follow free the entire journey.

Shara preened and looked over Brysen's head. When she tried to nip at his hair, one quick whistle warned her to stop. Brysen had mastered her well, but the thought was not a comfort to Kylee. Shara had taken him years to train, and she was as much like a ghost eagle as she was like a handsaw. Brysen was hardly great with a handsaw, either.

A vein in her brother's tight jaw was pulsing, and Kylee felt the rhythm of his heartbeat in her own. How could they be so far apart when they were so close together? How could she, in moments of fear and anger, speak unknown words to birds of prey but couldn't find the right words to say to her own twin?

"I said stop looking at me like that," he told her. "I'm not an idiot. I've got a plan."

He started assembling a second pack with iron stakes for the snare lines and a net, each strand inscribed with words in the Hollow Tongue, whose presence on a trap was supposed to bring luck.

Kylee couldn't take it anymore. He'd rely on dead languages and half-mad birds, but wasn't going to ask her for help? His stupid pride.

"I'll come with you," she offered. "I can help you. I can at least watch your back."

He stopped packing and froze, a coil of spider-silk binding rope halfway into the sack.

"I'll come with you to the mountain," she said. "I can get someone else to look after Ma. That Crawling Priest will check in on her."

Brysen took a deep breath. "You'll come with me," he repeated.

Kylee nodded, but Brysen wasn't looking at her. "Yes," she said.

"What about the business?" he said. "What about making enough bronze to shut down for good?"

"Dymian can look after the business. He owes us that much. And—" She cleared her throat. "If we have to stay open longer, then we will. What's another season or two?"

"You don't want to do that." Brysen dropped the rope into the bag and cinched it shut. He moved for the door, but she stepped in front of him, forcing him to look at her. Brysen's ice-blue eyes made her flinch when they met hers, filled with a too-familiar fury.

She did not look away. "You're right," she said. "But I *want* to come with you more. I want to help you."

He clenched his jaw. The muscles bulged all the way down his neck, and he took a deep breath in, held it a moment. "You're too late," he said at last. "Way too late."

He left her there, letting the door of the mews slam behind him as he stomped away without a good-bye. Kylee felt herself reeling. The invisible tether that bound them to each other snapped back, and she felt the strain on her heart, the pull as she was tossed, like a falcon from the glove, back in time, back to before, back and back and back, and the brutal magic of memory left her no escape.

The past pinned her in its talons, mantled its wings over her mind, and would not release her until she lived it all again, that one night, two seasons before their father went up the mountain and didn't come back, the memory as fresh and brutal as it was the first time, as it was every single time.

12

BRYSEN WAS CRYING WHEN HE RAN ACROSS THE YARD TO KYLEE, stones clicking under his feet until he hit the grass and sprinted.

She'd been practicing her knots under the shade of the wide ash tree behind the house. Valyry the Gloveless had written that there was no greater magic than the knot. With a simple twist of hand and rope, one could bind any creature to oneself at will and unbind them again just as easily. To the unmastered, a strong knot was as impenetrable as the most ancient Hollow Tongue incantation.

Kylee could secure the jesses on a hawk's ankle to her glove one-handed without even looking now, and she could've even tied the thick leather anklet on an eagle, if only her fingers were bigger. She could dream the whole world and more, but her hands were too small to hold it.

As her brother ran to her, she shoved the knots into her pocket. Brysen struggled with his knots and often got a smack in the ears for making them so sloppy that one finger could loosen them. He could dream the whole world, too, but couldn't wait to grab it. More often than not, all he got was a handful of air and a fresh welt on his back.

Their father still had him spending days and days making tiny slits around the edges of leather anklets so they didn't rub the birds' skin raw, while Kylee got to learn birdcalls and hunting techniques. She didn't want Brysen to feel dumb by seeing how much further along she was than him.

He dropped to his knees in front of her, tears streaking his dirty cheeks. "I messed up bad," he cried. He wiped his nose on his sleeve. His black hair was disheveled, twigs and leaves tangled in it. "Really, really bad."

"What happened?" she asked.

"I was playing in the mews—"

"Oh, Bry, why? You know Da doesn't like—"

"Shh, okay? I know. It's just, I wanted to see if I could make Silva jump to my arm the way Da does. I practiced the whistle the same way he does it. Exactly the same. I didn't try with Silva until I was ready. I swear."

Kylee's heart sank. Silva was their father's newest catch, a male painter's eagle, brightly colored and extremely rare. He planned to sell to a special client, a convoy master willing to pay a hundred bronze for such a find. It had taken Yzzat the better part of three weeks just to get the bird to jump to his arm without bating from the perch, shrieking, or plucking its own feathers out. Painter's eagles were notoriously difficult to train. They'd often die rather than submit.

"I wanted to show Da I could do it," Brysen said. "He always tells me I'm a good-for-nothing scuzz-guzzler, but I was *sure* I could do this. I can make Shara jump whenever I want. I put the big glove on and everything, but I left Silva on his leash. I didn't want him to escape."

Kylee felt her heart slow down again. At least the bird hadn't escaped.

"So I came up to him and whistled," he said. "But Silva panicked." Brysen bit his lip. He was fighting tears again. "He bated straight off his perch and then flew at me, like he was gonna attack. I ducked, and he dove for me . . . and . . . and . . ."

"What?" Kylee grabbed him by the shoulders. "What happened?"

"When he dove, I dropped the leash. He . . . he flew off with it still attached. Right out of the mews! He's gone! With his leash on!" He was sobbing now.

"It's okay," Kylee comforted him. "It's okay. We can find him. I'll help you. You know what to do: Listen. Listen for the crows."

Brysen shook his head. He was crying so hard, he couldn't speak. He couldn't stop. Kylee told him to wait, to calm down while she got the eagle back for him. She ran down to the mews, click-clicking along the stones. *Click click. Click click.*

She stood at the door and looked out, tried to imagine where the eagle would go. She listened for the sound of frightened crows. That was the trick. When a bird of prey was around, crows and ravens got frantic, calling out warnings to one another in shrill, agitated tones. Brysen was bawling too hard to hear from where she'd left him under the ash tree, but just up the hill, the crows were screaming. Kylee ran up and saw the mob around a juniper tree, screeching and flapping their black wings wildly.

An eagle could certainly defend itself, even against a small murder of crows. The situation couldn't be *that* bad.

As she drew closer, Kylee saw it *was* that bad. Worse.

Bright feathers littered the ground below the tree, and

through the riot of crows, she saw the eagle itself hung upside down in a spiderweb of leather. The leash had tangled in the gnarly branches, and in trying to fly off, the eagle had wrapped its legs and tangled its wings. As it tried to escape, it made the tangle worse, breaking its feathers and choking itself on its own leash. The eagle hung like a cutpurse from an executioner's tree.

It was dead.

Their father's hundred-bronze eagle was dead.

And now the crows were tearing it apart.

Kylee's hands shook, and she felt the burning wind grow inside her. Her whole body tingled and her heart raced. She knew what was coming, could feel it, but couldn't stop it. The air scorched her lungs, and she had to let it out. She opened her mouth.

"*Shyehnaah,*" she whispered. Suddenly, a mature male peregrine screeched down from the pure-blue sky. The crows scattered. The wild falcon flew through the flock like demon's lightning, striking one crow instantly dead with the impact and swooping up as the others gave chase. The enraged birds followed the falcon higher and higher and away over the jagged ridge line, seeking vengeance. Crows are quick to scatter but quick, too, to regroup. Resilient birds, far more than falcons. *I'd gladly join a murder of crows*, she thought, frightening herself with her brief blasphemy. The devilish mob had left the eagle hanging alone in the juniper tree, mutilated, with one dead crow lying beneath.

Kylee leaned against the trunk and wept. She wept for fear of the word she'd spoken without knowing why, without knowing how, and she wept for her brother and the suffering that was sure to come. From her pocket, she pulled the expertly tied knots and tossed them away, disgusted with herself. If she'd been with Brysen, he'd never have gotten Silva tangled up. He'd never have been playing in the mews in the first place. She should've been protecting him instead of playing with knots.

When Kylee came back to the old ash tree, her brother wasn't there. She found him at the hearth shoving candied ginger into a sack, along with a child's blade, a fire-starting stone, and the moth-eaten blanket he slept under.

Shara watched him pack, perched on a dangling frying pan. Her eyes followed his finger, mouth open, ready to play their little pecking game.

"Prrpt," she said.

"Not now," Brysen told her.

"Prrpt."

"Not. Now." He glared at her, wiped his eyes, and then went back to shoving things into his bag.

"What are you doing?" Kylee asked.

"I'm going," he said. "I'm running away."

"You can't run away! Where will you go? The ice-wind's starting any day now. You'll freeze. You'll starve."

"I'll make a fire. I'll hunt. Shara will help me."

"You don't know how to do any of that! You've never even flown her free."

"You're good at that stuff," he said. "Come with me."

"What?" Kylee swallowed.

"I can't stay here. Da's gonna—" His voice cracked. "I can't stay. Come with me. We'll cross the mountains and join a hauling convoy. See all the places we've talked about: the Sky Castle, the crimson sands of Parsh, the bronze pits at Rishl!"

He'd stopped crying and he smiled, like he was already watching the great Parade of Masters along the Sky Castle's battlements or stargazing from the back of a three-humped camel strutting over a dune in the Parsh Desert. Like he was already gone. Already safe.

But he wasn't safe.

Kylee loved the stories they dreamed together, but she knew the real stories, too, the stories Ma told them, about when she came to the Six Villages, before she met their da. About slavers who prowled the oases on the edge of Parsh, looking for thirsty Uztari runaways and snapping them up like a kestrel eating gnats. About the Tamir orphan houses, where poor children were sent to earn their keep at the mercy of twisted adults, or the convoys of children sent up into the mountains never to be seen again. About hunger and rot foot and scorpionflies. About desert winds that stole your fingers and snapped off your ears. Not only would Brysen's beloved bird not survive—he wouldn't, either. None of them would. Their mother had fled that life for a reason!

No. Kylee couldn't run away. She couldn't run to unknown terrors when at least the hurt they knew kept them fed, kept them warm.

"Beg for mercy," she told her brother. "Maybe Da had a good day at the pits. Maybe he'll forgive you. Or just . . . just give you . . ." She couldn't believe what she was suggesting. "Just a *little* whipping."

"I can't go alone," her brother whispered, holding his bag in his little rope-burned hands.

Kylee felt another burning inside her, but it wasn't the swell of a mysterious word in her lungs; it was the cry of a word she knew too well, the same as Shara's plaintive *prrpt*.

Please, she wanted to beg. *Please don't go.*

She thrust her arms out and hugged him. She didn't want to run away. She didn't want him to run away, either. He was her best friend. She didn't need to say it. The hug told him.

As she pressed her chest to his, she felt their hearts beat

together, like one heart right in the middle, a heart they shared. But Brysen broke the hug. He pulled away.

Some falconers love their raptors so much and feed them so often from the fist that the birds forget they can fly away. On the hunt, such birds will see prey in front of them and will rouse, flapping their wings, eyes fixed to attack, but they won't fly. They won't leave the fist. Although the jesses are loosed and they are free, the birds remain, by a kind of broken love for their bondage, fistbound.

Brysen looked at Kylee the way a hunter looks at a fistbound falcon. Then he dropped his runaway bag right in the middle of the floor and, without a word, walked from the house.

Click click. Click click. Click click.

He crossed the yard, climbed the hill, and returned with the eagle's body in his arms. He sat with it in front of the eagle's empty cage in the mews to wait for their father to get home. The sun set bloodred behind the mountains.

Their father arrived home soon after dark, carrying a torch to light his way. He went straight to the mews.

Click click. Click click. Click click.

The shouting started within half a heartbeat.

Ma stood by the hearth, looking in the direction of the mews through the open door.

"Ma?" Kylee asked her, hoping she'd go down and calm their father.

Her mother shook her head, clucked sadly, and sat in the chair by the fire. When Brysen's screaming started, she held her arms out to Kylee.

"Not Shara!" Brysen shouted. "She didn't do anything! It was me!"

Kylee rushed for the door, thinking to take the blame herself, but her mother moved faster than she thought possible, grabbed her tight, and pulled her back.

"Seeing you will make it worse," she warned. Kylee struggled against her grip but couldn't break free. "Shhh, shhh." Her mother tried to soothe her, covered her ears, muffled the screams.

"*Lay la li, lay la lu, never old and never new, lay la li, lay la lu . . .*" her mother sang. Through the cracks between the mismatched wooden slats, Kylee saw the torch light, dim at first, then flaring brighter. Even through her mother's fingers and over her mother's song, she could hear Brysen scream as their father burned him.

"I'm sorry," Kylee whispered. "I'm sorry, I'm sorry, I'm sorry."

After Brysen healed, the pink scars covered half his body,

and his black hair grew back ash-gray. Shara survived the fire unscathed. He hadn't let a single spark touch her, which was more than Kylee had done for him.

The memory released her.

She opened her eyes and saw Brysen's silhouette hiking up the path above their house and into the wilderness, toward the Cardinal's Crest Ridge and the high pass above. She watched him until he disappeared around a boulder and then she watched the sky beyond. A swirling flock of blackbirds whirled and pulsed in the air, like a living cloud.

Kylee knew she was going to follow her brother, even though it meant their debts wouldn't be paid and their business would have to stay open for several seasons to come. She knew she was going to follow him, even though it meant saving that scuzzard Dymian at the cost of her own freedom, and she knew she was going to follow him whether he wanted her help or not. This time, she would not let Brysen down. Some journeys no one should have to take alone.

And besides, she'd been in those mountains before.

13

BRYSEN WOULD HAVE A HEAD START ON HER, BUT SHE COULDN'T JUST run off unprepared. She'd have to get her own supplies for the climb. She'd have to convince Dymian to look after their business as much as he could, despite how little she trusted him. She'd also have to ask someone to check in on her mother.

This was how her dreams of freedom fell apart—not in some dark debtor's dungeon but in a flurry of errands. As she returned to the market, the thought of the seasons to come landed heavy on her, and she had to lean on a fence post for a moment, take a deep breath, and stop herself from screaming. *It's not Brysen's fault*, she told herself. She wanted to believe it.

The sun had already peaked by the time she got back down to the market. Dymian, his leg wrapped in a splint, had just finished flying the dovehawk and, Kylee noticed with some surprise, had already sold the pair of kestrels.

"Nyall helped me out." Dymian pointed at his leg. "He's a good one, that kid. He also told me what Brysen is doing for me . . ."

"Mm-hmm," Kylee said without comment. "How'd you get those kestrels to fly?" She changed the subject. Both kestrels were overweight—no matter what nonsense Brysen had written in the log—and if they'd flown at all, they probably wouldn't have come back. They'd have no reason to. They weren't the least bit hungry.

Dymian grinned. "Folks are nervous to get back on the road fast. Buyer never even saw them off my glove. Just offered me ten bronze apiece. I got her to thirty for the pair." He gestured at the receipt book. "All accounted for."

"Good," she told him. "That's the least you could do."

"I know." Dymian hobbled closer to her, leaning heavily on a stick he'd turned into a crutch. Well, more likely that Nyall had. No way Dymian was that good a craftsman at his best, and he was currently far from his best. He was pale as an ice-wind sky and his hands shook as he popped another wad of hunter's leaf into his mouth. "I can't tell you how grateful I am. I don't deserve what your brother is doing for me."

"No," Kylee agreed. "You don't."

"I care about him a lot," Dymian said. "I really do."

"If you cared about him, you wouldn't have let him do this. You wouldn't have risked our future for your own."

"You know no one can stop Brysen when he's got some heroic notion," Dymian said. "It's one of the great things about him. Like Renyard wrote, 'A bird is safe in the nest, but birds are born with wings. Better to risk flying than miss out on everything.'"

"Do not recite poetry at me right now," she snapped. "Thanks to you, I have to go up after him, and I need you to look after our tent and our ma. Make sure she eats. And keep her from giving what we earn here away to the Crawling Priests."

"I'll do right by you," Dymian promised. "I'm really grateful that you're looking out for him up there. He needs you. Everyone knows he can't do this without you."

"'Everyone knows'?" Kylee frowned.

"I'll look out for Skybreaker and for your ma," Dymian assured her, and did not address her question. "They'll be in better shape than when you left them. I owe you that."

"You owe us so much more than that." She left him in the

tent with their entire livelihood. Her brother's recklessness, it seemed, was contagious.

Nyall had frowned at her as she'd passed by, but he was busy with a crowd of customers, and she didn't feel the need to stick around to tell him what she was up to. He'd try to talk her out of it, just like she'd tried to talk Brysen out of it. But the events had become an avalanche, and there was no stopping them now that they'd picked up speed. She had to let them carry her on and hope she could ride them without being crushed beneath.

"So you're really going after him?" Vyvian said, striding up beside her on the road as she made her way back toward home.

"Who said anyone was going anywhere?" Kylee responded. Vy was her friend, but that didn't mean she was trustworthy. She had her own family business, too.

"Come on, Kylee, the deal Brysen made with Goryn Tamir is a secret, which means everyone's placing bets on whether or not you're going to follow him, and I'd like to increase my odds."

"You don't gamble."

"Well, maybe I plan to start."

"When you send your report back to your family's masters, you can tell them I'm going, too," Kylee said. "We're taking the Blue Sheep Pass up to the Nameless Gap."

"And which route are you really taking?"

Kylee hesitated.

"Come on," her friend said. "This one's between us. I won't put it in the letter."

"I really have no idea," Kylee said. "Brysen's leading the way. I'm just following."

"He'll take the Cardinal's Crest Ridge," Vyvian suggested. Kylee shrugged. It was the most likely because it was the most difficult climb, and that was just the sort of challenge Brysen would add to an already impossible task, but Kylee wasn't going to give Vyvian more information than she needed.

"Like I said, I'm just gonna follow. The rest is up to him."

"So you won't help catch it?" Vyvian cocked her head. "He'll never be able to do it without you."

"He's a good trapper," she said.

"But you've got the—"

Kylee cut her off. "I'd prefer if we got nowhere near this eagle."

Vyvian sighed. "Not really an option anymore."

"No," Kylee sighed. "It's not."

"Bry's already got a pretty good head start on you. Some herders said they saw him halfway up the Sunrise Slope. You better get going, or you'll never catch up."

"I'm on my way now," Kylee told her. "Just . . . Vy, could you do me a favor?"

"I'm yours."

"Make sure Dymian doesn't do anything stupid while we're gone? If we survive, I'd love to have something to come back to."

"Of course I will." Vyvian made the winged salute across her chest. "You'll survive, by the way. I've—" She leaned in close, whispered in Kylee's ear, "I've seen what you can do."

Kylee tensed, pulled back, and looked her friend in the eyes. Shook her head. "Don't. Please. Don't say . . . anything about that."

Vyvian frowned. "I'd never betray your secret like that."

Kylee looked at her carefully. They both knew she was lying, that she'd certainly betray Kylee just *like that*. It was her livelihood and her family's tradition to betray Kylee's secrets like that. The only question was whether she had already or was about to.

"I'm not the only one who was at the battle pits, though, Kylee," Vyvian warned. "You won't be alone on that mountain. The prize you're after is too big to go uncontested. Look out for yourself, too, okay?"

"I always do," Kylee said, and left her friend in the road,

picking up the pace for home so she could pack and say good-bye to her ma.

"You're going after it then, just like your father?" Her mother was sitting in her chair in the center room, by the low-burning fire in the hearth. Her dark hair hung in long, loose coils, framing the sharp features of her face, her dark eyes blazing in the stillness of the rest of her, like twin flames dancing against a black sky. She wouldn't dare say the words *ghost eagle* aloud, not even before one had killed her husband. That made Kylee want to say the words even more.

"I don't give a scuzz about the ghost eagle," Kylee said, but didn't look at her. "I'm going after Brysen. I'm going to keep him safe."

Her mother leaned forward and stood slowly from her chair, letting her hair fall in front of her face. She placed the cup of mint-grass tea she'd been sipping onto the table, then pulled her long hair back over her shoulders. Kylee went rigid as her ma crossed the room and grabbed Kylee's biceps. Their eyes locked. "He'll never be safe with this longing for what he should not have. Nor will you. As long as you are bound to this creature, you are bound to death. When the Kartami come, this whole cult of sky lust will be wiped away. Repent it now, my daughter. Denounce it and be saved."

"I'm not like you," Kylee replied. "I can't just stop caring."

"But I *do* care," her mother said. "My sin is my own longing—my longing that you be *saved*. Redeemed. I *should* curse you, should leave you to your damnation, but I can't. I thought your father's cruelty would poison the cult of Uztar for you forever, but it didn't work. I should have taken you away. You know you can save yourself from the blasphemy of Uztar. You can simply . . . *stop*. Let your brother go. Be free. I know that is what you want."

Kylee felt her insides cracking, like a long-melting glacier finally breaking off and collapsing. She did want freedom, from the raptors, from her father's debts, and from her brother's oaths, but not on these terms. Not like this.

Kylee pulled from her mother's grip and backed toward the door, shaking her head. Her mother shook her head, too. "The Hollow Tongue's not meant to be spoken by those who walk the dirt," she said as her daughter retreated. "That's what it is, Kylee. The Hollow Tongue is a sacred thing not meant for you. No good's ever come of speaking to the sky. You, I hoped, might escape."

Kylee found the handle to the door and wrenched it open,

backing outside. Her mother collapsed to her knees, not to beg, but to stare at the floor and pray.

"Empty the skies so my children will fall; empty their hearts so they have space for the truth; empty the skies and their hearts and their sin before misery mantles over them unending; empty, empty, empty . . ."

Kylee closed the heavy door so she couldn't see or hear her mother anymore. The woman had made her choices.

Brysen was in danger. And not from some abstract superstition. His body could be destroyed by a thousand things in the mountains, from the ghost eagle to other trappers or even a fall off a cliff. Her mother had never protected Brysen's body before and would not start now.

It would be, as it always was, up to Kylee.

She hoisted her pack and made for the mountaineers' trails behind their house and the start of the ascent toward the ghost eagle's eyrie. She knew a hundred different pairs of eyes were watching her from the Villages below, but she kept hers fixed upward. Up was the only direction that mattered to her now. She had to catch up with Brysen before the sky fell down around him.

14

KYLEE HIKED UNTIL DUSK, FOLLOWING THE WELL-TROD TRAPPERS' trails, until she turned off the main route for the steeper slopes that led to the rocky ridges of the Cardinal's Crest.

The sun sank between two jutting peaks in the distance, the sparkling snow that blew off them bejeweling the air. The light had dimmed perilously by the time she reached the misty lowlands, where the stands of ash, juniper, and cypress trees grew sparse, where large boulders littered the landscape and sheer cliffs rose straight up at odd intervals, like the jagged teeth in a giant's broken grin. Above her, over a lip of sharp rock, was the blood birch forest, thick with trees that needed almost no soil but were said to grow wherever blood had been spilled.

As she rounded one wide outcropping of stone, she finally saw Brysen, high above on a flat gray rock face, climbing the vertical. As the bird flies, he wasn't too far ahead of her now, but the height of the sheer cliff must have slowed him down considerably. If he'd planned his route more deliberately, he might have found easier paths instead of climbing the first rock face he saw, but Brysen was a believer in running headlong into . . . well . . . everything. Kylee was a strong and deliberate climber. She'd plotted a smarter route, and she might catch up to him before midnight if he rested and she didn't.

Her brother had flown Shara up with a long leash tied to her jesses. The other end was tied to his belt. If he fell, she'd stay bound above him to mark his body. Either someone would see and recover him, cutting her free, or she'd starve there, tied to him. It was a selfish choice not to let her fly on her own—*she would surely follow Brysen without being tied to him*, Kylee thought—but she understood why her brother did it.

If he fell, he didn't want to be left all alone.

He had on just his vest and leather pants; he'd tied his packs and coat to another spider-silk rope so he could climb up the sheer face, looping it over outcroppings as he went, then hoisting the bags after him. It was a slow process but one that gave him periodic chances to catch his breath. He was two-thirds of the way up this cliff face and moving very slowly, toehold to toehold, muscles tight and shining with sweat in the last light of the sinking sun.

Weaker climbers hauled themselves up by the arms, but Brysen knew that the real power came from the legs. He never looked lighter or more graceful than when he was climbing, freeing himself from gravity and from all the worries that waited back in the dirt. Climbing used to be one of their favorite things to do together, but he hadn't done it for fun in a long time. She always offered to bring him along on her morning climbs, but he always refused, choosing to sleep in and then go down to the Broken Jess.

Kylee had found solace in climbing. It was calming, the simple search for toeholds and handholds. Plotting the vertical path was like putting together a puzzle where the solution truly mattered. Your life and death were in your control. It was almost a pleasure watching Brysen do it with such confidence.

Then his foot slipped, and Kylee's heart beat like the wings of a startled dove.

He slid down along his belly, a torrent of loose stone cascading around him. His fingertips caught a jagged outcropping and stopped his fall, but his legs dangled and his other arm swung free, flapping like a useless wing.

"Scuzz!" he shouted.

"Scuzz . . . scuzz . . . scuzz . . . scuzz . . ." His voice echoed down to where Kylee stood.

From above, his goshawk watched the struggle. Her line still had slack, so she felt nothing of his fall. To her, this brutal drama was the tedium of a life among the wingless. Brysen's fingers clung, bony knuckles clutching, tight tendons straining, grasping, fighting gravity. It hurt Kylee to see her brother fling himself back against the rock, hard, gasping and scrambling. But he held on. He steadied. He climbed again.

He had scraped the side of his face, and now, foot over foot, handhold to handhold, he ascended through the bloody streak he'd painted on the rocks above him. It took him until the moon was perched above the far ridges to reach the point where Shara, by that time, had been waiting for hours. Kylee covered most of the distance in half the time, careful to keep out of his sight line, but pushing herself relentlessly after him.

Long ago, the ancient caravans from the steppes followed the migration of birds from lands of ice and dust to the lush plateau, where they'd built the Uztari civilization. But to follow the birds, they had to cross the mountains—these mountains. The humans scrambled and struggled, seeking the gaps and passes. Those they found living here already, the Altari, they fought and they subdued. And then, battle-bloodied, bone-weary, and half-frozen, they had to keep climbing down.

What took them generations to traverse, the falcons flew in minutes. For the Uztari, the birds led the way to salvation. For the Altari they chased down into the desert, the birds were a portent of their exile. No wonder Kartami fanatics hated the Uztari and hated the raptors that served them. The birds had flown over the peaks and brought cataclysm with them.

Now, Brysen repeated that ancient journey in reverse, straining to leave the safety of the hills and make the treacherous ascent into the brutal wild, led, once more, by a bird.

At the top of the cliff, Brysen collapsed onto the ledge beside his hawk, stroking her wing gently, which she seemed to enjoy, and playing his finger-pecking game on the ground between them. When she'd tired of nipping at him, he rolled flat on his stomach, bruised, bloody, and exhausted. He tilted his head over the edge without moving his body and, loudly, lavishly, barfed off the mountain.

The sound echoed.

Ugh. Kylee cringed.

Brysen spat and rested his head on his hands, facedown. He'd kept a good pace, given the condition he'd started the day in, but he wouldn't be able to make his deadline if he kept going so slowly up cliffsides. He needed to find and follow the ancient goat roads. They were winding and longer than the straight ascent but far easier. He was straying from any known route and entering a wilderness whose pitfalls Kylee couldn't anticipate and for which Brysen was definitely not prepared. The blood birch forest loomed over the direction he was heading, and no Uztari had ever charted a route through those woods. If Brysen just stayed near the ancient paths, Kylee could catch up to her brother without scaling a cliff in the dark, and once she was at his side, he'd have no choice but to let her help. She knew better ways up than he did, safe ways that steered clear of known dangers, and climbing together, they could watch each other's backs. He couldn't refuse. Anyway, it was better to apologize than to ask permission.

She'd find a path up to him and lead him from there. He'd strayed from the route to the Cardinal's Crest Ridge, but she could guide them both back. She'd already begun to plot a likely way, when her eyes caught something moving on the ledge just above Brysen, and she stopped, squinted up, trying to make out the shape of the movement in the moonlight.

At first, she saw only the scraggly brush of the overhang, but her eyes caught the movement again, a shadow in the shape of a cat—a big cat, lean and purple-black as the lips on a corpse. A rock panther.

The great beast lowered its head, eyes fixed on Brysen's lithe back. Had he mustered himself to build a fire, the panther would never have dared come so close, but he hadn't. Had he been sitting upright, it might have stayed away, as rock panthers prefer to take their prey from behind and rarely attack when they can see its eyes. But Brysen was asleep, exhaustion having hooded him before he bothered to make camp. If Kylee were closer, she'd probably be able to hear him snoring.

If she were closer, she'd have been able to help.

The panther lowered itself nearly flat against the ground, creeping to the edge of the outcropping directly above Brysen.

"*Get up,*" Kylee whispered. "*Get up, get up, get up.*"

If she shouted, would he hear? Would it scare the cat away?

"Get up!" she yelled.

"Get up . . . ," echoed back at her. "Get up . . . get up . . . get up . . ."

The angle of the cliffs and the direction of the wind blocked the sound. Brysen heard nothing. The panther heard nothing. Whatever Shara heard, she did not move. Shara was looking out over the valley, her back to the rocks, unaware that a predator was stalking in her blind spot. Rock panthers knew how to stalk raptors. Wild hawks were a staple of the big cat's diet.

Kylee felt helpless down below, as helpless as when the

long-hauler held his knife to Brysen's throat in the battle pit. She felt that tug on her heart, a thrumming pulse in her ears. She closed her eyes, breathed deep, and tried to light the air in her lungs aflame, tried to find the words her mother had called blasphemy, the words of the Hollow Tongue.

She pictured her brother being torn apart, pictured the cat's paw tossing him over, ripping his belly, the blood on its teeth as it tore his entrails out.

"*Shyehnaah,*" she said, but it had no effect, no meaning. She could make the sound on purpose but couldn't make it work. She couldn't command it, couldn't control it. She exhaled feeling nothing but cool night air.

She took another breath; the cat crept forward, poised. She pictured her brother in the mews at home with her father and his torch, blue eyes looking into blue eyes, one pair wet as ice-melt lakes and the other cold and hard as glaciers. And the light of the flame reflecting off both, inching closer and closer. She made herself see the fire touch his skin, she made herself hear the sounds and smell the burning cloth and flesh and hair. The fire lit in her lungs, and she spoke the word again.

Shara's head turned. The panther's lips pulled back from its bone-white fangs, its muscles quivered beneath the taut, corpse-colored fur. There was a jolt as Shara saw the predator, a lightning shock of instant action, eye to wing, wing to beak.

"Ki ki ki!" Shara shrieked, launching herself from the ledge, the leash unspooling behind her.

Shara's outburst startled the panther and woke Brysen at the same time. Brysen saw Shara sky out, and a heartbeat later, he spun toward what had scared her.

The startled panther swiped, but Brysen rolled out of its reach toward the precipice of the ledge.

He had no escape, and when the second swipe came, he rolled under it, toward the mountain and below the overhang. He drew his blade as he rolled and released the knot that tied Shara to him.

The panther leaped down to maul him but instead found itself impaled on the curved black-talon blade of Brysen's knife. Brysen whistled, and Shara spun, then dove for the panther's back, sinking her talons in just below its skull.

A hawk knew in its blood that the panther was an enemy. Shara squeezed the cat's spine from behind as Brysen jerked his blade upward, into its heart.

The squeal of the big cat echoed around the mountain.

Its blood poured down past Brysen's elbow, over his chest and stomach. Brysen shoved it off and drew himself back against the rock, holding his bloody blade in front of him and staring at the dead panther while Shara proceeded to peck at it, tearing the gray-and-black fur apart with beak and talon like a mad butcher's apprentice. She broke into its flesh and stuffed her crop with the pulsing, hot meat.

If Brysen didn't stop her eating, she'd fill up so much that she wouldn't fly in the morning. Brysen would need her keen for the next several days, or he'd never make it to the ghost eagle's eyrie and back in time for Goryn Tamir.

Then Brysen slumped, and Kylee shuddered. Had the cat clawed him somewhere Kylee couldn't see? Was he bleeding up there, his throat slit, his arteries open?

She sprinted toward the trapper's narrow path to make her scrambling way up the slope. She could stop his bleeding and save his life if she reached him in time. She'd have to run and climb faster than she ever had before, but her feet were sure, her heart pulling her on.

Only a few paces into her run, she heard a hoot.

"Woo-hoo!"

Kylee stopped and looked up at the ledge, and there was Brysen, standing up, dancing in a circle, his bloody arms raised in the air. He was hopping from foot to foot, his white grin and ashen hair gleaming.

"Woo-hoo . . . ," echoed around her. "Woo-hoo . . . woo-hoo . . . woo-hoo . . ."

"Ha-ha!" he shouted. "You'll have to throw more at me than *that,* you scuzz-guzzling carrion cruncher! You hear me?! I will beat you!"

"Beat you . . . beat you . . . beat you . . ."

She watched his dark form dance in the moonlight while Shara ripped into the dead cat at his feet. He was as happy as Kylee could remember seeing him in ages, celebrating a victory he believed was his own. Just like in the battle pits, he thought he'd saved himself. He thought he was still alone.

Kylee decided not to reveal herself. She would stay hidden. Give him his victory, give him his pride. She'd help her brother from a distance but remain invisible. She had to let him feel he was flying free if she had any hope he'd return when this was over.

15

THE MOON HAD NEARLY SCRATCHED ITS ENTIRE ARC ACROSS THE NIGHT
sky when Kylee reached Brysen's camp on the ledge. The
path had taken her on a winding route between boulders and
up rocky slopes. One moment she was scrambling on her hands
and knees, the next she was leaping gorges. She hadn't known
the path quite as well as she'd thought, at one point nearly
stepping straight into the opening of a deep bat cave from
which she would never have emerged.

At least the bats had already gone out for the night.

When she arrived on the very outcropping over Brysen's

camp where the panther had stalked him, he was asleep by the dying embers of a fire, where the panther's flesh spit and hissed over the coals. Kylee was tempted to slide down the ledge and steal some of it, but she didn't want to risk waking Brysen. If it weren't for her, he'd have been panther food and not the other way around, yet she'd eaten cold, pickled hen eggs for dinner.

Shara slept beside Brysen, her feet pulled up under her body into the downy warmth of her feathers. She shifted her weight from side to side to keep the blood flowing, and her head was tucked around nearly under her wings, but she remained un-hooded. Brysen would want to use her as an alarm if danger approached. Kylee stayed very still, very calm, and moved very slowly so she wouldn't wake the boy or the bird.

She pulled back from the ledge and slipped farther off into the dark. Brysen would begin his climb again after sunrise, hiking up into the blood birch forest over the next ridge. It would be easier to follow him but harder not to be seen.

She wondered who else was out there in the night below, making their way up the mountain after them, and what else was out there in the night above, watching and lying in wait. She shivered and knew she needed some sleep, but she had to find a sheltered spot.

On a nearby slope, two boulders had rolled together to form

a kind of lean-to in the space beneath. She could stretch out there, safe from predators and from Brysen's view but still with a clear sight line to his route in the morning. She laid some sticks across the path, precariously perched, so that if her brother left, he'd disturb the pattern and she'd know he'd gone already, even if she overslept. Beneath the boulders, she felt perfectly safe to close her eyes and let sleep obliterate her worries awhile.

The next thing she knew, dawn had broken like the pale yellow of overcooked eggs. She lifted her head, wiping a slash of drool from her chin, and studied the path. Her sticks remained undisturbed.

She crept on her belly back over to the ledge and saw Brysen still asleep below, snoring slightly. He'd draped the crook of his arm over his eyes, and his other hand was resting on the knife handle in his belt. His fire had gone out, and a sprinkling of frost had settled over him. If he didn't start sleeping under a blanket, he'd surely freeze to death when he got higher into the mountains. He'd slept blade-ready, but it would have taken an earthquake to wake him.

Taking a moment to stretch, she looked out over the vast landscape, the sun rising to the left and casting the long shadow of the mountain range over the Six Villages far below. The skies were clear, and not even the birds were awake yet. It was her favorite time of day in the Villages. Even the Crawling Priests hadn't begun their daily harangues.

At this height, no sound could reach her from the Villages, but she could see the clearing where their house sat and the steep path down to the Necklace. The Necklace rolled through the town and the high road ran alongside it, both disappearing around the mountain range on their long and winding way from the Sky Castle to the Talon Fortress. The trees and grasses and irrigated fields that ringed the valley edge where the Necklace ran soon gave way to the dry rock of the central flats, picked bare before the first ancestors by massive herds of goat and lamb and camel, and then to the vast desert beyond. Now only Altari nomads and long-hauler convoys crossed it. She could see their scattered fires burning, smoky lines rising into the sky like banners all the way from the pale-green edge to the empty red dirt and golden dunes of the Parsh Desert. Somewhere in that desert, the Kartami were building their war barrows, stringing their battle kites, and saying their prayers for an empty sky.

From this height, people's wants and wars seemed totally insignificant. The only thing real was the landscape: rock, snow, grass, and sand. It was a view like the one she and Brysen used to daydream.

Over the desert, she could just make out the purple outlines of the eastern mountain range—the Lower Jaw, they called it. They lived at the base of the Upper Jaw. There were older names for the mountains that ringed the high steppe and sheltered them from the killing winds off the surrounding steppes, but Kylee always liked the idea that Uztar was a great open mouth on the face of the world, and their entire lives were spent between two massive sets of teeth. Every day held the possibility that the jaw would slam shut on them and their entire civilization, so every day was an act of mercy. With every sunrise, the world gave them another chance instead of swallowing them whole.

She liked the idea of another chance. She could do things right this time.

She crept back to her burrow beneath the boulder, rolling her supplies up in her rug and cinching the bundle with a leather nomad's strap. The people of the Villages owed so much to those they'd expelled to the deserts, yet most Uztari loathed them. Her father, though he'd married one, loathed them with a special fury. He never missed a chance to call anyone he didn't like a glass grinder within their mother's hearing, whether they were Altari or not. Often it got him a punch in the jaw, but that didn't stop him from slinging the slurs. He was the sort of man who'd rather take a punch than let go of his hate. The provocations only made her mother pray harder for his business to fail and the skies to fall empty around him. He'd then accuse her of birthing Brysen *on purpose*, as if Kylee's twin was a curse on the family.

Some people lose a family member and permanent clouds descend on them. For Kylee, when their father died, it was as if the clouds had finally parted and she could see all the vastness of the world he'd hidden from their view. Was it a sin that she'd never felt the slightest need to mourn him? Her fondest memories were of the daily flocks of mourners' crows, whose somber songs promised the arrival of cakes and sweets and countless gifts her mother wouldn't touch. She and Brysen could eat their fill and then some.

Her thoughts were suddenly cut short when a shadow passed over the opening of her sleeping cave. A shadow in the shape of a person.

She scurried out the opposite side of her shelter and swung around the boulder, but saw no one. She moved around the other way . . . still no one. Then she crouched, creeping along the edge until she found a handhold and, with one thrust of her legs, sprang up to the top of the boulders and tackled the hooded stalker from behind. As he fell, she drew her hunting knife and pressed it against the side of his smooth throat, right along the big artery. She jammed her knee between his thighs, slamming him forward and flat onto his belly.

"Ah! Kylee! It's me! Please! It's me!" he cried out. The figure held his hands open at his sides, his body rigid and still beneath her, and she yanked the hood from his head, freeing a mop of tight curls.

Nyall.

She pulled the knife from his neck and got off his back.

"Shhh!" she said. "Be quiet and get down here."

She dropped back to the ground and waited for him in between the boulders. It took him a second to recover—more from the knee in the crotch than the knife to his throat, she figured—but he dropped down eventually and squeezed himself into the small space.

"What in the flaming sky are you doing here?" She forced herself to whisper.

"I heard what Brysen was doing," Nyall said. "It's all anyone is talking about."

Of course, Kylee thought. Anyone who wanted to steal Brysen's catch—in the unlikely event that he actually succeeded—would have plenty of time to prepare an ambush.

"Everyone said you'd be on the Blue Sheep Pass," Nyall told

her. "So I knew you wouldn't be. The more people know a thing, the less likely it's true."

"How did you find us? It's a big mountain."

"Vyvian told me the real route you planned to take."

"She just *told* you? For nothing?"

"No." Nyall looked away from her. "Not for nothing."

"Oh, you peacock!" Kylee shoved him playfully. He smiled, his dimples explaining Vyvian's fee. "So you followed me up here to . . . what? Warn me that Vyvian's a spy? I knew that already."

"I followed you to watch your back," Nyall said. "When I saw you leaving the Six, I knew you'd come up here to look out for Brysen, but no one would be looking out for you."

"*I'd* be looking out for me," she replied.

"So you don't want my help?" Nyall looked hurt, but what was he expecting? That he'd show up uninvited and she'd *thank* him for it? She didn't need a hero or want a lover. "You can't go up against the world alone," he added.

Kylee wanted to tell him that she absolutely could, but she stopped herself short. Only chicken-brains like her brother looked at kindness and called it a curse. Accepting help wasn't a sin, and having the company of a friend wouldn't be the end of the world.

Nyall opened his arms, waiting. Unlike the other battle boys, he had only one tattoo: just a few lines of illuminated poetry that wrapped around his wrist and forearm like a coiled rope: *The starling sings love's agony, the dove sings its humanity, but one and all will fall the same when pinioned by love's gravity.* He was an unrelenting romantic, like her brother, but he was loyal and kind and good in a tough spot—also like her brother. The hunt for a ghost eagle was sure to have more than its share of tough spots.

"Fine," she said. "Stick with me. That way we can sleep in shifts . . . but *do not* give us away on the hike like you just gave yourself away to me, okay? I don't want Brysen to know we're following him."

"Because he'd never accept help?" Nyall grinned widely, brushed the hair from his eyes, and let his dimples linger.

"I'm aware of the irony, finch-face." She shoved his shoulder again, and he lost his balance, falling out of the space between the boulders and landing on his back, where he looked straight up at the sky. His smile collapsed and his dimples vanished. He raised his hands, palms open.

Kylee shook her head. "You don't have to surrender. I'm not gonna hurt you again. I swear . . . knee a guy between the legs just once and he becomes jumpy as a chickadee. I should tell the village girls; we'd start a revolution."

Nyall didn't look at her, though. He was still looking up, unmoving, unsmiling.

A shadow fell behind Kylee, blocking the other way out of the hollow beneath the boulders. "Come out now," the shadow commanded. "And watch where you put your knees, or your brother and your boyfriend die right here."

16

KYLEE PRESSED HER HAND INTO THE DIRT AND CURSED, BUT SHE crawled from between the boulders and pushed herself up to standing. The Orphan Maker, backed by his two friends, sucked his teeth in front of her, spat on the ground between her feet. His brown-striped kestrel once more perched on his fist.

"Took all night to find my little one," he grumbled, then looked from the kestrel to Kylee. "Move too fast, and she'll dig a talon in your eye."

One of the other long-haulers had a bow pulled tight with an arrow pointing straight at Nyall's face. It was so close, he could've licked the arrowhead. The other long-hauler had

Brysen kneeling in front of him with an ax blade against his neck. Shara was pinned down in a net snare, which was staked hard into the rocky slope. She struggled and tried to flap her wings but couldn't escape, and she called incessantly.

"Ki! Ki! Ki!" she shrieked. "Ki! Ki! Ki!"

"Nyall?" Brysen said, puzzled, then slumped on seeing her. "Kylee?"

Her brother actually had the nerve to be disappointed that she was there. He should have been more disappointed about the wooden block that the copper-haired long-hauler threw down at his knees, because they clearly meant to behead him on it. Brysen never was good at keeping his priorities straight.

"Ki! Ki! Ki!"

Kylee stared at Brysen as the executioner grabbed his neck and shoved it down to rest in the groove of the chopping block. This wasn't a block used for livestock, stained from the viscera of a thousand meals. This was an ornately carved executioner's block, covered in scenes of crime and punishment with channels to flow the blood away and deep gauges in the slot where other unfortunate necks had rested before. There was a rough and brutal justice among long-hauler convoys, and Kylee had no way to know if these men just meant to frighten them or if they truly planned to kill. The ax blade gleamed, well sharpened. Brysen's hands were bound behind his back.

"Ki! Ki! Ki!" Shara screamed and flapped frantically under the net.

Kylee couldn't find the wind to burn a word through her body. She searched her breath, her heartbeat; she focused on her fear . . . nothing. An exhausted quiet had overtaken her.

"Ki! Ki! Ki!"

The long-haulers turned Nyall toward Brysen with the arrow pointed at his back. They wanted him to watch his friend's head come off.

"You Six Villagers think you're so much better than us," the Orphan Maker said. "Life on the mountainside has made you weak. We risk Kartami attacks when we cross the desert to bring you the grains you glut yourselves and grow soft on, but we who cross the valley know what it is to go days without water, weeks without food. One drop of our blood is worth ten of your lives."

"Then I guess your face is priceless now," Brysen replied.

The Orphan Maker touched the wound that Shara had given him, then bent down in front of Brysen, nudged his hawk off his fist and onto the ground, so she stood just in front of Brysen's nose. "She's keen," he said. "Maybe keen enough to take a bite out of your face."

"What's the point of killing us?" Kylee shouted, trying to divert the attention away from Brysen and whatever smart-ass comment was forming in his mind. "Have you no honor?"

"Honor," the Orphan Maker sneered, leaving his hawk on the ground in front of Brysen as he turned on her. "A pretty word for a pretty village girl. Let honor sleep indoors. When his soul can't see its way to sky, *then* I'll think about honor."

There was no crueler punishment than to separate a head from its body and keep them apart in death. When the vultures came to devour the dead in sky burial, the head of a corpse had to "see" the sky, or the soul would rot instead of rising into the blue. This was as true in the Villages and mountains as it was in the plains and the desert, in her mother's faith and her late father's. Kylee didn't care much about superstitions, but Brysen was a believer.

A sound escaped Brysen's lips, involuntary. A whimper. The long-hauler licked his lips, nearly panting with excitement.

"Ki! Ki! Ki!" Shara cried.

Brysen's eyes still met Kylee's, but the anger had left them and the momentary flash of fear had turned to something else. It was a look she hadn't seen from him in a long time but one that she would always understand: the look of her twin in cahoots. She nodded slightly in return, and he blinked once, breaking the stare, accepting her help.

Nyall was ready. She was ready. They had no weapons to hand, and she couldn't count on her mind to conjure up the right words on purpose. They had only each other's speed and guts. The chances were good that not all three of them would survive this.

"Hey, Kylee—one question for you?" Nyall said. His voice was calm and casual, as if they were still back down in the market tent, haggling over how many cups of tea she had to drink with him to get one of the bird boxes.

"What is it?" she replied.

"Did I stand a chance with you?"

She had to laugh. "I don't know, Nyall. I'm not a game of chance you can win or lose. But I do like spending time around you."

Nyall smiled his dimpled grin. "I guess that's better than nothi—"

"Enough!" the Orphan Maker cut him off. "Word is the girl's got some talent . . . might make her worth keeping around. You." He pointed his knife at Nyall. "I'm selling you to the slavers. You're pretty enough to be a catamite. But first, we'll take off this little bird's head."

He wasn't talking about Shara.

The executioner tapped his ax once on Brysen's neck to get his aim, then raised it high. Brysen kicked his bound legs out, tripping the would-be executioner, and rolled off the chopping block. The sudden movement spooked the kestrel, which jumped back crying, opening her wings and launching herself off the ground.

At the same instant, Nyall bent his knees, arched his back, and flung his arms forward as he jumped into a backflip, hitting the archer's arm. The arrow fired just under him and snapped harmlessly into the dirt. As he landed, he lashed out with a fist and knocked the archer sideways.

He was a battle boy through and through.

Kylee aimed her first kick at the fateful point between the Orphan Maker's legs, but he blocked her before it connected, which drew his focus down, so she could chop hard at his throat, a much more vulnerable spot. He gasped but caught her with a jab in the teeth that knocked her onto her back. She scrambled away, but he charged at her, wheezing, as he pulled his blade and found the breath to whistle for his hawk.

The bird dove at Kylee, harrying her face, blocking her view, and forcing her to shield her eyes from the flurry of talon and feather. As Kylee backed up, she bumped into Brysen, who was trying to free his wrists, while backing away from the executioner.

"Ki! Ki! Ki!" Shara flapped and twisted against the net.

"Ya! Ya! Ya!" the little brown kestrel screeched. Kylee tried to knock her away, but she kept coming. A talon cut the back of Kylee's wrist, and she felt the bird's beak nip at her hair.

Nyall wasn't faring so well, either. The archer had recovered from the punch, and though he'd lost his bow, he still had an arrow and over a hundred pounds on Nyall. He had Nyall's hair in one hand and was about to slam an arrow through his eye with the other.

Except, with a flash of white, the arrow was snatched from the archer's grip and carried aloft by a massive, snow-white owl, gliding silently. The archer still clutched Nyall with his free hand but stood utterly still, his mouth hanging open.

"Ki!" the small kestrel shrieked, and then whirled, racing away for safety. From just over the snowy ridge above them, a second owl shot up, just a shadow against the rising sun. It intercepted the kestrel in midair, snatching her in its talons and dragging her, crying, back down behind the other side of the ridge. It was gone nearly as soon as it had appeared.

A third owl, a great gray with bright yellow eyes alight, glided over the Orphan Maker and appeared almost to hover above him, then dropped, snatching his blade hand in its talons with such force that it knocked the knife free.

Then the great gray owl flapped away without a sound.

Shara had fallen still below her net, huddled against the ground with her head tucked back. She looked more like a shuddering stone than a bird of prey. It was clear that she was desperate to avoid the same fate as the little brown kestrel.

Brysen had sawed his wrists free on a stone, but the executioner had him leaping and diving away from the ax. He'd have been split in two if the snow-white owl had not come between them, slipping around the ax blade like its feathers were fog, and pushing the executioner back.

The whistling arrow made the first loud noise since the owls' arrival, and it appeared so fast, it didn't look like it had been fired at all. But there it was, sprouting from the executioner's chest. The black feather fletching gave him the look of a molting bird with but one plume left. And, like a bird's broken pinfeather, the wound began to squirt blood.

The long-hauler fell.

"I think I found the Owl Mothers," Brysen announced as if it had been his plan all along.

17

THE TWO REMAINING LONG-HAULERS LOOKED AROUND TO SEE WHERE the arrow and the owls had come from, but the brush and stones were silent as morning.

And then a voice spoke with the thunderous melody of the earth herself: "Kneel."

"Who's there?" the Orphan Maker called.

The archer dropped Nyall and drew an arrow, bending in the same moment to pick up his bow. He didn't stand again. An arrow passed through his throat without slowing.

So Kylee knelt.

Brysen knelt.

Nyall knelt.

The scab-faced Orphan Maker hesitated. An arrow seemed to sprout from his thigh, and it forced him down with a scream. No sooner had his knees hit the ground than five women appeared from beneath cloaks of earth and stone, not spitting distance from where they all knelt. How long they had been there, perfectly camouflaged, was impossible to know.

Beneath the cloaks they wore thick-feathered robes cinched with leather belts from which hung blades and climbing gear. They had black-and-white sable scarves wrapped around their necks and fabric for climbing wrapped around their wrists and palms. All of them had snow-fox-silver hair worn short, and their faces were rugged as the mountain itself.

Two of them held beautiful walnut crossbows. The other three simply raised their left fists, and the silent owls returned to them.

Owl Mothers.

This was their ridge. This had always been their ridge. The Altari feared them, the Uztari avoided them, and only a fool disrespected them.

Brysen had veered off the known routes through the mountains and walked straight into them. It was a deadly reckless thing to do, but it might have just saved their lives.

The woman who looked to be eldest crossed the ground to

Kylee, removed a sharp dagger from her belt with her right hand, and extended it, handle-first. Her face was tanned and windburned, broad and flat as her owl's, watching Kylee just as impassively. Two of the younger women looked just like her, while the other two had hawk-sharp features and skin as dark as Nyall's. All five of them stood solid as stone.

Kylee wasn't sure what was expected of her now. Should she take the blade? Bow? In the Six Villages she might give the winged salute, but that didn't seem to be what was expected of her here.

Under the net, Shara returned to screeching, red eyes darting with her whole head from owl to owl. This was not a position a hawk preferred. Brysen's face was etched with pain for his trapped bird, but he didn't dare move to set her free.

The Owl Mother nodded, and Kylee took the knife.

Then the woman pointed at the kneeling long-hauler. "They'd've taken yours," she said. Kylee understood the words if not their meaning. "Yours," the woman repeated, waving one hand at Brysen and Nyall. "Your men." She snorted, reconsidered. "Boys."

"They're not *mine*," Kylee explained, but in a way, they were all bound to one another. Did that make them hers?

The woman helped Kylee up from the ground and guided her in front of the long-hauler, who knelt in a growing pool of his own blood. The woman gestured again to the blade and to the man. "Take him. He deserves it."

She hesitated. The blade shook in her hands. She'd never had another soul so fully at her mercy. She was used to violence but only in flashes, like a hawk in a dive: the sudden screeching terror and then quiet, maybe a whine, maybe a tear. But this? The man was no danger anymore. This wasn't the quick clash of a falcon and a hare, or even the ale-lit cruelty of her father's brutal nights. This was cold-eyed murder.

"I'll do it," Brysen said, rising to his feet. The man had nearly cut his soul off from the sky and buried his head in the dirt, but her brother had never killed anyone before, either, not as far as Kylee knew.

"No!" the Owl Mother shouted, and raised her left arm. Her owl rose from it and flew over Brysen, hovering with silent wingbeats. He stopped moving. "Life and death aren't yours." She looked again at Kylee. Her eyes were black and cold but gentle, like a deep mountain lake. "Blood belongs to us."

Us.

"Man can't take what he can't give," the Owl Mother explained. "Only we shed man's blood here."

Kylee's blade hand didn't move, and the woman reached out, wrapped her fingers around Kylee's, and took back her knife. She smiled; the skin around her eyes crinkled with it and

Kylee felt the fear leave her chest. The Owl Mother radiated warmth and power, her face a fortress wall and her smile a hearth behind it.

And with the same empty silence as an owl hunting over a snowy meadow, the Owl Mother swiped the blade across the long-hauler's throat and kicked him backward down the slope to the cliff's edge. The Orphan Maker plummeted over the side and was gone. The great gray owl circled back from Brysen and settled silently on the Owl Mother's fist again, wide yellow eyes blinking one at a time at Kylee.

"You come with us," she said. "We'll hear what breeze brought you; we'll see what wind will carry you on."

Two of the women started walking up the mountain single file, two more gesturing for Nyall and Brysen to walk between them, with the last waiting for Kylee to go in front of her.

"Ky," Brysen whispered with pure, desperate terror. He didn't move to his place in line. He looked at Shara beneath her net.

Kylee understood. He would never leave his bird.

"Excuse me? Um . . . uh . . . ?" Kylee called.

The Owl Mother who had killed the long-hauler turned her head but not her body. "My name is Üku."

"Mem Üku." Kylee bowed her head and gave the winged salute across her chest. "May my brother bring his hawk with us? They are . . . dear to each other." She looked at the desperate goshawk in the net. "Her name is Shara."

The Owl Mother smiled, realizing surely that Kylee had mentioned the *female* hawk because she understood something of the Owl Mothers: Men and boys had their uses, but it was women who ruled here.

"Nothing's dear to a raptor but its own life," Üku said. She touched her index finger to the cheekbone just below her eye, a gesture Kylee didn't understand. "But he can bring her."

Brysen scrambled to cut Shara free, cradling the hawk against his chest and whispering comforting words but tying her onto the leash on his belt quickly as he did. He knew she'd fly away the moment he let her go. There was only so much punishment a hawk would take before it abandoned you. A strong knot was a more reliable bond than affection.

"Don't worry," Brysen whispered at Kylee as he passed her to take his place in line. "All part of the plan."

He nodded briskly over the mountain, and Kylee saw a line of climbers far below them, no larger than ants, marching single file toward Blue Sheep Pass, which was slow and long and avoided the Owl Mothers' territory completely. At least Vyvian had spread the right rumors back in the Villages. She'd bought their little expedition time.

There were over a dozen figures making their way up—
trappers and porters together. Even from this far, she could
see the weapons they carried—long bows and heavy swords.
These weren't mountaineers or Six Villages trappers. These
were mercenaries, and someone had hired them.

"Let's go." Üku nudged Kylee forward, and they began their
own single-file march up into the blood birch forest.

THE DIRT'S MERCY

THE MORNING MIST OVER THE GRASSLAND PLAIN HAD ALREADY BURNED away, and there wasn't much game for the hunt. Sylas's peregrine had bagged a grass hen early, while his son Victyr's little desert falcon had nearly taken a sand weasel but lost it down a hole and caught only a footful of dirt instead.

The boy had complained all morning of boredom, and neither the servants nor their work dogs could flush much game out from the low scrub. He'd hoped to take larger prey to teach the boy how to dress it, but at this point he'd settle for as much as a vole in the boy's game bag.

The desert falcon sat hooded on the T-perch his son's valet carried. Victyr wanted to stop for an early lunch.

"It's like all the game's run off, Kyrg Sylas," one of the guides apologized, mopping his forehead where the sweat was beading over angry, red sun blisters. "Might be good to take a rest and travel on after we're fed. Maybe some migrating river gulls will make good sport later. It's the season for it."

"Please, please, please," Victyr begged, hopping up and down. Windblown sand speckled the boy's rich brown skin. One of the valets rushed over with a cloth to wipe his arms and legs off before they began to itch.

Sylas exhaled but couldn't refuse his son's pleading little face. His own parents had never given in to a single one of his pleas, and he'd vowed not to be so hard on his own children.

His mothers' harshness had, of course, been born of their positions on the Council of Forty. They were both kyrgs, each busy with official duties, which meant he'd hardly known them. He'd been raised by servants and sent away for study and training. Yes, that had prepared him for his own service as one of the Forty—how many men could claim to have had both parents serve?—but it hadn't done much for his enjoyment of childhood. He meant to be warmer to his son, and besides, what harm could an early lunch do? They would hunt gulls later. That'd be far more exciting for hunter and falcon alike.

At least the boy would know a thing or two when they got to the Six Villages, and maybe those schemers wouldn't be able to rip him off so easily. Sylas had lost his fair share of pocket money as a boy visiting the Six Villages Hawkers' Market. Once, he bought racing pigeons that were hardly more than flying rats. He suspected his own boyhood valet had been in on the scam.

No valet would raise his son. He and Victyr would hunt together, eat together, and talk together. Victyr would grow up strong, but he'd grow up loved, and *that* would be a fine inheritance to leave him in addition to a position on the Council.

He rested his hand on his son's back, watching the servants set up the picnic. There was a basket of flatbreads, cardamom rice with barberries and chili, and cold roasted rabbit with saffron oil. Honey cakes and sweetroot pies for desert. The boy would have hearty goat's milk, while the servants had brought a low mountain wine for Sylas and the two minor nobles who'd joined him for the hunt. They scurried over, leaving their falcons on the square carrying frame with their own valets.

"My proctor has decided it's lunchtime"—Sylas grinned at Victyr—"and I am sworn to obey his commands." He pretended not to see the eye roll that passed between the two nobles. He could scold them for the disrespect of their betters, but that would make for a long remainder of the journey. He let the slight go and invited them to sit with him for the meal.

"The guides think we'll have more luck hunting gulls this afternoon," he said. "Better sport in the air, anyway."

"Humph," one of the nobles grunted, tucking into a rabbit leg and getting grease all over his wispy red beard.

"I think we might have a flock to take right now!" The other noble stood, excited. He pointed toward the horizon, where, indeed, they could make out the dark shapes of a vast flock sweeping toward them. The noble smiled from ear to ear and ran to get his falcon.

"Lunchtime's over, kid! It's time to hunt!" The other noble dropped his rabbit leg on the basket and nearly toppled the whole picnic running after his friend.

"Da!" Victyr whined. "I haven't eaten anything yet!"

Sylas hadn't moved. He and his servants looked at the approaching flock in awe. There were hundreds of dark shapes in the sky, moving in a formation like geese . . . but they looked far too large to be geese. They were coming much faster than geese, too.

"What birds do you think those are, Kyrg Sylas?" one of the nobles shouted back, nudging his lanner falcon to the fist and taking off its hood.

"Those aren't birds . . ." Sylas's voice was no louder than the creak of a bedroom door.

The ground below the massive flock was a cloud, like the sort of nuisance dust storm one dealt with in the deeper desert but not here in the grasslands. There wasn't enough dust, especially at this time of year.

In the heart of the cloud, Sylas saw the shadowy shapes of war barrows rolling, two figures standing on the back of each, clutching guidelines in one hand and in the other, blades. The guidelines rose from each barrow to a dark shape in the sky above: a large kite hung with straps.

"Kartami," Sylas said aloud, his voice breaking. "Kartami!" he shouted now, at full volume.

As the horde of kite warriors sped in, each barrow driver released a line, and the other line furled upward, carrying the second warrior aloft. They rose on their lines like spiders to a web, and before Sylas could take another breath, each kite had a warrior strapped under it, clutching a bow or double spears, and the speed of the wind pulled the barrows they were tied to straight at the hunting party.

"Arms!" one of the guides shouted before Sylas could find the words. "To arms!"

Sylas grabbed Victyr and hauled him to his feet, spilling wine all over the picnic rug's pattern of songbirds in a garden.

He shoved a dagger into the boy's belt and hung two skins filled with milk over his shoulders.

"Run, Victyr!" he commanded. "Do not look back. Run straight for the convoy and warn them. Tell them the Kartami are here. Tell them . . ." He looked up and saw that the two nobles had already unleashed their falcons to fly at the kite warriors and try to harry as many as they could from the sky. "Tell them we've been overtaken."

"But—" Victyr objected.

"No." He cut him off, hugging him close. "We will hold them off as long as we can. But you *must not* be taken yourself, you hear me? No matter what. Do not let them take you. You're my sky, understand? My soul flies to you. Don't let it be lost."

Victyr nodded, and Sylas turned him around. He couldn't look into the boy's eyes, couldn't bear the good-bye. He nudged him and Victyr ran, straight away toward the far horizon. He just hoped the convoy could outrun the oncoming horde. It was up to Sylas to give them time.

He turned away from his son, took his falcon on the fist, and faced the rolling attack.

"Utch!" he shouted, tossing his peregrine skyward as he drew a blade from the sheath his valet presented him.

The valet's hand shook. "They say the Kartami bury the heads of any who won't submit."

Sylas nodded. "They do say that."

"And they spare any who pledge to join them without re-sistance," the valet added.

Sylas didn't look at him, though he'd heard such rumors, too. "Those are lies," he told the frightened man, and assessed the cloud of dust that seemed to span the entire horizon. "Sur-render is death to us and to the others back in the convoy. We fight. We give them time. Draw your blade."

"There's no hope in this fight," the valet said, going pale.

Sylas didn't have a chance to look at him before the valet's blade plunged into his spine. His knees gave out and he drop-ped, eyes forward, as the horde of kite warriors slashed through the first two falcons. They'd been trained for hunting but not for combat. His own peregrine had gone up and taken a stoop, diving straight and fast for a kite in the middle of the line— just as he'd trained her.

The silk ripped around the bird, and the weight of the war-rior immediately pulled the kite twirling to the earth. The barrow driver lost control, spinning and flipping. It took two other barrows out in the crash, rolling over their warriors.

Only two. One of the survivors looked to the body of her dead kite warrior, then drove a sword into her own belly.

The others steered around the dying woman as smoothly

as water around a stone. They raised two fingers at her as they passed.

A servant had flown Victyr's little raptor up, and it'd made for the face of another kite warrior. A crossbow bolt from the barrow driver below snatched it out of the air, and when it hit the ground, the wheels smashed its tiny body without slowing.

Sylas felt nothing. There was no pain when the valet's knife slid out of his back again. The valet's arm wrapped around him. He couldn't move.

"Sorry, Kyrg Sylas," the valet said. "They have to see what I'll do for them. They have to see. I swear it will be painless for you."

"If Victyr is caught," Sylas pleaded, "protect him. Please."

"He will not suffer," the valet assured him as he held Sylas in place.

He watched from his knees as his falcon rose again, then dove and clipped a kite warrior, but it wasn't hard enough to shake the warrior loose or break his kite. When the bird turned to make another pass, the warrior hurled his spear, a direct hit. Even from this distance, Sylas heard his bird's shriek when the spear point broke its body and it fell.

He'd lost falcons before; they'd flown off or been killed by crows or mountain cats. One even died in a lightning storm. This was not the first he'd seen die, but a tear fell from his eye because he knew it would be the last.

The warriors reached the men of the hunting party. One noble caught a kite warrior's spear through the top of his head. It went straight through and into the ground, holding his lifeless body upright as a bird feeder. The barrow driver below the kite sped past with his blade out and took the noble's head off without slowing.

The other noble and two of his servants dodged the first volley of spears and arrows, but the second came on them immediately after the first, and they all went down. Sylas saw the entire hunting party slain in the space of a dozen breaths. Soon they reached him where he knelt in front of his valet.

Still they didn't stop.

"I surrender!" his valet cried over the din of their wheels. "I'll join you!"

The rolling barrows didn't slow. They clamored past him by the hundreds, pulled on by the unrelenting high wind over the plain.

He waved his blade up in the air. "I renounce Uztar! Look what I will do for you!" He lowered the blade back to Sylas's neck, but before he could deliver the killing slice, a spear from the sky pierced his chest and knocked him off his feet. The kite's barrow driver rolled past without slowing and tore the spear out of the valet's chest with a wet crunch. He left Sylas on his knees to choke on the dust.

The cold sweat that had broken the moment the kite warriors appeared on the horizon hadn't even raced all the way down his back yet, and they were gone. He could still hear their rolling wheels, the groan of their ropes, and the snap of the wind against their silk kites, but he couldn't turn to see them leaving.

His vision narrowed to a pinprick and he wanted desperately to turn. He didn't know how far his son would run before they caught him.

He did not want to see. He wanted to see.

Victyr could never outrun them. He shouldn't have sent his son off alone. His wife would never forgive Sylas for doing that. He wondered when she would be visited by the first of the mourners' crows. Would she be in the Council of Forty when they came or at home, looking out over the bluffs and watching the black flock approach in maudlin formation, their tail whistles wailing as they descended to her? Would there even be anyone left to report his death and dispatch the crows?

Desert vultures were already circling overhead. *At least I'll have a proper sky burial,* he thought, *unless they take my head too.*

Maybe our boy won't be captured, he prayed. *Maybe they'll let him live.*

The Kartami rolled on like a wave, the blessed vultures diving to the feast left in their wake and carrying him into his eternal breeze bite by holy bite.

BRYSEN

DIFFERENT VEINS

18

THEY HIKED FOR A FULL DAY UP TOWARD THE BLOOD BIRCH FOREST, single file along knife-thin spurs of rock and on hands and knees up loose stone slopes. Brysen had to unleash Shara so she could follow on her own, flitting from boulder to boulder overhead. She flew back to him every few minutes, pecked nervously at his glove, and kept a wary eye on the owls, who each slept serenely on their Owl Mother's fist as the sun burned down the day.

When they reached the snow line, they stopped to stuff fur and feathers into their boots, then hiked on, crossing a series of ice bridges over deep gorges, until they finally reached the dim forest. They stopped in a clearing of skinny white trees. There were taps scattered among a few of their trunks, collecting the red sap, drop by drop, into jars. A few small boxes were nailed high up for fledgling owls. Nothing made a hoot, however. The forest was silent as the sun set behind the western slope, drenching them almost instantly in white darkness.

Brysen knew his life, and therefore Dymian's, depended now on the Owl Mothers who'd captured them. Not *rescued*—despite the unmistakable relief he felt at having not lost his head to those long-haulers—but *captured*. He was a prisoner, but the best path to the ghost eagle was through his captors. They knew where the ghost eagle hunted; they knew the best routes to its eyrie in the Nameless Gap. They were the key to his success, and they had come to him. He felt a rush of pride.

His plan was still working, although it'd had a few surprises and a lot more violence than he'd hoped. Still, he could picture Dymian's face awash with relief when Brysen strolled down the mountain with the giant black eagle secure in a net across his back. He could already hear the cheers from the battle boys and feel Dymian's hot breath on his neck when they embraced. He was perched on the edge of glory. He'd be a hero! A legend! He'd probably be able to run the business without Kylee, if she still wanted to leave it. He could set her free, just like she wanted, and he'd be her hero, too. He could be everyone's hero.

"The covey will look after these two," Üku said to Kylee, not deigning to pay Brysen any attention. It was going to be hard to bring her around to his cause if she wouldn't even speak to him.

"If I could just ask you a few—" he began, but the woman pursed her lips and held up a hand to silence him. She turned back to Kylee. "He'll be safe with the covey. You'll come with us for a while."

"Where's the covey?" Brysen asked, trying hard to assert his right to speak. He looked for some kind of mews or cages where the Owl Mothers might keep a flock of birds, but he saw none. Just more bone-thin birches, their smooth trunks rising up the slope as far as he could see. Baby owl eyes blinked at him from boxes, and he slipped Shara's hood over her head, then drove the small folding perch into the rough soil with his boot and leashed Shara to it. He didn't want her shrieking or skying out when the owls roused themselves for the night. If she went after a baby owl, the parents wouldn't be far behind. They'd make short work of a hawk like her, tough as she was.

Üku looked at him but didn't bother to answer his question.

"I don't want to leave them," Kylee told her. "We're on a journey together. We have to trap the—"

"Shh," Üku hushed her. "There will be time for that later."

Kylee looked at Brysen, uncertain. He hoped she'd be able to convince them to help. She'd made the biggest wrinkle in his plan. If she hadn't come along, the Owl Mothers would have had no choice but to talk to him. As it was, *he* now had no choice but to let his sister do the talking while he stayed with the covey, whatever it was.

"It's fine," Brysen reassured her. "Nyall and I will be fine. Just . . . you know, explain to them that I need their help, that I'll do whatever they want, but that they have to help me. I'm trying to save someone's life." He looked at Üku. "Can you tell them that?"

Üku glared at Brysen, obviously annoyed. One of the other Owl Mothers moved toward him, fist balled, but Üku raised a hand, stopped her.

Her silver hair was shaved on the sides, so she had a kind of mane swooping from her forehead down between her shoulder blades. She was solidly built, and in her looks she was more mountain goat than bird. In his mind, he named her Goat Mother, but he didn't dare say it aloud. He wasn't stupid. She could break him in half and break those halves in half if she chose to.

"We hear you," she said coldly, raising a finger and pressing it to her cheek just below her eye again. Then she turned back to Kylee. "The covey will look after them with care while you have a talk with us. Come."

The Owl Mothers surrounded Kylee and moved her on up

the slope, into the forest, leaving the boys alone in the clearing. Unguarded.

"So, this is not what I expected would happen when I woke up this morning." Nyall swiveled his head all around, looking at the taps in the trees, looking for footprints on the ground or the feathery remains of prey, the castings of undigested bone and fur that predators left behind—looking for any sign of this covey that was supposed to look after them. "Like, are baby owls guarding us from those boxes?"

"We're no baby owls," someone said, and both boys whirled toward the sound.

What they saw in front of them was not a bird. It was a boy, of sorts, yet there was something of an owl about him and something of a phantom. He was wide-eyed, white as powdered snow, and shirtless in spite of the cold mountain air. His stark-white skin was tight over his muscled chest and arms, which were tattooed with calligraphy that went from his left wrist all the way up his arm and halfway across his chest to his neck, then tapered down the left side of his rib cage to vanish below loose, feathered pants that draped over his hips. The feathers were the brown and white and gray of the owls, and he had a matching scarf over his shoulders. His feet were bare, and the left one was also covered in tattooed words. The markings looked something like the symbols of the Hollow Tongue on Brysen's black-talon blade, but these were more intricate, ornate, and far more beautiful.

The tattoos' positions were also a mirror image of Brysen's burn scars, hidden below his clothes. The coincidence made him flinch, more so than the sudden appearance of the phantom boy.

"We're the covey." Beside this phantom appeared a larger, older, stronger boy, and then another beside him—a flock of them materializing from behind the trees and within the shadows of trees. All of them had words and symbols tattooed on their snow-white bodies. A few of the oldest ones were covered from head to toe in tattoos, while the youngest, little boy phantoms, had only a few marks on their slim wrists. Even the oldest of them was no more than Dymian's age.

"She yours?" The boy who'd first appeared gestured at Shara on her perch. Brysen nodded, still speechless. Then to Nyall, "You have one?"

Nyall shook his head. He hadn't brought a hawk with him. Wisely. Brysen feared he shouldn't have brought Shara after all. The phantoms might feed her to an owl.

"Relax," the boy said. "You're all safe here. We're told to look after you, and we will. No lie." Just like the Goat Mother, Üku, had done, the boy pressed his index finger to the cheek under his eye. "You're our guests. Make yourselves comfortable."

"So you're the covey, huh?" Nyall asked.

The boy grinned, his lips and gums flashing pink while his pale eyes shined. "Who'd you think we were?"

Nyall looked at Brysen, and Brysen shrugged. The truth seemed the best approach here, so he offered it. "We honestly don't have any idea what's happening right now."

That provoked a round of laughter from the entire covey. "Right. Well, to explain: You're guests of our Mothers until they decide what to do with you. So *what's happening now . . . is dinner.*"

He laughed and pointed Nyall and Brysen to a spot in the forest where two birch trees leaned together like a new couple holding each other up after too much wine, and the rest of the covey peeled off and climbed to it. As they stepped below the arch the trees made, they vanished underground.

"Maybe they're ghosts," Nyall whispered.

"Boo!" the boy said, laughing. "Maybe we are . . ." Suddenly, he burst into song:

"To live and die, then live some more,
without our bodies to come along,
would be an awful wretched boor.
What good is living without your don—"

"*What* is going on?" Nyall whispered over the crude rhyme, but Brysen could only shake his head. He'd planned to make a plea for safe passage to the Owl Mothers this morning and be on his way toward the Nameless Gap by now. Instead, he was being invited to dinner by a group of rhyme-spouting mountain wraiths. He was losing time that he and Dymian didn't have, but he picked up Shara and her perch and followed the boy toward the arched trees and the cave below.

"You're Nyall, eh?" the boy asked as he led them down the sloping path that cut into the mountain. "And you're Brysen?"

"How do you know our names?" Brysen stopped walking. Nyall bumped into him from behind, and the boy turned around, cocking his head.

"You don't recognize me?"

"Why would we recognize you?" Nyall wondered.

The boy shrugged. "We grew up together."

Brysen looked at the boy closely, searching for something familiar.

"My name's Jowyn," the boy said. "I lived in the Villages until my legs were long enough to run."

"Jowyn?" Nyall gasped. "Jowyn *Tamir*?"

The boy touched his finger to the skin below his eye again. "See for yourself."

Brysen looked him up and down. He had known Jowyn

Tamir, Goryn's younger brother. They were the same age. Sometimes they'd played bone dice together outside the Broken Jess while Brysen's father gambled inside. Some days Jowyn had shown up with new bruises from his siblings. Some days Brysen had shown up with new ones from his father. Some days both of them had shown up wounded, but neither of them spoke about it. They hadn't needed to. There were no secrets in the Six Villages, not even for little boys at playtime.

And then one day Jowyn hadn't come to play. He hadn't come the next day, either. Rumor said he'd gotten ill. Goryn told everyone that he'd died of frost fever. The mourners' crows came. Even Brysen's father sent one to the Tamirs.

Brysen saw it now, in the boy's face. His coloring was different—an unnatural white—and his head was shaved, but he had those same broad Tamir features that his brother and sisters had. Goryn had lied. His little brother was standing right there in front of Brysen, transformed, but very much alive.

"You've . . . uh . . . changed . . . ," Nyall noted.

"New pants," Jowyn said.

They stared blankly at him, and then he exploded into laughter. He amused himself to no end.

"Seriously," he told them after he'd calmed down. "My brother and sisters would've carved me hollow before I grew my first armpit hair. I had to leave. I ran for the mountains, thought I could cross over, find the heroes of the old stories on the other side. But a little boy alone is no match for the winds of this world. I starved, mostly froze, and nearly broke every bone I had on the climb. After a full moon's turning, I finally caught a vole in a snare. Just before I snapped its neck to eat it, the Mothers found me. They gave me a choice: Kill the little vole, eat, and be banished from their mountain . . . or spare it and carry on. I was near dead with hunger, but I let the vole go. The Mothers melted away like fog. It was another few days of brutal hunger and loneliness before they appeared again, offered me sanctuary, gave me sap from the blood birches to fortify me for the mountains."

"The sap did this to you?"

"*I* did this to me," Jowyn replied. "The sap was just the means. It bled me, broke me, battered and rebuilt me. Now I can walk barefoot on a glacier or roll nude in burning coals."

"Are you all runaways?" Brysen wondered.

"Not all." Jowyn didn't offer any more explanation.

"What's with the tattoos?" Nyall asked.

Jowyn looked down at his markings, ran his hand across his chest. "Gifts from the Mothers. There is a story in these mountains older than can be told, bigger than can be told by one teller. But we all get to tell parts of it—the truest parts we can. They write 'em down for us once we find them out for ourselves."

Brysen felt like his scars had tightened over his chest and side, pulling so hard that his bones might break out. What story did his burns tell? Whose story was it?

They had reached the end of the passage. It opened into a large cavern, where the covey lounged in little groups all over the floor, sharing some sort of bright red beans served on large flatbreads they used as platters. The air smelled sweet with sweat and spice and smoke.

Over their heads, the roots of the blood birches made a massive crimson filigree that arched across the ceiling. Torches burned along the stone walls, and mineral deposits in the stone made them sparkle like starlight. The far wall of the cavern had a large fire pit, with a stone chimney leading aboveground. A group of the youngest boys ran back and forth from the fire, bringing dinner to the older boys. They reached barehanded into the fire and carried red-hot clay bowls. None of them had so much as a scar.

What would it be like, Brysen wondered, *to have a body free of scars and skin impervious to wounds? Does that sap heal wounds that go deeper than skin?*

"So no women in the covey?" Nyall wondered, looking around. Brysen hadn't thought to ask.

Jowyn laughed again. "There are girls training with the Mothers. They come and go as they please. They're always welcome, and we are always glad to see them. But we make do among ourselves just as well."

"Some of us more than others!" another of the pale phantoms laughed.

Jowyn grinned and waggled his eyebrows. "A heart's like a bird; who can tell a bird on which branch to land?"

"We know which branch you like birds to land on!" the other boy shouted.

"My branch is big enough for any bird who wants to perch on it," Jowyn laughed.

Nyall and Brysen looked at them, stunned.

"What?" Jowyn chuckled. "You thought we'd be chaste as Crawling Priests up here?" He shook his head. "The sky makes rainbows same as clouds."

"So the Owl Mothers don't . . . *keep* you here?" Brysen wondered, changing the subject away from the boys' branches. His eyes were tracing the strange writing over Jowyn's skin and the taut muscle beneath. Everything in his own body tightened further. He felt hot and, at the same time, ice-cold. Sweat beaded on his upper lip. He forced himself to look away.

"Keep us?" Jowyn wrinkled his forehead. "It's a gift to live on their mountain. It's a gift to have the illusion of our differences blown away. Who runs away from a gift?"

Brysen met Nyall's eyes. If they weren't prisoners, that

meant Brysen and Nyall could just go. Jowyn, however, caught their glance.

"Sorry, friends," he said. "I should've been more clear. *We* aren't kept here. You two . . . would not get very far if you tried to run."

"We just want to know if his sister is okay," Nyall pleaded. Brysen felt a stab of guilt. He hadn't been wondering that at all.

"Kylee is more than okay," Jowyn told them. "She's up with the Mothers. No sense worrying. Might as well eat."

They dug into the food and Brysen watched Jowyn carefully. If the Owl Mothers wouldn't talk to him, maybe Jowyn would help him reach the ghost eagle's eyrie, as long as Brysen didn't mention that he planned to hand it over to the big brother who'd tried to kill Jowyn as a child. He might be hard to convince.

Shara would need to eat something soon, but Brysen decided not to feed her yet. If she stayed hungry, she'd be able to help them fight when the time came. Maybe *he* couldn't shed blood on the mountain, but not even an Owl Mother could stop a hawk who was keen for blood, and if Jowyn wouldn't be an ally, then he could become a hostage. He made sure she was untethered to fly.

19

BRYSEN TORE OFF A PIECE OF THE STEAMING FLATBREAD AND USED it to scoop up the beans piled on the platter between Jowyn, Nyall, and himself. It smelled like a dish his mother used to make: heavy with mountain onion, sweetroot, and deep dirt chilies. His father would rage that there was no meat in it, but this version tasted thick and hearty and exploded with flavor. Something in the stew made his tongue tingle and his head feel light. As he ate, the dim room brightened. It felt like hunter's leaf felt the first time but clearer, sharper, cleaner.

He couldn't get enough.

"Eat slowly," Jowyn warned. "It can be intense if you've never had it before."

"Had what?" Brysen asked, scooping up another mouthful.

"There aren't enough nutrients in the soil here, so we supplement with a little tree sap . . ."

Brysen stopped with the glob of beans halfway to his mouth. His eyes widened at the pale boy. Brysen did not want to be broken, battered, and reborn as a phantom.

Jowyn, who was never too long a walk from laughter, laughed again. "Don't worry, a little of it isn't going to change you. It's how folks have survived up here since forever. You'd have to drink a lot more of it, fresh from the tree, to get as pretty as I am. And you'd need permission for that. Can't suck the sap from any tree you please up here. Gotta ask first." He winked, then slapped his knee at his own joke.

"You laugh a lot for someone living half-naked on a mountainside," Nyall observed.

"I wasn't supposed to live at all," he replied, not laughing. "My siblings wanted me dead; this mountain tried to kill me. But I still get to laugh because I'm alive. I get to laugh and cry and love and sing, and every time I do, I tell death she hasn't got me yet."

"You learn that from the Owl Mothers?" Brysen asked.

"I learned that"—Jowyn leaned forward—"by trying the other way for long enough, believing what the world told me about myself, and dying every day because of it. Up here, I learned that I get to tell the world about myself, not the other way around. You should try it, Brysen."

Brysen wanted to answer, to deny that he let anyone tell him how to feel, but he couldn't quite find the words. Nyall could sense Brysen's mood turning and changed the conversation. "Is it true that the trees only grow where someone's been killed?"

Jowyn touched the cheekbone below his eye.

"What is that?" Brysen asked. "Why do you keep doing that?"

"It's a reminder to see," he said. "If you've got eyes but won't use them, you might as well not see. When something's true and you don't see it, you gotta look closer."

"So you're saying it's true about the trees?"

"There was a war on this mountain." Jowyn pointed to his wrist, where the strange words looped and tangled, crashed into each other.

Brysen couldn't read the words, but they looked like a war. As Jowyn spoke, he moved his finger up his arm, narrating the pieces of the story that were written in ancient calligraphy on his skin. "The people who think they're Uztari fought here against the people who think they're Altari, before either of them had those names for themselves. Sky-bound, Mountain-bound. The war made the words. The two peoples named themselves for what they yearned for. They believed the lie that what you want is who you are. But death doesn't care what you want. These slopes ran red with the blood of men, women, and children who wanted to be alive but died anyway. Every death fed the seed of a tree, and the forest grew from murder's soil."

He touched his shoulder, where the lines of the text ran vertically, like the trunks of the blood birch trees.

"Yeah, but those are just stories," Nyall told him. He showed his own tattoo, the line of the old poem. The tattoo that had seemed so ornate down in the Villages suddenly looked paltry and plain beside Jowyn's. "It doesn't mean they're real."

"The forest is real," said Jowyn. "The struggle between Uztari and Altari is real. What makes the story not real?"

"It's just something people made up to explain the world," Nyall explained. "It didn't happen."

"So everything that's real must happen?" Jowyn touched beneath his eye again. "What's the difference between Uztari and Altari?"

"Where we live." Nyall shrugged. "How we hunt. How

we use birds. Our words, our food . . . I mean, it's who we are."

"And you're real?"

Nyall looked at Brysen and laughed, but the laugh had a blade in it. "Is this guy ill?"

Jowyn laughed, too, but his laugh was smooth and clear as a mountain lake. Brysen could've bathed in it. The thought of bathing with Jowyn made his ears burn.

"I mean, if you left where you lived," Jowyn said. "And you let go of your beliefs. If you stopped telling the *Epic of the Forty Birds*, stopped hunting with falcons, learned a new language, ate different food, would you become Altari?"

Nyall shook his head.

"He can't change his history," Brysen added. "Who we are is as much what's happened before us as it is what we do."

"What you *believe* happened before you," Jowyn corrected him. "You weren't there when the mountains were born or when the first hawk flew over them. You weren't there when the people followed. You decide to believe the stories you've been told, and what you decide to believe makes you who you are—about your people, about yourself."

"You talk like a mountain mystic," Nyall grumbled. "Who cares what we believe? What matters is what's true."

"You're up here chasing the ghost eagle," Jowyn observed. "A bird that can change the fate of kingdoms if it can be controlled. I'd say what you believe matters a great deal, if you plan to wield that kind of power."

"How do you know that?" Brysen asked.

Jowyn touched his finger under his eye again. "Only ones who come up here are running from something or running to it and runaways come alone. You are not alone."

Brysen glanced at Nyall. "Maybe I meant to be alone."

Jowyn shrugged. "So you aren't after the ghost eagle?"

Brysen didn't deny it. "I am."

"Why?"

Brysen took a deep breath, looked for an opening and saw the futility of evasion and went with the truth.

"Because I believe in love," he said.

Jowyn raised a pale, white eyebrow, surprised.

"I'm not looking for wealth or glory or power. I'm trying to save someone's life. The person I love. And my sister followed me because . . . well . . . she loves me. And Nyall followed her for love, too. We're all here for love." He felt like a fool saying these words out loud, but he needed help, and the only weapon he had to get that help was the ridiculous, embarrassing truth. His voice caught in his throat and he coughed. "I know it doesn't make sense, but I know I can do this. I know that my father died believing this same dumb thing, but I know I can capture this eagle, because *I'm* not doing it for the wrong reasons. I'm doing it for love."

Jowyn stared at him. An uncomfortable silence lingered. He rubbed his palms on his knees and leaned back. "The ghost eagle doesn't care why you're after it. It kills lovers just as well as hunters."

"You *just said* it matters what we believe."

"To me, it matters," Jowyn said. "Not to the eagle."

"Well." Brysen tried his luck. "Will *you* help us?"

"I can't take you to its eyrie," Jowyn said. "Not until the Mothers allow it."

"Forget this," Nyall stood. "I say we leave this cave, get your sister, and go on ourselves. I'm tired of sitting around being lectured."

"You can't go yet," Jowyn said.

"I dare you to stop us," Nyall told him. "I'd love to see you try."

"We don't bring violence here," Jowyn answered, rising to stand in front of him.

"That'll make it easier for me to smash your face in," Nyall growled.

Everyone turned to them and silence as sharp as a falcon's

beak snapped over the cavern. Nyall's jaw tensed, muscles tightened, and his fists flexed. Brysen got ready to spring to his feet for the fight.

They were outnumbered fifty to one, and every one of the covey looked like his skin had been carved from stone. If it turned into a brawl, there wasn't much of a chance Brysen and Nyall could win.

He slid his glove on, reached to the perch where Shara stood, and touched the back of her foot; her cue to step onto his fist. Once she was there, he stood and unhooded her. She screeched with surprise at her underground surroundings.

No one else moved.

"We're going," Brysen said. "I made a promise that I have to keep."

"You can't," Jowyn replied.

Nyall took a deep breath. "We'll cut through you like a fart through fabric."

"Do what you have to," said Jowyn.

He put his body directly in their way, opened his arms wide, tattooed chest rising up and down with his breath. He looked Brysen straight in the eyes, firmly rooted as a blood birch tree but completely vulnerable, undefended. If he was a tree, Brysen and Nyall were the ax.

Nyall moved to knock Jowyn down, but Brysen held him back. They didn't need to hit the boy; they could just go around him. When they turned, Jowyn pivoted to block them. Still, he did not raise a fist.

Nyall shook his head. "Get out of our way, or I'm gonna break all your branches and use them to light a fire."

"Do what you think you have to," Jowyn replied. "But remember that stronger winds than you have tried to break me."

Nyall drew his fist back and punched Jowyn in the stomach. The boy grunted but didn't bend or flinch. Nyall had pulled the punch. He'd just wanted to send a message, but the message didn't make the boy move.

Nyall drew back again. The next punch was harder. It snapped across Jowyn's jaw and turned his head, but his feet stayed rooted. Blood beaded on his lip, but he stood straight. He looked at Nyall and then at Brysen. The joy, that inexplicable joy, was still twinkling in the pale boy's eyes.

Nyall cranked his fist back a third time.

Brysen had known violence. Victim, survivor, attacker, defender. He'd taken beatings from his father and from bigger boys and girls. He'd cut himself quietly in the dark, releasing his hurt with the clean slice of the blade across his thigh. He'd made violence a sport and bled for the thrill of it in the battle pits, and he'd stood side by side with Nyck and Nyall in the kind of scrapes battle boys were known for. He never doubted that he was in the right when he drew blood.

But this fight?

Jowyn had fled violence to live here, and it seemed like he was ready to take a beating before committing it himself. The others were just going to let him take it.

Brysen could've unleashed Shara on him. He could've punched him in the gut and doubled him over, or at least let Nyall do it . . . but instead he reached out, caught Nyall's shoulder, and pulled his friend back.

"Stop," he said. "Not this way."

Had he been charmed by the pale boy's laugh or fallen like easy prey to the way the lines of his hips slid in a migrating V beneath his feathered pants? Was his heart so easily swayed? He'd sworn to cut through armies and climb through hell to save Dymian, but here he was, faced with a ghostly pale, tattooed boy standing in his way, and all he had to do was move him by simple force, and he couldn't.

If he really loved Dymian, he'd do anything to help him, after all. He'd long ago learned that it was better to shed blood than tears, so he bit his lip. He clenched his fist. He leaned back.

At that moment, without a sound of warning, Shara shot from his other arm with a burst of power he hadn't expected, nearly dislocating his shoulder. As she flew toward the passage they'd entered by, Brysen saw the last flash of a snow rat racing ahead of her. Her first dive at the rat missed, and she tumbled head over tail against the wall.

"Shara!" Brysen tried to whistle her back, but she was up and off again instantly, with the unshakable tenacity that made goshawks infuriating to their trainers. A falcon that missed a kill would stand confused long enough for the hunter to track her, but a goshawk never ceased, never slowed when its blood was up and its hunger was keen. Brysen should have fed her when he had the chance.

She dove again, missed again, and the rat raced for the passage's opening. Jowyn and the other owl boys of the covey watched her shake her feathers out and launch herself after it in furious flaps, a tenacious hunter with more appetite than skill.

We're a lot alike, Brysen thought, and before he could whistle her back again, she was out of the cave and flying madly into the mountain night.

20

JOWYN HAD TURNED HIS BACK TO WATCH THE HAWK'S FURIOUS HUNT, and in that moment, Brysen shoved right past him and straight through the cave into the woods after Shara.

"Pfft!" he whistled. "Pfft!"

"Stop!" some of the covey shouted after him, but he sprinted harder.

His eyes scanned the dark trees and the frost-coated ground, searching for his hawk. It was common in the Villages to chase your bird through other people's property, to find yourself tangled in a thorny goat fence or wading knee-deep across the Necklace, because a hawk neither knows nor respects the boundaries people draw across the world. The demarcation of kingdoms, invisible lines drawn by war and language, treaty and betrayal—hawks erase them with a flap of their wings. Shara obeyed her blood and the tremor of her moods, and the hunt had called her.

He saw the white stripes of her chest flash from the corner of his eye and then glimpsed her in a blood birch, feet gripping the branch and back flattened, head low and level. He whistled her down, held out his fist, but she didn't even turn to look at him. She was focused on a small heap of frost-covered rocks, where the rat must have taken shelter.

Brysen whistled again. While he stood there, his eyes fixed on her and her eyes fixed on the rocks, Nyall and Jowyn and the others caught up to him, their breaths huffing out in misty clouds of damp air. The night temperature on the mountain had dropped well below comfort, and Brysen had left his coat and supplies back in the cave. He was amazed that Jowyn could run around shirtless, like he was in the blazing desert. Nyall had kept his coat on and was already shivering.

"It's not safe out here," Jowyn warned.

"That's why I have to get her back," Brysen replied just as Shara launched herself from the branch at the rat, which had bolted from its hiding place. It'd been flushed out by a deep-blue ice snake that now had the hawk's complete attention. The rat dodged a strike from the serpent, but before the snake could turn, Shara smashed onto it, snatching it just behind the head and pinning it down. Its body twisted and writhed, trying to free its head and snap its fangs into her, but Shara's grip tightened with every move the snake made.

An ice snake's venom was especially toxic at this time of year, when it had built up over the ice-wind, heating the snake from the inside and burning to get out. Ice snakes ended their hibernation when their venom's heat woke them to hunt, and they wanted nothing more than to expel the poison into their prey, cooking their meal from the inside out.

Brysen ran toward them, huffing his way up the snowy, wooded slope, muttering half prayers that the snake wouldn't get its venom into Shara before he could slice its head off. He drew his knife as he approached, but Shara had already crushed the snake to death and mantled her wings over its corpse. She didn't need Brysen's help.

As she bent down to break into the snake's meat with her sharp beak, Brysen's clumsy approach up the mountain froze her. She glanced over her shoulder at her master, saw him and his drawn blade, and then unceremoniously took off, the snake's corpse hanging from her talons like a flapping war banner. She weaved through the wood, wending and winding until Brysen couldn't see her anymore.

"Scuzz!" he shouted, stomping the ground.

He knew it wasn't meant as an insult, just goshawk instinct, but he couldn't help feeling stung by her flight away. Woodland hunters, goshawks preferred to eat in private, where other predators couldn't see what they'd caught or scheme to take it. It wounded him that she would think of Brysen as just another predator. It was irrational to expect that she would treat him differently, that she'd think fondly of all he'd done for her, that the ways of the world would make an exception just for him, but still, he wished they would.

Brysen tore off running again.

"Bry!" Nyall called up to him. "Bry! Where are you going?"

Brysen didn't answer. Shara had flown across a low sloping field shaped like a bowl. He skirted the edge, keeping to the lip and leaping over patches of slick ice, before finding himself back on the tree-covered slope again. As he ran, he caught a glimpse of Jowyn from the corner of his eye; he was cutting straight across the snow field, his skin nearly perfect camouflage in the icy moonlight.

Brysen stopped and listened. He heard Nyall panting and scrambling, feet crunching, but beneath those noises Brysen listened for the sounds of panicked woodpeckers or crows or anything that might give Shara's position away. He searched the dark wood for signs of feathers or snakeskin snagged on a bush or branch. A hawk always left some sign of its hunt if you knew what to look for.

Up to his right, the trees ended at a steep gray rock. There was a frozen waterfall pouring off the top and tumbling down in an unmoving crystalline crash. Behind the wall of frozen water was what looked like a cave. Some of the icicles at the edge of the cave's entrance had been smashed and their shards lay on the still, solid pool below.

Shara had to have broken them off while flying into the cave with the snake. A cave behind a wall of ice would make the perfect private place for her to eat in peace.

Brysen rushed over, determined to get her leashed to his arm before she could fly away again. He slipped a little as he crossed the ice, forced to widen his stance and shuffle to the edge of the frozen waterfall. He peered around the curtain of ice, searching the moonlit cave. Dim silver slices of light slipped through the frozen falls and cast shadows like the bars of a cage. In a corner, he saw the shape of Shara's mantled wings. Her head jerked upward with a tearing sound. She had blood on her beak.

Brysen let out a relieved breath. She was eating. He shuffled his way into the dark to reach her as calmly and quietly as he could. She was so fixated on eating that she didn't look up this time. He kept his eyes fixed on her gray wings, ready to dive at her if she tried to fly off again.

"Stop!" Jowyn shouted at him, his voice echoing inside the cavern. Shara flinched and paused, then returned to her serpentine supper. Brysen glanced behind him and saw Jowyn's shape on the other side of the icefall. His figure bent and wavered, backlit by the moon.

"I'm getting her now," Brysen said.

"Stop right where you are!" Jowyn repeated slowly. "And don't move."

Jowyn's voice wasn't a threat, Brysen realized. It was a warning, and it came at the same instant he heard a telltale *snap-pop-snap* beneath his feet. The sound of ice cracking.

He knew better than to run over frozen water during the ice-melt, but he'd been so focused on getting Shara back that he hadn't been careful. This was the kind of carelessness that Kylee always yelled at him about, that Dymian thought was so endearing. The kind of carelessness that his father had beaten him for, over and over again. Looked like his father was right: Carelessness was going to kill him.

"Scuzz," he said, and the ice broke.

21

BRYSEN SPREAD HIS ARMS WIDE IN PALE IMITATION OF A HAWK SLOWING
to land, but there was no wind to lift him or fist to catch him.
He crashed through the ice, and the cold dark closed around
him like a fist slamming shut.

The shock of the icy water felt like rolling on a bed of broken glass. It sucked half the air from his lungs, and the weight
of his clothes dragged him down, deeper and deeper. He flailed
his arms, tried to kick himself to the surface but then, in cold
confusion, doubted which way the surface actually was. The
frigid water burned his eyes when he opened them, but it hardly

mattered. There was no light. How could he get out if he didn't know which way was up?

Bubbles rise, he thought. Against all instinct, against every part of his animal brain that screamed at him to cling to his last bit of breath, he opened his mouth and let the air out. The last burst of life in his lungs floated away from him, and he followed furiously behind.

He couldn't swim fast enough. The heaviness of his clothes, of himself, pulled at him, and no sooner had his fingers grazed the solid underside of the ice than he sank again.

But he kicked through the burning cold as his lungs' hunger for air tore at him from the inside. His fingers found the bottom of the ice again. He tried to punch through, but the force pushed him back down. He kicked up again, burning precious energy. He couldn't find the hole he'd made when he fell in; couldn't see it, couldn't feel it. His fingers were numb and his vision narrowed. He sank once more, and this time he didn't fight it. He was so tired. He'd been struggling all his life, he figured—fighting against the weight of a world that dragged down boys who wanted to fly.

Maybe drowning was for the best. Maybe it was time to stop fighting.

The thought of surrender warmed him, wrapped itself around his body, and swaddled him in the loving hold of oblivion. He stopped feeling cold. It was peaceful below the ice. Quiet. Safe. So what if his soul couldn't find the sky and stayed frozen in that cold pool forever? The sky had never helped him before. He'd never been meant to soar. His father had been right about him all along. This was the kind of end he deserved. He'd been born to sink. He was ready now. He let his feet touch the bottom. He didn't struggle. He let his arms float up over his head. He relaxed into the void.

There was his father's face, floating in front of him, twisted in the rage and surprise of his last moments. Brysen had been there. Brysen had seen the ghost eagle take him. Their eyes had met one final time. The grimace now turned into a smile. This was his father's revenge.

Suddenly, he felt a hard hand grip him, lift him, pull him up. His father's face vanished. He couldn't see who had grabbed him, but with that touch, the cold rushed back through his body, the burn of his lungs screaming for air and the choking urge to live. He came back to himself and remembered that his father was dead and that he had lived. He'd survived beating and burning and more fights than he could count, and he was not going to die underwater. He was meant to see the sky again, to be reunited with Dymian in victory and glory.

He tried to kick his legs for the surface, but they refused to obey. He thrashed and flailed and the hand held him tighter. He needed air, but the struggle to stay alive . . . it hurt.

He screamed, and freezing water rushed in to fill the sound, choking him. He knew he was drowning; his brain yelled at him as his vision narrowed to a point.

You are drowning, you are drowning, you are drowning.

And then he was out of the water, felt himself being dragged by his belly along the ice, rolled onto his back, felt ice-cold lips on his, warm air blown into his mouth, and then he was coughing, throwing up in endless heaves.

"He's breathing," someone said. "I'll start a fire."

Nyall. It was Nyall scrounging around in the dark for scraps of birch bark and forest twigs to get a fire going. He saw his friend run off, but he still felt a hand on his back. He was sitting up, on the ground outside the cave in front of a long line of drag marks in the frosted dirt. Someone was holding him. Someone had dragged him outside. If Nyall was over there gathering kindling, who was . . . ? Oh, right. He remembered Jowyn, the boy as white as a snow owl. The laughing phantom boy whose body told a story. He'd wanted to punch him in the cave, to take him hostage, but that same boy had saved him, pulled him to the surface, breathed air back into his lungs.

For an instant, he couldn't remember why he'd needed saving at all, how he'd ended up underwater and out of air, and then it came back to him. "Shara!" he coughed, and his throat felt like shards of glass.

"She's fine," Jowyn said. "She's still in there."

Brysen looked up at the frozen waterfall, locked in its unmoving rush. He wanted to go back to get his hawk, to leash her, to hold her close, but at the first effort to move, he found his legs completely disobedient. They didn't hurt; they simply wouldn't move. He looked down at his fingers and realized they wouldn't obey him, either. He tried to tell Jowyn but found that his words came out as an unintelligible slur. His tongue was numb. His thoughts were, too.

Freezing, he realized. He had escaped drowning only to find himself freezing to death.

To his left, down the slope, he saw Nyall assembling the meager scraps of wood he'd found into a suitable shape for igniting, but he looked so far away, too far for his fire-starting to have anything to do with Brysen. Nyall seemed to realize only after he'd built a little pyramid of twigs that he had no stone to light it with. All their supplies were back in the covey's cave.

That struck Brysen as funny, like the personal disaster of his own dying was absurd compared to the disaster of Nyall's hopeless attempt to coax a flame to save him. He started to laugh, and the laughing started him shaking uncontrollably.

Jowyn said something to him, but he couldn't really even hear it. It was like he was still underwater and the phantom boy was shouting at him from the surface. Words couldn't warm him, anyway, so why should he try to hear what the words were?

He felt Jowyn pawing at him, tearing off his wet clothes.

He's trying to get me naked, Brysen thought. *Sorry, friend, but I'm taken.*

The thought set him laughing even harder, although a part of him knew his laughter sounded like gasps. He was, he noticed, having trouble breathing, gasping and not getting enough air.

At least he'd stopped shivering. That made it easier for Jowyn to get his clothes off. He was suddenly naked, and the phantom boy had wrapped himself around his body.

He'd never let a stranger see him like this before. All his scars were visible—the raised keloid trails across his back, the smooth tangle of burns up his side. But he couldn't make himself care to resist or to fight back. He saw his wet clothes in a pile beside him, but he made no move to recover them. If the pale boy with the strange skin wanted to mock his scars, so be it. What did Brysen's body matter, anyway? It was about to die.

Brysen had seen a man freeze to death in the Six Villages during the ice-wind when he and Kylee were small—an old hunter's-leaf fiend everybody called the Goldfinch. He'd talked endlessly but said nothing and had been tossed out of the Broken Jess for starting a brawl. Drunk, he'd stumbled into a snowbank and lashed out at anyone who tried to help him. He'd shivered for a while, then fallen asleep on the slope heading up the hill toward Brysen's home above town. The man froze there, dead, and Kylee and Brysen were the ones who found him the next morning when they went to collect their father. The man had looked so peaceful. Brysen wondered why his father never just lay down in the snow. He always seemed to pass out by a warm fire.

Freezing to death was, at least, a lot nicer than drowning. He felt the steady rise and fall of Jowyn's chest against his back. It felt good to be gripped in Jowyn's arms. Safe. Brysen closed his eyes. *So many different ways to die*, he thought, and wondered why he'd been so afraid to do it before now.

"How's that fire?" Jowyn shouted at Nyall.

"I can't get it started!" Nyall shouted back.

Jowyn cursed, and Brysen felt himself being laid down on his back. "'S all right," Brysen slurred. "Easy to die . . ." He opened his eyes and the boy was leaning over him, one arm raised, fist clenched. The stark-white muscles of his forearm bulged and his veins popped.

For a moment, he saw his father's face again, instead of the boy's. Maybe Jowyn *had* been a ghost all along, waiting for the moment to give Brysen one final hit, one last smack for daring to climb higher than he deserved, for trying to do what his father never could.

Strangely, the boy didn't hit Brysen. His gentle face was back and he pulled Brysen's curved blade from the pile of wet clothes and held it to the back of his own white fist. He drew a small gash with the tip across the back of his own hand. The red blood beaded against the white skin, glistening like jewels.

"Drink," he commanded, dropping the blade into the dirt and using his free hand to lift Brysen's head. He pressed Brysen's lips against the skin. The blood smelled like moss and metal and blazing bonfires. It smelled like sunlight and switchgrass and steaming cider. It smelled alive. "Drink," Jowyn repeated, and Brysen put his mouth to the wound, touched his tongue to the skin on the back of Jowyn's hand, and let the blood flow into his mouth.

At the first swallow, he felt cold again, started to shiver; then warmth blossomed in his stomach and radiated out, chasing the cold from him. His mind cleared; he was aware now, aware of the ground against his legs, the mountain wind against his back, the pain in his throat, but also of the heat returning, the rush and thrill of life in his heartbeat. His breathing calmed.

He'd heard of hunters drinking goat's blood to stay warm when they were caught out in the ice-wind and of desert convoys that ran out of water drinking the blood of their livestock. Blood was life, after all, and Jowyn was offering it freely.

He drank.

As he drank, the pain vanished, and although he was naked in the mountains with his best friend staring, slack-jawed, while he drank blood from a stranger's hand, he felt no shame. He felt amazingly well and whole and free . . . more so than he could ever remember feeling in his life. And the feeling flooded him so full that he cried, hot tears of pure joy streaming down his cheeks.

Jowyn began to pull his hand away, but Brysen reached both his hands up, grabbing his wrist and holding the hand against his face to get another gulp of blood.

"Stop," Jowyn warned, trying to pull away, but Brysen wanted more. All he wanted was more.

On a distant branch, an owl hooted. Brysen, with eyes closed, could see the owl perfectly in his mind. From the sound of its hoot alone, he knew exactly where it was, could hear its claws against the bark, its feathers moving in the breeze. He imagined what it saw, tried to see with its eyes and know what it knew. It was hungry; it was curious; it was patient. He tried to listen farther, to the distant peaks. Could he hear the ghost eagle's heartbeat? Could he see his way to its eyrie just by think-ing it? Could he call it to him where he lay right now?

"Stop!" Jowyn warned again. He yanked his arm free and used his powerful leg against Brysen's chest to push him back onto the frozen ground. The moment his lips broke from Jowyn's bloody fist, Brysen came back to himself. He couldn't see the owl or the eagle, didn't know where either were. His head cleared. He became deeply aware of who he was, what he could and couldn't do, and how he was now sprawled on his back, blood on his lips, stark naked on the edge of the blood birch forest, where this strange pale boy's blood magic had saved his life.

This was not exactly the heroic quest he'd envisioned when he set out.

22

BRYSEN SAT UP, DREW HIS LEGS UP TO HIS CHEST, AND WRAPPED HIS
arms around his knees, shielding as much of his body as he
could behind his skinny shins. His breathing began to feel
ragged again; all the euphoria he'd just felt was becoming
a hazy memory. He was not even the littlest bit cold, but
he began to shiver and wanted nothing more than to cover
his skin.

"What did you do?" Nyall spoke for Brysen as he came up
the slope, which was good, because Brysen couldn't quite find
any words.

"I did what had to be done to save him," Jowyn answered,

locking eyes with Brysen. "Your body temperature had dropped too low."

"Will it—?" Brysen wasn't sure how to form the question, wasn't sure if he wanted to know the answer. Jowyn's skin was unmarred, marked only by his tattoos, which he seemed to take great pride in. It was skin without anyone else's history carved into it, and Brysen wondered what it must be like to look at your bare skin proudly, as a thing earned rather than inflicted. On the other hand, was a life that left no mark any kind of life at all? The wound on Jowyn's hand had already begun to heal. "Will I turn into—?"

Jowyn shook his head. "You won't turn into one of us, no."

Brysen swallowed, relieved but strangely sad. He wiped the traces of blood from his lips. "I need to get Shara," he said, and he looked down at the exposed scars on his chest, at the rest of himself, just as exposed. "And I could use some clothes."

Jowyn smiled at him, gentle mirth back in his eyes. "Maybe not in that order, though?"

Brysen smiled, too, but pulled his legs closer to keep himself covered just as the other boys of the covey arrived. There were stones digging into his bare backside, and his knees ached, but he couldn't imagine standing up in front of everyone and strolling nude across the ice.

Jowyn looked at Brysen a long moment, then at the thin red

line on his own hand. He took a deep breath, like he'd decided something hard, and went over to talk to the others.

Sitting alone, Brysen raised his fist out to his side, holding his knees to his chest with the other arm like a shield. He whistled. If Shara was in the cave, she could certainly see him, even in the dark. She could at least see his silhouette. He imagined her in there, beak wet with snake blood, staring at his distorted form through the moonlit ice.

He could feel the stares of all the covey on his bare back, crosshatched with whip scars and burns like a wax casing stretched over ground sausage meat. His whole back tingled with the sensation of being seen, but getting his hawk back was more important. A falconer hunting a lost bird had no time for shame. The self was meant to disappear when a man called a bird of prey home. At its best, it was a moment of total selfless peace; at its worst, it felt like a crushing emptiness.

He felt his heart pulling out toward Shara, focused all his thought on her, gave no space to his own worries or plans or fears . . . but they made space for themselves. He felt totally exposed.

"Come on," he pleaded with Shara under his breath. "Come on, come on, come on . . ." He moved his fist up and down like he sometimes did in training when there was food on it and whistled again.

Still nothing.

If she wouldn't come to his whistle, he would have to go get her, no matter the risk. This time, though, he'd be smarter about it. He looked back over his shoulder. The covey boys were now locked in a full-blown argument with Jowyn, and it seemed like Nyall was trying to get a word in. They were pointing at the rapidly healing cut on Jowyn's hand, wagging fingers in his face. No one was looking at Brysen.

He stood quietly, trying to will himself invisible. His eyes searched for the thickest ice to cross, but before his bare foot set down on the glassy surface, three voices shouted.

Nyall yelled, "Bry, no!"

Jowyn yelled, "Don't!"

And from atop the icy waterfall, backlit by the moon, his sister yelled, "Brysen, what are you doing? And why are you naked?"

23

BRYSEN'S EYES DARTED UP TO HIS SISTER. SHE WAS BREATHLESS, panting, looking from him to Nyall to the bone-white, tattooed boys around them, puzzled. She glanced over her shoulder, like she was being chased. "Get your clothes! We have to go!"

"Where are the Mothers?" Jowyn called up.

Kylee ignored him. "Come on, Bry! Quickly!"

"Stay exactly where you are, all of you," a fourth voice commanded. Üku passed through the crowd of boys behind Brysen like sunlight through a cloud, carrying her huge gray owl on her left fist. Her eyes were red and irritated and the skin around them looked as if it had been burned. She raised her left arm as she walked and her lips moved, whispering a word to her owl. "*Thaa-loom.*"

The owl launched from her fist with two flaps of its wide wings and swooped up to Kylee, hovering just over her head, just out of reach. Its strong taloned feet extended down. She had enough force in those claws to open Kylee's scalp, and it was an uncanny ability of owls to hover over their prey in patient silence.

That the Owl Mother could send her owl to hover over a human target just by whispering a word chilled Brysen in a brand-new way.

More Owl Mothers emerged from the trees, and they, too, had owls on their fists or hovering over their heads, owls of different colors and sizes. At least now he knew why Shara wouldn't come out to him. She wasn't being cruel. She was afraid.

"I guess it didn't go so well with them, huh?" he yelled up to his sister.

Kylee shook her head, her face haunted. Something *had* happened, and it had shaken her. She wore a look Brysen hadn't seen in a long, long time.

"You should *not* have run from us," Üku called up to her,

and then looked at Brysen. He covered himself with his hands. The Owl Mother snapped her fingers.

Without a word, the boy nearest her brought Brysen a dry pair of feathered pants like the covey wore and his own coat from the cave. Brysen dressed, slipped on his still-wet falconer's glove, and, with the confidence of the newly clothed, turned to face Üku to demand passage up the mountain so he could complete his quest for love and honor. She, however, did not give him the opportunity to speak.

"*Shyehnaah-tar,*" she said, and like a stone from a slingshot, Shara burst from the cave, tucking her wings perfectly as she slipped between two icicles, then spreading them wide to land calmly on the Owl Mother's fist, where the great gray owl had been perched. The other owls watched Shara, blinked, but made not so much as a hoot or a ruffle of feathers.

"Don't move," Üku ordered Brysen, stroking his hawk's tail feathers with her right hand.

"I won't," he pleaded. "Just . . . please. Be gentle to her."

"Prrpt," Shara chirped, twisting her head sideways to look at him.

Though Shara clutched the cloth around the woman's knuckles, she might as well have been squeezing Brysen's bleeding heart in her talons. She'd obeyed a stranger before she'd obeyed him. They were at the Owl Mothers' mercy now, and the danger they were in was, for once, not Brysen's fault. He looked up at Kylee, whose wild eyes darted around like a trapped rabbit's. What had happened to her?

Üku nodded at another mother, who took Brysen's curved blade from where it still lay on the ground, wet with Jowyn's blood, and came to him. She stood about a head shorter and held him in the same impassive stare as an owl blinking from a hollow tree. She took his gloved left hand in her own, gently raised it, then turned and locked his arm in the crook of her elbow. She slid his glove off and pressed his own blade to his bare wrist. His *left* wrist.

She intended to cut off his falconry hand.

Brysen's heart pounded against his rib cage loud as a goose's wingbeats, and he tried to wrest his arm free, but the Owl Mother's grip was unbreakable.

"Don't hurt him," Jowyn pleaded. He touched his finger below his eye. "He means no harm. This is not necessary."

Üku glanced at Jowyn's bloody fist, then at Brysen, and then back to Jowyn. The rest of the covey tensed. "What have you done?"

Jowyn bowed his head. "He would have died."

Her nostrils flared, her jaw clenched. "Death is not yours

to give, and nor is life. We have very few rules here, but the ones we have must be obeyed."

"I know." Jowyn stared at his feet.

"You have bound yourself to *him*." She gestured to Brysen. "And so, as you have freely chosen, you are unbound from us."

Jowyn flinched and looked like he might cry, but instead he raised his head, puffed out his strong chest, and nodded. "I understand. I accept your justice and my"—his voice cracked, but he cleared his throat—"exile."

Jowyn had saved his life and was being punished for it, cast out. The blade pressed against the soft skin just below Brysen's hand, the curve of it seeking out the tight tendon. His knees felt weak.

"Please . . . no . . . ," he pleaded. He could handle the pain of a thousand whippings, of being cut and burned and broken down, but he couldn't bear the thought of losing his fist, the vital perch where Shara sat, of never calling her to sit on it again. Panic buzzed in his ears; he thought he might faint. "Please," he repeated. "Don't."

"This is our way," Üku said. The Owl Mother thought Brysen was pleading on Jowyn's behalf. In the pit of his stomach, he felt shame that he wasn't.

"Please," he whispered, disappointed in himself, looking away from Jowyn. "Don't cut me."

After all, he hadn't asked Jowyn to save him. He hadn't asked for *anyone* to save him, not for a long, long time. All he wanted from anyone was that they not hurt him. He felt like a little kid again, cowering beneath his father's rage, admitting everything, anything, inventing sins to confess, heaping whatever shame upon himself he could with the hope that it might make the hurting stop.

Then, as now, his pleas were not heeded.

The blade cut.

Brysen wanted to scream, but Kylee did it first, screaming from above on the frozen falls. Her scream was a word or a command or an avalanche made of wind.

When it left her lips, every owl in the clearing—even the one hovering above her—and every passage hawk and nesting pigeon and wild bird within hearing—Shara, too—burst into the air and formed a giant cloud of a thousand winged things, and then this massive midnight flock of feather and claw, beak and talon, swooped down upon them, sending the Owl Mothers and the covey boys scattering.

Brysen dove to the ground and rolled away, shielding his head with both hands, staining his gray hair red with the blood from his wounded wrist. There was a chaos of shrieking, honking, calling, and wings beating against the air. The frantic flock filled the sky so thickly, they hid the moon, the stars, even the trees of the forest. All was feathers. All was claws.

What had his sister done?

What could *his sister do?*

Through the melee, Brysen saw Üku standing straight and unafraid in the swarm, her eyes locked on Kylee. Üku was smiling.

MUD BETWEEN

THE FORTUNE WOULD BE NICE, OF COURSE. EVEN SPLIT UP BETWEEN the two of them, the kyrg's reward for the ghost eagle would give the Otak family enough wealth to match the Tamirs themselves. Goryn wouldn't like being beaten at his own game, but Kyrg Bardu had made it clear that she could protect them from the wrath of those Six Villages tyrants. She might even grant a title to the Otaks, which would elevate them immediately.

No more spying for other families. The Otak kyrgs would dictate their own destiny. *They* would have spies of their own. Wealth could be won by anyone with a will to do it, but nobility was the real lure that had called Petyr and Lyl Otak up the mountain.

Petyr knew the hazards, both physical and spiritual, that this journey entailed. His brother had been asleep when the long-haulers came for the twins, but he'd watched the scene unfold with a cold sweat collecting at the small of his back. He'd known those two since they'd been born, watched them grow in fits and starts. He'd felt bad for the boy, beaten all those years by his father, a petty man too weak to fight anyone his own age. Petyr'd been tempted to slug him countless times, but never had. He was a man who observed, not a man who acted on his observations—unless ordered to. Such was the duty of a spy.

After Yzzat's death, Petyr had watched Brysen train, sending off regular reports on his lout of a trainer back to that young man's family. The Avestris paid well for information on their son, Dymian, but Petyr had done his best to leave out the more lurid details of how Dymian carried on with Brysen. No sense bringing the amorous boy into the intrigues of a noble family. There was surely some noble boy or girl Dymian's parents would've preferred him with once his exile in the Villages ended. Brysen would've been an inconvenience, one they could have ordered vanished if they'd chosen to. Boys vanished all the time. In his way, Petyr felt he'd protected Brysen.

So it was hard to watch his head rest on the long-hauler's chopping block, hard not to intervene. He'd nearly charged up the mountain and come to their rescue, but the Owl Mothers' sudden appearance had put that plan out to roost. He'd been forced to follow them and wait, plotting a rescue if need be, but only so they could continue their quest for the prize.

Brysen was hopeless, but his sister's talents might be just the thing to bring the mighty bird down. Petyr and Lyl had pinned all their hopes to her and were rooting for her still, even though they knew, at the end, they would have to take the ghost eagle from her. Most likely by slitting her throat. Anyway, if they didn't do it, Goryn Tamir surely would when the twins returned to the Villages empty-handed, and Goryn would be far less gentle about it than Petyr would be. Petyr didn't want these kids to suffer, not more than they had to. How could a heart hold such contradictory things together? He wished them safety and success, knowing that he planned to rob them of both.

He wondered if, when the time came, he'd be able to kill these two children and their friend.

For riches alone, no. Never. But for nobility and respect for his family for generations to come? He could do anything.

When the kids went up the mountain with the Owl Mothers, he and Lyl followed.

"You go with the boys," he'd told his brother. "I'll follow the girl to the Mothers' camp."

Lyl had happily accepted the suggestion, which was a relief to Petyr. He was a better tracker than Lyl. And he hadn't wanted his younger brother getting too close to those women after seeing how brutally they'd dispatched the long-haulers.

He gave his brother the winged salute across his chest, then touched the charm around his neck, the Otak family seal: carved bone in the shape of a rabbit with eagle's wings and humongous talons. The seal had been a source of much mockery in their boyhood, but they'd both worn it proudly and thrown fists to defend it. The Otaks were like their symbol—easy to laugh off until they landed hard upon you with vicious claws and rabbitlike speed. He kissed the charm and his brother did the same to his own, and they went their own ways.

Petyr found a route up the east side of a spur along the edge of the blood birch forest. There were a few hairy inclines, a gorge he had to cross on a half-rotted trapper's rope that was older than he was, and one vertical he had no choice but to free-climb, but he kept up and kept track of them straight through to dusk. He passed the time imagining the inevitable future when he and his brother, elevated to nobility, would be invited to the Sky Castle: *Kyrg Petyr. Kyrg Lyl, the Otak Counselors for . . . what? Trade, weights, and measures? Breeding licenses. There was no limit to the fortunes a motivated member of the Council of Forty could make.*

So lost was he in the daydream that he didn't notice the loose stones falling down the slope in front of him, disturbed by figures moving into an ambush. Before he could reach for his weapon, one of them threw a heavy sack at him, hitting him square in the chest and knocking him flat on his ass.

The sack was wet and round, and lifting it off himself turned his hands a bright and angry red.

Blood.

The sack was soaked in blood.

"Open it," an Owl Mother suggested, standing above him with her tawny owl perched like a hungry ghost on her fist. It watched with unblinking black eyes as Petyr peeled back the fabric of the sack and then gagged at its contents.

His brother's face stared back at him, eyeless sockets in a head that had been roughly severed.

"Mud below and mud between. The dead can't rise to a sky unseen," the Owl Mother said as Petyr gagged again, dry heaving into the dirt next to his brother's face. "You two should not have interfered here."

There are moments when what you know of yourself and your world is shaken loose, sudden shocks, after which nothing can be the same. These moments send some men spiraling into the abyss, while others rise, soar, and are reborn stronger into new and unfamiliar lives, girded with hard-won wisdom.

Petyr Otak was not going to become a better man for having held his brother's eyeless head in his hands, but he was incandescent with rage and discovered in himself a feral thirst for vengeance he had not known he harbored. He wanted to tear the woman above him apart.

He sprang from the ground, drawing his dagger as he rose and rushed at her.

The tawny owl shrieked and jumped from her fist while she blocked the knife thrust with ease, using Petyr's own momentum to toss him sideways to the ground. She stomped the blade from Petyr's grip and broke every bone in his hand, then she kicked him straight in the teeth, shattering more than a few and cracking his nose. She bent down and rolled him onto his back, resting a knee across his chest to hold him.

Petyr tried to curse her, but all that came from his mouth were bloody choking sounds. Above him, the clouds had gone flesh pink with sunset, run through with veins of arterial red. The tawny owl glided down from that fleshy sky and landed on its master's fist. The Owl Mother set it across his breastbone and stood; the owl's hooked beak was poised to strike his face.

He tensed, tried to remain very still, fearful of provoking the bird. A breeze ruffled the feathers on the crown of its head.

"No," Petyr croaked. "Not . . . like . . . this . . ."

Two other Owl Mothers came into his line of vision, standing over him.

"You'll be coming with us," one of them said. "You've got a purpose yet to serve."

With a whistle, the owl jumped from his chest back to its master's fist, and the other two women lifted him from the ground, binding his hands.

"Consider yourself lucky," the first one told him as they led him away from the sack where his brother's eyeless head stared up at the sky. "Most men don't get to live through their own sky burial."

His knees buckled. They had to drag him up the mountain, each step bringing him closer to the night sky and whatever brutal end the Owl Mothers reserved for trespassers and spies.

KYLEE

THE HOLLOW TONGUE

24

KYLEE STOOD ON THE FROZEN FALLS, PUZZLING AT THE SCENE BELOW:
a boy whose skin was white as clean-picked bone, pleading for
her brother's safety. Her brother's hawk on Üku's fist, and a
blade pressed to the base of his own.

The Owl Mothers were not the benevolent guardians of the
mountain that they at first seemed. They were dangerous and
duplicitous, and what they had planned for her and her brother
was not going to end well. It'd been a mistake to head toward
their territory.

She knew the moment her brother was seized that she had
to find the searing words inside her, even as she knew that was

exactly what Üku wanted. The Owl Mother wasn't threatening Brysen because she wanted to cut off his hand. She was threatening Brysen because she wanted to provoke Kylee. But she wasn't bluffing. She *would* do it.

For a moment, Kylee tried to focus on her brother's hand, tried to imagine the pain he'd feel as it was severed from his wrist.

"*Shyehnaah*," she said, but nothing happened.

You have to mean what you say, the Owl Mothers had told her.

Brysen could still be a falconer one-handed. Some stories said Ymal the Cask-Breaker only had one hand, and he'd found a way to greatness. Brysen was afraid, but Kylee couldn't make herself feel his fear.

She had to find another way, another word. She had to *make* herself speak.

"Please," Brysen whispered below, the words carrying on the still night air. "Don't cut me."

Kylee remembered the stories she and Brysen used to tell each other about the distant lands that their imaginary birds flew over; the stories that gave them escape from their father's rages. She pictured the vastness of the world they'd invented and focused on how the two of them tried to awe each other with even greater feats of imagination. Hawks made of glass, goats grazing on clouds, winged youths who lived in the forests on the other side of the desert and whistled tunes that erased memory.

Where should we go now? Brysen would ask back then.

I don't know, Kylee would tell him. *Surprise me.*

And he would. He invented castles made of fur; he described giant birds who kept people on their fists; he created entire cities out of candied ginger.

Your turn, he'd say. *Surprise me.*

Their imaginations had been as big as the sky, untethered to what was real or what was possible in their ground-bound lives. Their imaginations flew.

Surprise me.

She closed her eyes and took a breath, then opened them and saw Brysen's terrified squirming, his panic, and the knife blade cutting skin.

The word burnt inside her, and she shouted it as loud as she could. It came without her knowing what sounds her mouth had formed, what word she'd spoken, but she knew precisely what it had meant as she screamed it.

Surprise me.

That was what she told the birds of prey, above and below— any that could hear her scream across the mountains.

Surprise me.

And they did.

Every owl, every wild bird swooped up and dove as one, a solid wall of feathers, a cacophony of calls. They scattered the Owl Mothers and those strange pale boys in every direction.

Üku was the only one not covering herself. She stood like a mountain peak in a snowstorm and looked up at Kylee, smiling.

"Brysen, Nyall, come on!" Kylee shouted down at them. Üku's smile was sharp as a beak, and she did not want to stick around for its first peck.

The boys scrambled to their feet as the Owl Mothers and the pale boys tried to regroup, harried by the flock, pushed down the slope in a riot of squawks and shrieks.

"My blade!" Brysen yelled, and tried to cross to the spot where the Owl Mother had dropped it, but a crossbow bolt cut the distance and snapped into the dirt just in front of his hand.

"Leave it!" Kylee said, and Brysen offered no argument. He and Nyall leaped to the icefall, climbing the slick surface as fast they could. Nyall had the sense to kick through the ice below him as he climbed, cutting off the fastest route on which they could be pursued.

When he reached the top and stood again, Brysen didn't look at Kylee. He turned back around and held out his fist. His face was pained but hopeful, and he looked at the wild flock, still driving the Owl Mothers and the odd collection of boys away. Shara was there among them, obeying Kylee's command.

Brysen whistled, and Kylee doubted the hawk would respond. She worried her brother would linger too long trying to call her and would get them all caught, but before she could warn him to just run, Shara broke from the flock and flew with furious grace to Brysen's bare fist. Her feet settled gently over his knuckles and though her grip surely stung, a small smile stole the corner of his lips. Weary as she was, Kylee smiled with him. His bird had come back to him on her own.

"What happened?" Brysen asked. He could have meant what happened with the birds or what happened with the Owl Mothers that could have gone so wrong, but she wasn't sure she could explain either, and certainly not right now. Nyall just gaped at her.

"You really going to stare at me like that forever?" she asked.

He shook his head, still speechless.

She rolled her eyes.

"He's just surprised," Brysen said. "We both are."

"You knew I could speak . . . this way," she said. "You've always known."

"I—" Brysen began, but then stopped. "I never thought you could speak . . . like *that*."

"Well . . ." She trailed off. She'd learned some things while they were separated, things she didn't want to think about. "We have to go now," she said instead of explaining anything, then turned toward the crush of boulders behind them to lead the way, leaping and hauling herself up a narrow crevasse. Brysen tossed Shara from his fist again, letting her fly to follow, like she'd been trained, so he could have both his hands free to climb.

It must have been hard for Brysen to let Shara off his fist so soon after nearly losing her, but he'd done it anyway. A falconer who wouldn't fly his bird free wasn't much of a falconer, and Brysen's faith in himself was as defiant as ever. Whatever had happened in the woods with those strange boys hadn't broken him.

When she'd reached the top of the first boulder, Kylee looked down and noticed the smear of blood Brysen's wrist left as he pulled himself up. Strangely, the gash on his wrist was already closing, although she'd bandaged enough wounds to know that this one should have been gushing dangerously. She'd want to take a closer look, but they needed to get some distance between themselves and the Mothers first.

After summiting the boulders, they ended up on a snow-covered slope, dimly lit by dawn's approach. The blood birch forest hooked around in front of them; they'd have to cross through a narrow stretch of it again before they'd be out in the open on the other side, and they'd likely be forced into harder climbing after that. The higher they got, the more jagged and treacherous the climb became. For now, though, they could run, and they ran for the trees. Without being summoned, Shara flew back to Brysen.

"She's afraid," he said.

They hadn't made it far before the hooting started. "She's got good reason to be," said Kylee. "Owls."

"Those aren't owls," Nyall whispered. He pointed to the left and they saw a flash of white between the trees. Another hoot and a flash of white behind them, a rustle of branches. More hoots.

The pale boys were following them, trying to flank them and coordinating their hunt with hoots and calls. Kylee changed direction, heading at an angle back down the slope, but saw more of the boys below. They turned and there were more.

And then the first owl appeared on a branch above.

Another fluttered down beside it. Kylee stopped, turned, but three more owls landed on the branches, and more hooting came from the boys giving chase. The Owl Mothers wouldn't be far behind. If they were caught again, Kylee feared that none of them would survive. Üku had demanded obedience, and Kylee hadn't given it.

Another owl landed. They were being surrounded.

And then Nyall vanished. And Brysen next.

"Down here!" Brysen whispered, and she saw his face in a small opening beneath the roots of a tree. She slid in and found herself face-to-face with one of the pale boys. He wore a woven shoulder satchel across his bare chest but didn't seem to be carrying any weapons. Her fists balled anyway. Better to be sorry than dead, but Brysen stopped her from lashing out.

"This is Jowyn," he said. "He's . . ."

"On your side now," the boy said, and though he didn't sound happy about it, he seemed to mean it. "I know a way they won't easily follow."

"He saved my life," Brysen told her, which wasn't the same as asking her to trust him, but going along with them was a better option than any she could think of at the moment, and so she followed through the dark and into a maze of caverns and tunnels beneath the forest. They crawled in the dark, smelling each other's feet and sweat and blood. Brysen stopped every now and then to comfort his bird, who he'd hooded but could still no doubt sense she was not somewhere birds were meant to be. They crawled on and on and on.

"Don't your friends know about these tunnels, too?" Nyall wondered when they stopped to rest in the close dark.

"We won't be down here much longer," Jowyn replied. "There's an opening ahead."

"And what then?" Nyall asked. "We're still on their mountain. They're still chasing us."

"They aren't the only ones chasing you," Jowyn explained. They heard him scamper away and then a shaft of brilliant light flooded the tunnel as he pushed open a snowy wooden door. He beckoned them up to the opening and the blessed fresh air.

They were on a low outcropping on the mountain's eastern slope. The sun was rising red and hiding the door in shadows. On a gentle incline below them was a campsite filled with a dozen mercenaries loading their packs, dousing their fires, preparing to continue their ascent toward the Nameless Gap.

"That's Yves Tamir." Kylee noted one of the figures standing among the mercenaries. "Goryn's oldest sister."

"And Jowyn's," said Brysen.

"Jowyn Tamir died," she said.

"And lived, too." The boy shrugged.

In the morning sunlight she got a better look at the pale boy. At first glance, he'd looked like a phantom or some deranged snow owl cultist, but she could see in the wide shape of his face, the heavy cast of his eyes, those familiar Tamir features.

Kylee didn't know what to make of this. Her brother had made an interesting new friend, and that friend had led them to a way out that might have been just as dangerous as the way back.

"What's Yves doing here?" Brysen asked.

"Probably trying to stop you from giving my older brother the ghost eagle," Jowyn suggested.

"Well, thanks for leading us here," Nyall scoffed. "Big help. How are we supposed to get past your dear sister? I'd rather fight a hundred of your covey buddies than Yves Tamir."

"You won't fight her," Jowyn said.

"Oh no, not more of this antiviolence scuzz," Nyall grumbled.

"We won't fight anyone," Brysen said, and the white teeth of his smile flashed widely. He'd sussed out Jowyn's plan and looked genuinely pleased with it, which meant, to Kylee, that it was probably reckless, foolish, dangerous, and had only the thinnest chance of success. Those tended to be the sorts of plans Brysen favored. It took her a moment longer to realize for herself what the plan was, and it was even more reckless than she'd imagined. It was also a bit of blood-soaked brilliance. "Though there *is* going to be a fight," he added.

25

KYLEE AND HER BROTHER WENT SIDE BY SIDE, BOOTS CRUNCHING through the sugar-thin layer of ice on top of the soft snow along the slope. The morning air was filled with wind-blown ice crystals, and Kylee hoped the effect of their silhouettes descending backlit toward camp would disorient Yves's mercenaries. They needed to be befuddled, distracted, and uncertain for a little while, just long enough . . .

"If this doesn't work, they'll use you as leverage," Kylee said as the figures in the camp began to notice them. "They'll take you hostage to get me to do their bidding."

"Why does everyone think you're the only one who can

catch a ghost eagle?" Brysen grunted as he tried to catch his breath. It was hard work going down the slippery slope without tumbling headfirst into the camp. "Not every great falconer could speak the Hollow Tongue . . . and you can *barely* speak it."

She didn't correct him. She didn't want to explain that she could speak it better now than she could before because of what the Owl Mothers had taught her. He'd never understand, just like their father never understood, why she didn't want to learn more, to do more. Everyone who learned what she could do wanted to use her gift for their own desires. She appreciated that, unlike everyone else, Brysen *didn't* want her to use her talent, even if it was because he was jealous of it. He wanted to be the hero of this story, and a part of her wanted him to be, too. She herself was no hero.

She remembered a flash of black wings, a blood-chilling scream.

No, not a hero at all.

She shook away the memory and focused ahead, squinting at the bright light shining off the snow. This high up they should have tied scarves around their eyes with little slits in them to prevent snow blindness, but it was too late for that.

"Who's there?" one of the mercenaries called. He looked more like a trapper than a soldier, ropes and nets tied to his pack, but at his side stood a woman who was definitely more the warring sort. She was one of Yves's "attendants," and her hand was already resting on the hilt of her sword.

"We want to talk to Yves!" Brysen shouted down at them. "She knows who we are!"

"But does she want to talk to you?" the attendant asked.

"Well, I *am* why she's here after all," Brysen replied, opening his arms wide, like he was showing off. With his feathered pants, falconer's jacket, blood-caked wrist, and wild gray hair, he looked something like a mountain hermit.

"Brysen? Kylee?" Yves Tamir called, hiking up to the slope to meet them. She had no bird on her fist, but three porters behind her each carried eagles in cages. Defense or bait, their purpose was unclear. Caged, they'd do Kylee no good if things went bad. She looked up but saw no other birds in the sky. Only Shara on Brysen's wrist, and the one hawk wouldn't be much use against Yves's mercenaries. "You seem to be hiking in the wrong direction."

"Does Goryn know you're here?" Brysen asked, and Yves's face tightened before opening into a smile.

"My brother has an independent streak that I prefer to keep in check," she said.

"So that's a no," Brysen replied.

Yves didn't answer. She looked at Kylee, still smiling.

"You've grown up quite impressively. If even half the rumors I hear are true, your little trek might just be a success."

"You shouldn't believe everything you hear," Kylee responded. "Especially not from Vyvian."

Yves laughed. "It does seem that what she told us about your route up Blue Sheep Pass was not entirely truthful, but one can't expect a spy to be completely honest, especially as I'm not her family's client. And yet . . . here you are. I can't help but wonder why."

"We need your help," Brysen said.

"Oh?" Yves raised an eyebrow. "But your deal was with my brother, was it not? He can be very stubborn when a deal doesn't go his way."

"I want you to negotiate for Dymian's safety," Brysen said. "In exchange for the ghost eagle."

"You don't trust my brother to uphold his side of your bargain?"

Brysen shook his head.

"A wise young man," Yves said. "But why would you trust me more?"

"We never forgot what you did for us after our father died," Kylee said. "We'd have never survived the first ice-wind without your charity."

"I'm sentimental," Yves said.

"No, you're not," said Kylee.

"No," Yves agreed, "I'm not. I've long known what you can do. Your father told me, did you know that? He wanted me to use you to fix fights at the battle pits in exchange for a cut of the winnings. Such a small man, he was. A gift like yours, and all he could think of was gambling." She glanced at Brysen. "He even offered you to me as collateral. Said you could clean our mews or work in a pleasure house. A wretched man he was, and you're better off without him." She winked. "But you knew that."

"Yes," said Brysen coldly. "I did."

"So you want me to help you reach the Nameless Gap, where you'll capture the ghost eagle and then give it to me in exchange for my intercession on behalf of Dymian?"

Brysen nodded.

"And yet, you don't have the ghost eagle, so you come to me empty-handed." Yves clucked. "This is not a negotiation, then. It is a plea. You're begging, not bargaining. And I could just as easily seize you right now and send Kylee to get the ghost eagle in exchange for your life. Wouldn't that make more sense? I don't understand why Goryn didn't do that in the first place."

She nodded toward her attendant, who stepped toward Brysen, drawing her sword. His hand went to his knife belt by instinct, but his knife wasn't there.

"We thought you'd say that," Kylee told her. "And I didn't think this was a great bargain to begin with."

"Then why'd you come to me?"

Kylee smiled. "You heard the saying about killing two birds with one stone?"

Yves nodded, eyes narrowing, calculating, but she had no idea what was coming. Kylee looked back up toward the ridge. Nyall and Jowyn were well hidden, but she wasn't looking for them. She had to stall a little longer.

"We're here because you aren't the only ones after us," she explained. "We're obviously no match for you—or for them— but we thought you might be able to keep each other busy."

"Who?" Yves snapped, eyes darting now. "Who?"

"*Who who*," Brysen laughed. "That's exactly right!"

Kylee would've loved to groan at his twisted sense of humor, but as realization dawned on Yves Tamir, the first owls descended, white feathers racing over white snow. They were invisible until their talons flashed, and then the crossbow bolts followed.

"Defensive positions!" Yves yelled, running for cover as Kylee and Brysen ran the other way, sprinting hard up the slope to round the upper crest of the rock spur while the Tamir mercenaries returned fire and unleashed their eagles at unseen enemies.

Over a dozen Owl Mothers charged from the lip of the slope, following their attacking birds and engaging the mercenaries in combat. Their birds clashed in the air as they fought on the ground, a mix of arrows, blades, and hand-to-hand brawling.

Kylee and Brysen had led the Owl Mothers straight into the mercenaries, and both would keep each other fighting for a while. Kylee didn't really care who survived as long as neither could follow them anymore.

She and her brother were breathless by the time they reached the top of Blue Sheep Pass and met up with Jowyn and Nyall again.

"I can't believe that worked," Nyall marveled, looking down. Yves's attendants had cornered two Owl Mothers but didn't see the great horned owl hovering above them, about to drop talons first. Kylee looked away before she heard the screams.

"A quest for the ghost eagle always ends in blood," Jowyn said sadly. He had created the opportunity for carnage between his estranged sister and former "Mothers," and he didn't look pleased with himself. "I hope our quest has seen its last."

He took Brysen's curved black blade out from his satchel. Brysen took it, and Kylee noticed their fingers touching as he did; Brysen's lingering on top of the other boy's for just a moment longer than necessary. Their eyes were locked. "Thank you," Brysen said.

Jowyn nodded once, then broke Brysen's gaze.

"*'Our* quest'?" Kylee asked the boy.

"I've been cast out," he explained. "I'll lead you to the Gap, where the ghost eagle is known to hunt."

"Why *did* you save me?" Brysen asked. "Didn't you know what they'd do to you?"

The boy nodded. "I knew, but I believe in saving who I can when I can. It's as simple as that."

"There is nothing simple about that," Kylee observed.

"No," Jowyn agreed. The screaming and clashing of blades echoed up from below. "I suppose there's not."

They spent the day hiking narrow trails and razor-thin ridges. Jowyn seemed to know every toehold and handhold, and he never grew winded, repeatedly climbing ahead and waiting for them to catch up. Once or twice Shara flew to where he stood and waited at his feet until Brysen arrived. Her brother didn't seem to mind when Jowyn picked her up—not the way he minded when anyone else did it.

The sun crossed its apex; they picked their way across a boulder field and then up another demanding slope where a lone blood birch grew. Kylee's legs were burning with the effort of the hike, Brysen was huffing and puffing his way along, and Nyall was doing his best to hide a limp. Neither of the boys would admit to their flagging strength, so it was up to Kylee to suggest a break on their behalf.

"We should stop here for a bit," she said. Nyall's back was slumped against the lone tree before she'd even finished the sentence.

"My legs feel like boiled noodles," he groaned.

Jowyn produced a lunch of cheese and bread from his satchel, and Brysen sat against a rock, feeding crumbs to Shara. He'd rest a crumb on one fingertip and then move it around in circles. The bird looked from the crumb on his finger to his face and back again intently until he stopped moving it and she could peck it off. Every time she plucked a crumb from his bare finger without breaking his skin, he smiled. She seemed to enjoy it, too, preening after each meatless morsel. For a little while, Brysen ignored everyone else. It was like only he and Shara existed.

"You're keeping secrets," Jowyn said to Kylee as she watched Brysen. "You should know that those secrets will come out. The ghost eagle has a way of revealing things we'd rather not have known."

"It's just a bird," Kylee grumbled, although it was obvious neither she nor Jowyn believed that.

"What happened with the Mothers?" Jowyn asked. Nyall had his eyes closed, but his head tilted toward her slightly. He was listening. Brysen's hand went still. He was listening, too.

She took a breath in. How could she tell them? What did they need to know? Both Brysen and Nyall loved her in their own ways, she knew, but she wondered what limit there was to that love. In her experience, no bond was unbreakable, no matter how complex the knots of time and affection that tied it. What she told them now might just sever them all.

She braced herself, took a breath. Remembered a flash of feathers, a scream. Blood was so much easier to spill than truth.

"I'm a killer."

26

AFTER THEY'D BEEN RESCUED FROM THE LONG-HAULERS AND separated from each other, the Owl Mothers led Kylee to their settlement, a flat patch of the mountain that butted up against a sheer cliffside. There were a number of caves cut into the cliff face, each of which commanded a view down over the blood birch forest, across the lower peaks of the starlit mountain range, out across the foothills, and into the valley. *Not much happening below would escape their notice*, Kylee thought. The Owl Mothers seemed all-knowing, but really what they knew was how to command a good view. A life in the mountains had taught her that perspective was just as good as wisdom.

Their cave openings were hung with heavy rugs to keep out the elements and there was a large circle dug into the ground in the center of the settlement, its sides sloping up just like the largest battle pit back at the Broken Jess, but this one had steps carved into its sloping edge.

After a hearty but silent meal around a stone oven, the Mothers assembled on those steps and directed Kylee to stand with Üku in the center. To her left was a tall wooden pole with a small hook on top, perhaps some kind of a perch. She felt like she was in a battle pit, but she had no falcon and no blade. She'd never wanted either before, but she felt helpless and exposed in front of them, lit by a too-bright moon.

"Kylee's come to us," Üku announced to the gathered women, "with some reluctance."

The Mothers laughed. Word traveled on the wind up here, and just as in the Six Villages, secrets were rare birds indeed, hardly seen and never kept long. "It is no accident, Kylee, that you are here. The wind that blew you to us has been buffeting you our way for a while."

"You know me?" She was stunned. Knowing about a ghost eagle expedition was one thing—the Owl Mothers could easily have seen her, her brother, and Nyall coming—but knowing her, *expecting* her . . . that was a different story.

"You've spoken in the Hollow Tongue since you were a child, have you not?" Üku asked.

Kylee didn't answer. *Let them know what they know and nothing more.*

"You've also resisted it for just as long, have you not?"

Again, she gave them nothing. She had a purpose here, and it wasn't this. "My brother and I are on a trapping expedition," she said. "With your blessing, we'd like to climb for the Nameless Gap."

"To capture the ghost eagle?"

She nodded.

"And you think you'll do it without our help?"

"We would appreciate your help," Kylee said. She was careful to say *we*, careful to show it was not her quest but her brother's and that he was essential to her. She would not accept any harm coming to him, wherever they'd taken him and Nyall. They would ascend together or not at all.

"And we will help you, Kylee." Üku put a hand on her shoulder. "We found you in order to help you. But for us to help you, you must learn to speak. You mustn't be afraid of the Hollow Tongue. You must master it, as birds of prey are masters of the hunt. They deal life and death as their appetites demand it, but unlike them, we choose. We—and only we—can choose when to create life and when to take it away. We can harm, and we can heal. We alone beneath this sky have the power to make those choices with reason and with care. Why should we fear it?"

Kylee crossed her arms. "Teach my brother. He's the one who dreams of commanding raptors from the sky. He's the one who wants to catch the ghost eagle."

"He doesn't have the words."

"You can teach him."

The Owl Mother swatted the air dismissively. "We can teach anyone the sounds. But making the sounds and speaking the language are not the same. Words have weight, wrought by history and memory. The weight of a word can only be held by the living of it. Your brother speaks many unspoken languages, and he will have to learn his own in time, but you carry the words for the Hollow Tongue, those that have not been entirely lost to time."

"I don't want them," she said. The Hollow Tongue was poison. It had only led her to trouble all her life, and not just because her brother couldn't speak it. She'd learned what believing life and death belonged to you could do, how thinking you could command the rulers of the sky curdled your heart like sour milk. "The Hollow Tongue is a dead language that should be left dead."

"The Hollow Tongue is a living language," Üku countered. "It is like a flame that must be tended. Each generation must preserve the language of their mothers, or it will be lost, and each generation must invent the language for themselves, or it will have no meaning. The language grows with all who speak it."

"Let someone else learn." Kylee looked around at the weather-worn women who'd taken her prisoner. "I can do enough damage with the language I speak already."

The skin around Üku's eyes crinkled with her smile. "Oh, we do teach others."

She opened her palms and gestured for a girl Kylee's age to come forward. She was dressed like an Altari merchant's apprentice, her long blond hair pulled back into a braid and wearing thick leather leggings under a colorful blouse, but over that she wore a padded leather vest and had thick cloth wrapped from her knuckles to her elbow for a falcon to perch on or to soften a punch. By the power in her shoulders and thighs, Kylee wasn't sure whether the former or the latter was more likely. She didn't love the thought of either.

"This is Grazim," the Owl Mother said. "She, like you, has some instinct for the Hollow Tongue and, like you, must learn to wield it. You will compete tonight."

Üku whistled and threw a small piece of meat on the ground

between Kylee and the other girl. A haggard red-tail, a small, wild, male hawk, flew up the slope from below and landed on the ground between Kylee and Grazim, snapping up the meat in its beak. It stood still equidistant from them both, and Üku backed away toward the edge of the circle.

Grazim widened her stance and wet her lips, eyes fixed on the hawk. The owls around the circle on their masters' fists shifted from foot to foot but otherwise did not move. The hawk, sensing the moonlight predators all around it, sank into itself, flattened its feathers against its body, afraid.

Kylee's first impression of this place had been correct. They *were* in a kind of battle pit, but there were no ropes, no knives, and only one bird. Grazim knew the rules already, but Kylee could only guess. Were they meant to command the bird to attack each other?

Üku waved and three Owl Mothers emerged from one of the carpet-covered caves above them. They hauled a limp figure, a man who could hardly keep himself standing. His hands were bound and he had a rough hood over his head. The women dragged him to the wooden post at the edge of the circle and hung him by the binding of his hands on the hook at the top. Then they tied his legs to the pole with a thick rope and swiped the hood from his head.

Kylee gasped. She'd known Petyr Otak her whole life. He and his brother were spies for one of the kyrgs. They claimed it was Bardu, but most people thought they were paid by a lesser member of the Forty. They'd never had the devious talent necessary to rise up in the ranks, not like Vyvian and her family. Either way, the Otaks had always been fairly harmless, but they *had* seen her at the pits when she'd called Shara from the sky in the Hollow Tongue.

"He followed you into the mountains," Üku said. "He and his brother meant to rob you."

"Where is Lyl?" Kylee asked.

"Dead." Üku showed no emotion.

"Kylee . . . ," Petyr murmured, looking at her through bruised, swollen eyes. His nose was broken, his face bloodied. "Kylee . . . ," he repeated.

"There were traditions in the ancient sky cults from which we all come—your people and Grazim's, and ours as well," Üku said, beginning a lesson Kylee did not want to hear. "They involved sacrifice to the raptors. Human sacrifice. We honor those traditions. Grazim will command the attack; you, Kylee, will control the defense. You may not touch each other or the sacrifice directly but act only through the bird. It's that simple."

She stepped farther back, out of the circle. "You believe the Hollow Tongue is good for only destruction. Perhaps you're right, perhaps not. Now is the time to find out."

"*Shyehnaah*," the other girl said, and the hawk launched itself at Petyr.

27

AS THE HAWK ATTACKED, PETYR SQUIRMED BUT COULD NOT BREAK free. The bird flapped in front of him, talons scratching at his face, screeching.

"Ah!" he screamed. The Owl Mothers and the owls on their fists watched with equal impassivity.

"Stop this!" Kylee cried.

"The Hollow Tongue word for a bird of prey is *shyehnaah*," Üku lectured her, voice heavy with urgency. "The word itself is just a sound. Like any word, it is a carrier for the stories that make it. In the old stories, the *shyehnaah* was one great bird that summoned all others to it. Many were lost on the journey. Pretty birds had their bright plumage burned away by the desert fires; shy birds feared to fly in flocks and lost their way alone in storms; and brave birds saw themselves in the clear waters of the endless lake, and cowered at their smallness, and flew too low in order to make themselves seem bigger in their reflection. The waves crashed over them. Of all the birds that left to find the *shyehnaah*, only forty survived, which is what the Uztari reference with their Council of Forty. But the suffering and the longing—the hard journey to find the self— that's the word. Only when you know yourself can you mean the word you speak."

"*Shyehnaah!*" Kylee yelled. "*Shyehnaah! Shyehnaah! Shyehnaah!*" It made no difference. The bird clawed and pecked at Petyr's face. He couldn't defend himself. He was counting on Kylee to defend him.

"Do you want to help him?" Üku asked.

"Yes!" she said.

"I don't believe you," Üku said. "The hawk does not believe you."

Kylee whirled to the girl, fists up, although she knew to strike the girl would be to summon her own punishment. "Call it off!" she pleaded. "Call it off."

The girl shook her head. She was fighting a smirk at the corner of her mouth. She knew she was winning.

Kylee turned back toward Petyr and the hawk.

Petyr had stalked her and Brysen into the mountains, had worked against her. Worse, he was a man her father's age who knew her father's cruelty and yet had never raised a finger or a word to help. They'd probably been drunk together at the Broken Jess. Patted each other on the back on the way home. In her heart, she knew, she didn't much care what happened to Petyr Otak.

But she did not want to be that person. She was not someone who'd watch a man suffering and do nothing to help him. She could feel the heat inside her, the breath beginning to burn. This was not about Petyr. This was about her.

"Teach me a word," she called out to Üku.

"What word do you want?"

"How do I call it to me?"

"Use the word for the place to which one is bound. It is in the name of your people," Üku said. "*Tar.*"

"Ahhh!" Petyr screamed again.

Kylee closed her eyes. She thought of herself at her favorite moments. Climbing alone in the morning as the sun came up, hot on her back. Reaching a peak just at the moment she thought her legs would give out on her and finding she could make the last push. Taking in the view of the Necklace and the Villages below. Seeing her home in the golden light of morning and knowing it was safe and she was free.

"*Shyehnaah-tar*," she said, and the hawk dropped to the ground, turning its head nearly upside down to look at her. It took a tentative step, then another, and then it beat its wings and thrust itself up, flying to her fist and settling with a fluff of its feathers. Her arm shook, which caused the bird to spread its wings and rouse, but it did not take off again, and it calmed as soon as she did. The hawk looked at her expectantly, without shock. Her face surely showed enough shock for both of them.

"Thank you." Petyr's tears streaked the blood on his face. "Thank you, Kylee. Thank you."

Usually, when Kylee blurted out a Hollow Tongue word in desperation or terror, she felt diminished afterward, relieved but empty, like the breaths that come after sobbing. But now she felt the warmth of the word lingering on her tongue. She felt a connection to the wild hawk on her fist, something precious in knowing she had spoken to it in its language, not hers, and it had understood.

She hadn't known until that moment that she hadn't ever felt truly understood before. Her father had thought she was withholding her talents out of stubbornness; Brysen was jealous of her; and her mother thought her talent was blasphemy. Everyone looked at her and saw what they wanted for themselves. But this raptor had heard her, seen her, and come simply because she asked it to. She said exactly what she meant and meant exactly what she said.

"You've called the hunter to you," Üku said, "but its nature is not your nature. Be careful what you tell it now, because truths traded between such different bloods as yours cannot be undone."

"*Shyehnaah preet*," Grazim snarled, and Kylee didn't need to know the meaning of the second word to understand its cruelty. The hawk dove from her fist, swooped low, and grabbed onto the belt of Petyr's pants with its talons, flapping to keep itself steady.

"*Kraas*," the girl said, and the hawk's head shot forward with lighting quickness, its beak puncturing Petyr's belly and breaking into his flesh.

"Ahhh!" he wailed, and the hawk pulled away with a string of flesh hanging from its beak like a fresh-caught worm. It swallowed and dove in for another bite.

"*Shyehnaah-tar*," Kylee said, but the hawk did not respond.

Petyr shrieked as he was ripped open alive.

"In the Hollow Tongue, some truths are stronger than

others," Üku shouted over his screaming. "*Preet* is the word they know for prey. *Kraas* is the word for 'eat.' The basic animal urges of the hunter will always cling to it harder than a command attached to human truths." Üku paused and watched Petyr writhe, blood pouring out of his gut. "Unless those truths are bigger than the animal's urges. Whoever speaks the truer words can command the hunter. That is the challenge of the Hollow Tongue. That is its demand."

"Kylee!" Petyr cried, looking at her through a veil of blood. Her hands shook; her mind was blank. What truth could she find stronger than a hawk's instinct to kill and eat? She had nothing. With every passing heartbeat came another blood-curdling scream from the man on the post. She'd lost too much time already. She'd never save him now. Even if the attack stopped, he wouldn't live. His screaming scattered any clear thought she could find.

"I'm sorry," she muttered. "I'm so sorry."

The hawk flew to the top of the post and jumped down onto Petyr's head, talons clutching his skull, digging into his scalp. It bent to set its beak to his eyes.

"No!" Petyr's voice was shrill. "Not that! Please!"

Grazim smiled, but Üku looked grim. "You can stop this, Kylee. The tether that ties thought to feeling is the bond that makes language possible. Use it."

She remembered her brother's screams the night when her mother held her and sang, the night when Brysen was lit on fire. She remembered the screams, and she remembered running to the herbalist afterward to get a salve to rub across his skin, to soothe the heat and stop infection. She couldn't undo the burning, but she could provide the salve.

This time, she did not need to be told the word. It rose up in her on its own, pulled from some place inside her that knew things she didn't know she knew. Her heartbeat slowed, and the heat inside her built. She harnessed it and spoke it like breathing fire. "*Iryeem,*" she called out. "*Iryeem.*"

From above, there came a strange rattle. The hawk stopped pecking, looked to the night sky as the first vulture dropped to the ground in front of Petyr, then another and another. A wake of vultures surrounded the unfortunate man.

They were huge birds, the mountain vultures, with pale blue faces on downy white heads, the rest of their feathers somber browns and grays. The hawk, outnumbered by the larger birds and calmed by what Kylee had called, took off, skied out, and vanished over the mountain.

Grazim's smile bent into a frown, and she shook her head, looked to the Owl Mothers for guidance. While most whispered among themselves, Üku nodded approvingly at Kylee.

More vultures descended, called from the wild on whatever

wind Kylee's word had flown. They flocked around Petyr, then rushed him, wings open in a curtain of brown and gray and white that blocked the fatal feast from view. Petyr's screaming stopped a few moments later as the vultures put him beyond pain. Kylee shuddered; the warmth of the word had left her feeling chilled.

Üku was at her side now, having fluttered up as silently as an owl, and her voice was soft as mist in Kylee's ear. "Do you know what it means, the word you spoke? *Iryeem?*"

Kylee shook her head. The word had come to her the way breathing comes when a swimmer breaks the surface of the water after too long below.

"It means 'mercy'," Üku said.

28

"I DIDN'T WANT TO KILL HIM," KYLEE CONFESSED, TEARS IN HER EYES.
She wasn't sure how much time had passed. She'd dropped to
the ground after the battle and had doubled over, throwing up.
She couldn't stop shivering and she wondered if she'd fainted.
The moon had sunk lower in the sky and the feasting vultures
had turned Petyr into little more than meat on a hook.

She tried to stand, but her knees wobbled, her feet were
numb. "I didn't know they'd do that," she added.

Üku squatted down beside her, pulled her hair back, and,
when she was finished retching, handed her a flamestone cup
of hot tea. "Great poems know more than their poets, but they

cannot exist without them. This is the art of the Hollow Tongue as well. Sometimes a novice will hit on a perfect word, but the lack of control can be dangerous to both the speaker and the spoken to. That's why we'd like you to study and to train with us. We can learn from each other."

"But he's dead; I won!" Grazim objected, still standing tense in the battle pit, looking ready to fight Kylee herself to prove her victory.

"Yes," Üku said. "He's dead. You won. And you will be trained, too. But Kylee has shown us something valuable." She helped Kylee to her feet, nudged her to sip the tea, which warmed Kylee instantly and cleared her head at the same time. She felt calmer and clutched the cup with both hands but resolved not to sip again. Whatever they'd put in it, she wanted no more. "She showed the kind of creativity under pressure that will be required in battle."

"In battle?"

"In service of the kyrg," Üku said. "For whom we have promised to train you."

"You sold me out to the Sky Castle?"

"Sold you out?" Üku shook her head. "That's dramatic. We are helping you get what you want: to command the ghost eagle from the sky."

"That's not what I want," Kylee said. "I want to help my

brother. *He* wants the ghost eagle and only so he can save someone he thinks he loves."

"Interesting way to phrase it."

Kylee shrugged. They didn't need to know Brysen's business. "I'm not doing this so that a kyrg can just take the eagle from us once we catch it," she said.

"A war is coming, Kylee," Üku said. "The Kartami are growing and moving fast, and they are coming to tear every bird from the sky. Our interests and those of your kyrgs in the Sky Castle are the same. What good will saving Brysen and his lover do if the Kartami cut all of your heads off?"

"What do you care? Why would you serve the kyrg?" This time Üku offered no information. Kylee had to puzzle it out for herself. "Because they stand between you and the Kartami . . . ," she said. "The Kartami are as much a threat to you as to the Six Villages . . . but they have to go through *us* first. The lowland foothills are your first line of defense."

Üku didn't deny it, but there was more. Kylee couldn't quite figure it out until she looked around and realized there were only women and girls here. To survive, they needed outsiders . . . outsiders that the Uztari kyrgs provided. Boys disappeared all the time.

"We'll survive," Üku said. "You can help us all survive."

"Catch the ghost eagle yourselves," Kylee grunted.

"We cannot," said Üku. "It has no interest in hearing us . . . but it has long been interested in you. In your family."

"Interested enough to kill my father," Kylee said.

Üku nodded thoughtfully. "That is one way to see it, but perhaps the ghost eagle has more perspective than you can know. From high atop its perch, it sees more than you can imagine. Its will is its own, but you might persuade it to serve yours. To serve all of ours."

Kylee shook her head. She was not a warrior, and she would not become *their* warrior. She had seen what violence did to bodies, and she wanted nothing more to do with it. Birds of prey killed to eat, but, as the Owl Mother had said, only humans could choose to kill. Or choose not to. She would not let them turn her into a killer.

Into more of a killer than she already was.

"I'm going to find my brother," she said.

"We will not simply let you walk away from this." Üku cracked her neck and stood in Kylee's way. "One who speaks the Hollow Tongue irresponsibly cannot be allowed to roam free. You might fall into the wrong hands. Imagine what our enemies would do with you. Not everyone has your interests in mind, Kylee."

"You don't, either."

"Our interests align. That should be enough."

"Just let her go; we don't need her," Grazim spoke up, but a harsh glare from Üku silenced her.

"You should listen to her," Kylee warned, and strode for the edge of the circle. Üku was in front of her again before she'd made it three steps, and two other Owl Mothers flanked her just as fast. Behind her, the rest of the Mothers had stood from their seats along the mountain slope. Kylee felt a tingle on the back of her neck, a sense that untold numbers of owls had their wide eyes fixed on her. "Let me go."

Her eyes darted quickly to the sides of the pit around her, confirming what she'd feared: crossbows pointed at opposing angles between her shoulder blades. If they fired, the crossbow bolts would make an X right through her heart. She looked at the vultures, who were still feasting. Could she find a word to command them? Would Üku counteract whatever she tried? And what would become of Brysen if she died right here, right now, and left him on the mountain?

In front of her, Üku raised an eyebrow, asking a question of her own. *What now?*

One thing Kylee and her brother had in common—a great gift of their family perhaps—was a refusal to back down in the face of total hopelessness. It had to be an inherited trait, she figured, because Kylee had never before imagined herself doing something as foolish as what she did next.

"Thanks for the tea," she said, and then, raising the cup as if to toast her captor, she tossed the hot liquid into Üku's face. As the woman grabbed at her eyes, Kylee did a forward somersault, knocking past her. The crossbows bolts flew, one grazing Üku's head, the other zipping harmlessly over the side of the mountain and toward the treetops below.

Kylee was already running at full stride, taking controlled falls down the dark slope and hitting her feet just in time to scramble over boulders and along the lip of a narrow gorge, running straight for the blood birch forest.

"And that's when I found you," Kylee said to the three boys sitting around her. "The Owl Mothers sold us out to save their own skins."

She waited for Jowyn to defend them—the women to whose cult he'd belonged until recently—or for Nyall to comfort her, or for Brysen to tell her she did the right thing and that Petyr Otak deserved it, but none of the boys spoke. Each was lost in his own thoughts, she supposed, changing what he thought of her, deciding if she was a danger, maybe, deciding if she'd always been a monster or had just become one on the mountain.

She knew the answer to that question, of course, but none

of them asked it. Instead, Brysen stood and offered her a hand up from the ground.

"So it's true," he said. "About the Kartami? They really are coming."

"The Owl Mothers think so," Kylee said.

"And so must Goryn," Nyall added. "That's probably why he wants a ghost eagle. For defense?"

"The ghost eagle does not defend people," Jowyn said. "And neither does my brother."

"I don't care about the Kartami's war with the Sky Castle or Goryn's plans for the eagle," Brysen told them. "I care about doing what I promised. I care about Dymian."

Kylee noticed her brother looking at his feet, avoiding Jowyn's or Nyall's gaze. Avoiding *her* gaze, too. Some part of him had to know how reckless he was being. Some part of him had to think of the bigger picture here.

Whatever part that was, he'd squashed it when he looked up again, resolved. "I'm doing this. That's the deal I made. Jowyn will lead me to the Nameless Gap. If I can make it by nightfall, then I think I have a plan to catch the eagle." He looked at each of them in turn. "But I could use some help." Her brother stepped to her, squeezed her hand. "I won't force you to use the Hollow Tongue," he added. "I know how hard it is for you."

She gave his hand a gentle squeeze back, glad to have her brother's kindness after so long without it, glad he was finally asking for help. But even as she nodded at him, all she could think was *You have no idea how hard it is for me.*

They formed a line and climbed single file toward the ragged edge of the Demon's Beak, a high traverse of stone with a giant hooked peak above it. They climbed until well after nightfall, then woke to keep climbing. It was nearly a whole day before they finally reached the narrow pass below the Beak, pressing their backs against the snow-blanketed stone to shuffle along the edge of an endless fall. Once they passed the traverse, it was a quick climb over the lip to the rough slopes of the Nameless Gap, where the ghost eagle kept its eyrie. It watched all who approached. They would be no bigger than rats in the eagle's eyes.

Kylee knew this climb. She'd done it once before.

Petyr Otak had not been her first kill.

THE SAPLING FOREST

A MESS OF BLOOD AND FEATHERS LITTERED THE SNOWY SLOPE. PACKS were scattered among the corpses of human and eagle and owl alike. Gray-haired women lay sprawled, throats sliced, staring dead-eyed at the sky, their beloved owls lying bolt-blasted beside them. Uztari mercenaries lay mangled as meat, their corpses strewn with crossbow bolts and feathers. *What a sickening waste of life*, thought Yval Birgund, *but battles always are.*

He'd seen a few in his time as a soldier, fewer since he'd been the defense counselor of the Forty. For more seasons than he could count now, he'd spent his days explaining provision allotments and expenses for the movement of falconry officers to the cloistered kyrgs and their attendants. It'd been a relief from the tedium of courtly life when he was dispatched to the Six Villages for the market and even a delight when he'd been informed that he was required to attend to an expedition in the mountains above the Villages.

That was before he knew he'd be chasing children into the clouds. After a few words with the many village spies, he'd learned of the children he was meant to pursue and the lofty, if absurd, task they'd set for themselves. He'd also learned that he'd encountered the boy before, that gray-haired eyas who'd come to the aid of a street urchin. He hoped at least for the chance to deliver that boy a whipping. No one made him look like a fool, especially not some smooth-cheeked hatchling from the Villages.

When his retinue had found the bodies of the long-haulers, he took it for the sort of mountain brigandage that Six Villagers had a reputation for. Brutal but nothing un-expected. Standing before this second scene of carnage, how-ever, he had to revise his expectations. These young ones had unleashed a massacre.

"A new forest will grow here," Üku, the Owl Mother, told him, stoic as ever in spite of the injuries she had received.

"I will mourn to see many of these saplings grow." She kicked at the body of one of the mercenaries. "I will spit at the base of others."

Yval Brigand sighed. Üku had lost a lot of her people. So far, Yval's men had not found Yves Tamir's body, which was for the best. Her mother would demand retaliation, and Kyrg Bardu had made it clear that the Sky Castle's alliance with the Owl Mothers was a priority. So, too, was the bronze the castle received from the Tamirs' vast and varied businesses. War required wealth to win, and the Owl Mothers weren't the most affluent of allies.

"You have to admit," Yval told her, "these children have shown resourcefulness, turned their weaknesses into strengths."

The woman merely grunted agreement. The red burn on her face and irritated eyes spoke to why.

"When the time comes, we will still rely on you to train the girl," he said. "Grudges aside."

"I do *not* hold grudges," she told him. "But I *do* have a memory. A very good memory."

The last remark might've been aimed at him as much as at Kylee. He'd known Üku long enough not to turn his back on her when they were alone.

"Do you think she'll be able to bring down the ghost eagle?" he asked.

"That will be up to the eagle," Üku said. "Her talent is raw, which makes it unpredictable, and there is much we don't understand about it. She's protective of her brother, which might be a help or a hindrance."

"That's not an answer."

"And I'm not a mystic," she snapped at him. "You want fortune-telling, study augury. I deal in what is knowable."

"Well then, tell me what you do know," Yval said. "Or consider our alliance at an end."

"Our alliance did not protect my family," she said. "Our alliance, so far, appears rather one-sided."

"When my forces keep the Kartami off your mountain, speak to me again," he growled. "There will be plenty of bloodshed to share when these shards blow in from the desert with their kites. Unless we can control her."

"And unless she can control the eagle," Üku added.

"Yes, unless that."

"So, you'll want to make for the Nameless Gap?" Üku asked him, and he turned his eyes, squinting, toward the snow-capped peaks of the Upper Jaw range. High above them, past the Demon's Beak, he could just see the cloud-shrouded dip into the Nameless Gap, a narrow gorge that formed a jagged, lonely U and rose to the summit of the range, where only the ghost eagle flew.

"No." He shook his head. "They've a guide?"

Üku nodded. "He's a good boy. It pained us to lose him."

"There'll be others," Yval snorted. "We always see that there are." He found the business of their covey distasteful, and their strict views of male and female bewildering, but it was not his place to rewrite the traditions of the Owl Mothers. They had their ways, Uztar had its ways, and they needn't care much for each other as long as they could work together.

He turned the discussion back to the twins. "With their head start, we'd risk missing them on the way down if they succeed, and if they fail, it won't be worth the effort to make the climb."

"If they fail, we'll surely hear their screams," Üku observed.

"I think I have a different plan," Yval said. "But it will require more of you than you want to give, perhaps?"

"The sacrifices I've made so far demand that I see this to the end," she said. "If more is required of me, more will be given, but I will not have sacrificed in vain, understand? Not even the walls of the Sky Castle will keep you safe if all this comes to nothing."

"Funny you should mention the Sky Castle," Yval told her, and her stoic frown slipped as he explained the rest of what he required of her. Owl Mothers, he knew, did not like to leave their mountain.

In war, a lot of people had to do things they didn't like. And this war was only just beginning.

BRYSEN

WINDS AND WOUNDS

29

"YOU LOOK SICK," KYLEE TOLD HIM. "YOU OKAY?"

Brysen leaned his head against the closest rock, breath clouding in front of him, eyes closed. They'd stopped to rest. "It's the altitude," he said, which could have been true. This high up, everyone had a little trouble breathing, everyone felt a little sick. Well, everyone except Jowyn. Whatever the blood birch sap had done to his body had adapted him to thin air. Brysen hoped Kylee wouldn't look at him too closely, because some of that sap's properties were in him now and he wasn't really feeling the effects of altitude, either. He was troubled by a different sickness as they huddled halfway up the steep slope leading into the Nameless Gap.

Memory.

A short run down the slope from where they were, past abandoned packs and tents and ropes from ill-fated expeditions past, a few scrubby bushes had taken root, growing up through the rocky ground and patches of snow that clung stubbornly against the whipping winds funneling through the gap. He knew those bushes, remembered the feel of their scratchy branches on his face as he cowered behind them, how their tough leaves rattled when he shivered, giving him away. How the sounds of what had happened next echoed off the high sides of the Nameless Gap for a long time after.

He'd been here before.

At the moment he'd nearly been caught following his father. Yzzat's breath had been bated and his blade drawn, and Brysen had known he was about to die. He'd been certain that, instead of gratitude that he'd come to help—to show he *could* help—his father would finally kill him, and he'd known he wouldn't fight back, couldn't.

He'd imagined the curved, black-talon blade entering him, could practically feel how it would part the scarred flesh of his side to slide between his ribs, the twist of the blade and the cold flood when the razor tip touched his heart. He hadn't been afraid; he'd been relieved. Finally, there would be no more fear, no more waiting for the brutal end. It was here, it was now.

And then it wasn't.

He'd come expecting death and had been given life. The ghost eagle had saved his life that night.

Better that Kylee didn't know. He'd always told her that he stole their father's knife before he left for that final expedition, and that he'd wanted it as a keepsake afterward, and she'd never questioned him. She never questioned him about that time at all, when he said he'd spent a full moon's turning in hiding *after* stealing the knife, afraid of what would happen to him when their father returned. He'd only come home once everyone knew Yzzat wouldn't. What Kylee had done while he was gone—how she and Ma had gotten on without him— he didn't ask and she didn't bring up. And Ma only ever prayed at them, never asked questions. Of all the silences in their lives after the ghost eagle killed their father, the silence around that time was the heaviest.

But here he was again, like a hawk circling its hunting ground, flying the same circle again and again, but at a greater height with farther to fall.

His own hawk shifted from foot to foot on his fist, shrinking into herself. The Nameless Gap was not a comfortable place for her, either. Her head dipped and turned, snapped around as she tried to see in every direction all at once. He set her on the ground, left her unleashed. She would need that advantage if she had to escape quickly. He wouldn't tether her this close to the ghost eagle's eyrie. If things went wrong, she'd have a flying chance.

"We could all use a rest," Jowyn said, eyes on Brysen. He was playing along, but there was a question on his face, a question Brysen had no intention of answering. Yet he felt like he could, like Jowyn might understand. Jowyn had fled to the mountains once, too, after all. The only difference was that, unlike Brysen, he'd found what he was looking for. Brysen hadn't yet but was poised to.

"We'll have to get into position before sundown," Brysen said. "I'll need each of you to play a part in this. I lost my nets and snares back with the covey, but I've still got enough spider-silk rope to tie the eagle once we tackle it."

"'Tackle it?'" Nyall gasped. "You sure the height hasn't cooked your brain? No one can tackle a ghost eagle."

"No one can," Brysen said. "But a group together might. Think about it: Did you ever read the stories of the old trappers—Ymal the Cask-Breaker, Valyry the Gloveless, the Stych Sisters?"

"Not much for reading, Bry," Nyall scoffed. "And last I checked, neither were you."

"Exactly," said Brysen. "Because nothing written about those legends is true. If it were, everyone who followed their paths would've already caught a ghost eagle."

"So the fact that nobody's written about a group taking down a ghost eagle makes you think it can be done?" Nyall shook his head.

"You're saying you don't trust me?" Brysen asked. He hadn't asked Nyall to come on this journey. Hadn't invited him, in fact. They both knew he was only there because he was in love with Kylee. Nyall would go along with whatever she said. Brysen turned to her.

"It's not impossible," she told them. "I *have* read all the fragments of the old stories. They contradict each other. It doesn't mean they aren't true, but it could mean the truth is maybe more complicated."

"Complicated," Nyall repeated, looking between Kylee and Brysen.

"The stories all talk about these great heroes," Kylee said. "But they all leave things out, skip parts, try to make the trapper they're writing about sound like the greatest person ever. But no one real is perfect. No one real can do everything themselves."

Brysen felt like her last words were aimed straight at him. She was taking his side, but somehow, he found it annoying.

"Anyway," Brysen added, "every trapper who's come up here alone has died. So our chances are better if we work together. It's pretty simple. We lure the eagle down, grab it by the legs, and tie it up—just like we do with passage hawks we want to train."

"Passage hawks aren't the size of a grown man," Nyall objected. "Passage hawks can't snap the arms off their prey with one bite."

"So you're saying you're too scared?" Brysen spat at him. "You don't want to be here? You're fine to sing outside our window and argue about bird boxes, but when we really need your help, you've got all kinds of reasons not to?"

"Hey!" Nyall growled right back at him. "I'm trying to protect you, here!"

"It was never *me* you were trying to protect," Brysen replied.

"Don't get mad at Nyall," Kylee cut in. "He's just asking questions. We're all on your side. We *want* to help you."

"About time!" Brysen grunted.

"What's that supposed to mean?" Kylee snapped.

"You know exactly what it means," he told her.

"Well, I'm here now."

"Exactly!"

"You don't want me here?" Kylee stood. "After you asked

for my help? You think you don't need me now?" She pointed a finger in his face. "You'd already be dead if I hadn't come after you!"

Brysen knocked his sister's finger away and stood up to look her square in the eyes. "I know you're better than me, okay? You don't have to stuff it down my throat all the time!" He yelled at her with a rage that made him shake and set her back on her heels. His voice echoed off the high ridges on either side of the Gap. It sounded like his father's voice.

"Don't you dare yell at her." Nyall stood now, too, putting himself between Brysen and his sister. "She's done nothing but defend you since we were kids, and you've never shown any gratitude. You chew hunter's leaf and fool around, and you don't do *anything* to help your family. Your sister is the most amazing person I've ever known, and you treat her like a bait pigeon while you worship the sweat that drips from that bird-nester, Dymian. It makes me sick. There're times I want to punch your face in."

"Do it then," Brysen said, putting his face nearly against Nyall's, so close their foreheads almost touched. He'd always known his "friend" secretly hated him, was only using him to get close to his sister—just like everyone else did. She was the special one, the one with talent, the one with brains. He was just the screwup, the poor, put-upon boy they could cluck and shake their heads at, never believing he could do anything great.

Nyall shoved him. "Maybe once I break all your teeth, Dymian'll like you more."

"Maybe with your skull bashed in, Kylee will pay any attention to you at all."

"Don't make this about me, Brysen," Kylee growled. "You're the one who got us into this. It's your fault."

"You don't think I know that?" Brysen was crying now, but his blade was out, and his rage stretched wide like wings. He wanted to smash Nyall's face in, and his sister's face, and even Jowyn's face, though Jowyn hadn't said a word and was still sitting against a boulder with his eyes closed and his fingers intertwined in front of him. Was he *praying*? Or was he trying to distract Brysen from his goal, trying to steal him from Dymian so he could turn Brysen into a freak like himself?

And who was Brysen to think that boy a freak? *He* was the one covered in scars, the one who loved the wrong people and made crazy promises and followed phantoms into the clouds, and the one who would never do anything in life worth remembering and he'd fail and fail and—

"You all need to take deep breaths right now." Jowyn's calm voice sliced through the riot in Brysen's mind. "The eagle is nearby. It's in all of your heads." He looked at Brysen.

"Whatever thoughts you're thinking are not the truth of you. None of you. Look at one another. *See* one another. You're more than what you're feeling right now. You are more than your worst thoughts. These thoughts are no more solid than a cloud. Remember that. You have to remember that, or it will tear you apart one by one."

Brysen saw the boy's calm, and it infuriated him. He didn't need to be lectured.

"Prrpt," Shara chirped.

"Shut up!" he yelled at her, raising a fist. Shara flinched, and the blood left Brysen's face. He nearly fainted, had to hold himself steady. He would never hurt Shara. Could never. This wasn't him.

He looked up at Kylee, her face twisted with anger and hurt, and that wasn't her, either. She was tough and loyal and had smarts and gifts to spare, and everything she'd done had been for him. And Nyall was loyal and fun and generous, and he never shrank from a fight. He was here now.

They were both here now. With Brysen. *For* Brysen.

The ghost eagle couldn't plant thoughts in their minds; it could only distort what was already there. But like Jowyn said, they were all more than their worst thoughts. Maybe there were pieces of truth in everything they'd just yelled at one another, but only the most jagged pieces. No one was only the sum of broken things inside themselves. Anyway, what were breaks if not openings?

"I'm sorry," Brysen said, and felt his thoughts clearing, the act of apologizing helping him feel the truth of the apology. "That . . . that's not what I think about any of you . . . not really."

Nyall nodded. Reached a hand out. Brysen flinched at the motion, but Nyall just squeezed his shoulder. "Same," he said. Kylee didn't say a word, just embraced her brother, held him tight.

"I told you I wouldn't ask you to speak the Hollow Tongue," Brysen said to her. "But that doesn't mean I don't need you. I *do* need you. I always have."

Kylee wiped her eyes. "I wish I could speak the right words to do this," she told him. "But one thing I learned from the Owl Mothers is that it's dangerous when I can't control it. I don't know what I might make the eagle do if I tried."

Brysen was, in a way, relieved. He'd come to capture the eagle himself, though no one had believed he could—not Goryn or the Owl Mothers or Yves Tamir—but he was going to. *They* were going to.

He felt a grim determination, a swell of pride, and he had to wonder if that was the eagle's trick, too. Was he deceiving himself into confidence? Was the eagle guiding him straight into her talons?

It didn't matter. It had to be done. He had to do it. Dymian's life was on the line, and all of theirs, too, now. He was responsible, and he would not fail. He picked up Shara.

"For this to work," he said, "we'll need bait." He held Shara against his chest. Her soft feathers warmed his hands, and he could feel the delicate flutter of her heart beside his. He clarified: "*Human* bait."

30

"I'LL DO IT," SAID KYLEE.

"I'll do it," said Nyall at the same instant.

They both looked at each other, each wanting the other to back down.

"No." Jowyn stood and came to Brysen. "I have to do it."

"You led us here," Brysen said. "But I can't let you do this. I've cost you enough already."

" 'Cost'?" The boy shook his head. "This isn't the market. What I give, I give freely. When I saved your life, I bound myself to you like a falcon to a falconer. I'm not tethered; I choose where I fly. And this is the only way it makes sense." He looked around the group. "You three are all experienced in trapping birds of prey. I'm no falconer—I haven't held a bird on the fist since my childhood in the Villages. I'm no use to you when it comes to pinning the eagle down. But I'll stand out in the darkness. I make a great lure."

"A lure?" Brysen looked him up and down. As the sun dipped below the high mountain range, darkness purpling the Nameless Gap, he saw Jowyn's point. His bright white skin did stand out.

"I can be very *alluring*." Jowyn winked. Brysen hadn't seen that joyous glimmer since the Owl Mothers had expelled him. It was an odd time to be making jokes, but everyone managed fear in their own way.

Brysen consented. They didn't have much time, so he asked Kylee and Nyall to use some flat stones to dig three shallow pits for hunting blinds. When the time came, Jowyn would stand in position in the center between them. It was an old method, older than any fancy nets or snares. This was how the first falconers had caught birds of prey to tame. They'd dig pits within arm's reach of a wounded bait pigeon, and when a hawk or eagle or owl descended to kill the pigeon, they'd grab it by the ankles and wrestle it to the ground, then tie it up with a length of spider-silk rope and haul it home to begin the training. It was a good thing hawks didn't hold grudges, or the first falconer would never have tamed the first falcon.

"You must really be fond of him," Jowyn interrupted Brysen's thoughts, while Kylee and Nyall grunted through the effort of digging shallow pits in the rocky ground. The boy offered one of his befuddling smiles.

"What?"

"This Dymian person," Jowyn said. "You must really care for him to give him this kind of gift. A little songbird would've been easier."

"Are you making jokes?" Brysen smiled back. "Right now, when your life is in my hands?"

"Our world weighs a feather; our world weighs a stone," Jowyn recited with a smirk. "Make the world you've wanted, or take the weight alone."

"Aaaaand . . . now you're a poet?"

"All romantics are poets," Jowyn replied, and he looked at Brysen without blinking. "You are, too."

He held Brysen's gaze for way too long, until Brysen broke the stare, feeling his skin spark like the windblown embers of a campfire. It was an unfamiliar burning from an altogether new direction. He snuffed it out as quickly as he could. "Yes," he said. "I'm very fond of Dymian."

"Well then, we better get to it," Jowyn said as the others finished digging. He pointed at Brysen's hand. "You'll need to use that, I suppose?"

Confusion turned to clarity when Brysen realized he was holding his blade. "Right," he said. "Yeah . . . uh . . . you'll need to look wounded. There needs to be . . . uh . . ."

"Blood," Jowyn said. "I know."

The boy rolled one of his pant legs up to his knee, and Brysen bent down, taking Jowyn's leg in his hand. The calf muscle was thick and strong, bright white against Brysen's dirty fingers.

"Do it," Jowyn said. "Don't worry. I heal fast."

Brysen nodded, took a deep breath, and then sliced the blade across Jowyn's skin. Jowyn winced, and the thin line across his white skin turned red, and the red began to flow. It flowed over Brysen's fingers, down the calf to Jowyn's ankle, over his foot. It covered Brysen's fingers. He remembered the taste of it and shuddered.

Jowyn's hand was suddenly on top of his. He looked up.

"Go," the boy said gently. "Just make sure you don't go far."

Brysen nodded. He stood up, sheathed his blade, and retreated to a boulder far up the icy slope, where he'd set Shara. He picked her up again and set her in a deep crack in the boulder. He put his finger out in front of her, and she pecked at it. He moved it, and she pecked again.

"You stay hidden," he told her, as if she could understand him. "I'll come back here for you, but you fly if you need to. You fly away if you need to, okay?"

He looked at her intently and she back at him, thinking whatever thoughts floated through the mind of a tired hawk at the end of a long day.

He smiled at her, then settled into the shallow blind Kylee and Nyall had dug for him.

Jowyn looked up to the sky, feigned a weak leg, and waited in the open, stone-faced.

The spider-silk rope felt smooth in Brysen's hands as he prepared the lasso and then lay down with it resting in front of him. He covered himself over with dirt. Kylee and Nyall watched him from their own holes, ready to jump when he made the first move. It all rested on him now; their lives were bound to his boldness. They trusted him, and he trusted them. That was real. Whatever else the eagle showed him, this was real.

Full dark had fallen over the gap. Above, the stars winked bright; they crowded the night sky for a view, whirling and turning in the passing dark. One would fall, blazing, every now and then.

Brysen felt like he was waiting out the night inside a grave.

He wondered, darkly, if this ghost eagle was the same one

that had killed his father. Would it remember him? Or maybe these thoughts were just the eagle in his head again. He let them pass. He would think of them like Jowyn said: clouds drifting by with no more weight than air. He had to keep his focus keen and sharp, so he'd be ready when the eagle came.

If this was a grave he waited in, it was one he intended to climb out of.

31

THEY WAITED IN THE DARK, APART, BUT INTENT ON ONE ANOTHER. Just after the moon had started its slow arc to the opposite horizon, Jowyn tensed like he'd seen something in the sky, and he glanced toward Brysen's dugout. When nothing happened, he half laughed at himself and his nervousness, startling at shadows.

And then the shadow fell, screeching.

"REEEEE!"

The ghost eagle swooped just over Jowyn's head; its body was large as an ox with wings wider than a man's height. The boy ducked to dodge, but the eagle didn't strike him. It flew up again and was lost in the dark. Brysen followed its flight by the stars that vanished in its shape, the void it carved in the sky. It came around, dove low, but then, instead of taking Jowyn where he stood, landed in front of him.

Jowyn fell backward, jumping out of the way, and the ghost eagle stood where he had been. At its full height, the ghost eagle was taller than a horse, with two black legs thick as tree branches. The eagle was a shadow made of flesh and claw.

Before Brysen could spring from the hunting blind to grab it, the eagle snapped its head around and stared straight at him, spread its wings wide.

"REEEEEE REEEEE!" the bird screamed, and every hair on Brysen's body stood on end. The cry was so high and horrid, it could've cracked the stars. He wanted to dive forward and snare the beast, but his legs wouldn't move. Panic seized him.

Coward, the eagle seemed to say.

Coward, he heard in his father's voice.

The ghost eagle settled its wings, lowered its head, and stepped toward Brysen's hiding spot. Its massive talons crunched the ice and stone. In the eagle's face, Brysen saw bright blue eyes, ice-on-the-mountain eyes. His own eyes. His father's eyes.

"Move!" he shouted at himself, and finally, breaking the trance, he sprang from his hiding spot and dove straight for the eagle's glistening black beak in a shower of dirt. The eagle raised a foot to strike him, eyes dark as onyx once more. Just then, Nyall and Kylee sprang from their holes on either side, behind the eagle's back. It saw them instantly and reacted just as fast but was already standing on one foot. In trying to launch over them, it tilted itself to the side.

Nyall's full body weight slammed into the bird, knocking it over, while Kylee wrapped her arms around its wings as it tried to thrash free.

Brysen was on it a heartbeat later, the loop of his lasso sliding over its feet and pulling tight to lock its legs together, but the eagle jumped and slipped the knot before it tightened. It threw Kylee to the ground before rising into the air and whirling on them, beating its wings, snapping at Nyall so he had to roll away. It turned on Brysen, settling in front of him with wings open wide and harrying him backward up the slope away from Kylee and Nyall. Stones slid out from under him, scraping his hands raw on the icy slope until his back hit a boulder and he and the eagle were alone.

He was trapped. It snapped its beak, and he dodged left. Snapped again, he dodged right. Its breath smelled like blood and meat, its feathers like ice and fire together. With a lunge, its beak caught the edge of his ear, sliced a notch into the thin flesh, but missed his skull. His quick moves learned in the battle pits were the only things keeping this game going.

And that was what it was to the ghost eagle: a game. For the bird of prey, the hunt had already ended. It was just toying with Brysen. He thought of Shara pecking playfully at his fingers, playing their game. She was able to hurt him but chose not to. The eagle met his eyes now, locked gazes with him, and he knew this was the same game but with a different conclusion. The moment the eagle decided to kill him, he'd be dead. That was how this game would end.

He looked down the slope to his sister, hoped she might summon the Hollow Tongue, might find the right word to save him, because at that moment he felt the most basic, most ancient of animal desires, free of pride or shame or jealousy: The eagle was going to kill him, and he did not want to die.

Kylee was far down the slope, trying to get back to her feet, climbing on hands and knees to where he'd dropped the rope.

Jowyn had climbed the slope and was trying to distract the bird from behind. It knocked him back with its tail and a swipe of its wing. In that flash of distraction, Brysen pulled himself up to scramble around the boulder, but the eagle blocked him, lunged not with its beak but with its head, and hit him in the chest. The wind left Brysen as he fell onto his back. He gasped, he gagged, and the eagle hopped to his side and pinned him to the ground with one deadly foot on his shoulder. A talon pierced him, thick as a dagger.

Brysen screamed. The eagle reared back, mouth open. He saw its slug-gray tongue, the tiny gleam of the razor hook at the end of its beak. He wondered if he'd feel it when the bird tore his throat out, or if it would go for his stomach instead, disembowel him like some birds of prey preferred to do. He tried to punch it with his free arm, but the quick beak snapped at him, and he drew back to protect his hand. He tried to kick free, but the eagle's other foot slammed down onto his right thigh and squeezed. He froze, knowing that if he moved again, the game would end, the eagle would rip him open.

Kylee had reached the rope and was racing up the slope with Nyall close behind, but they were still too far away. They wouldn't get to him in time. They couldn't save him.

Maybe Kylee should have stayed with the Owl Mothers, Brysen thought. *Learned a little more.* He could have used her new knowledge now that he was about to die.

"Ki! Ki! Ki!"

Just then, Shara bolted from the crack in the boulder where he'd hidden her.

The eagle cocked its head and saw the bird coming for only a moment before the hawk's talons crashed into its face.

"REEEEEEE!" the ghost eagle shrieked. It flailed its head to shake Shara loose, then snapped at her as she flew free, snared Shara by the leg, and threw her to the ground. The hawk landed hard, stunned, and the eagle lunged at her prone body.

"Fly, Shara! Go!" Brysen yelled, and at that moment his sister yelled something, too. Whether it was his words or hers or some vital burn of Shara's to live, Shara came to and dodged the first strike, flapped hard and launched herself up, into the sky. She flew crooked and one leg hung limp, but she was airborne.

She was too slow, though. The eagle would be on her with just a hop and half a wingbeat. Already, it was poised to snatch her down again.

But that was as much time as Brysen needed. His shoulder and his leg were free.

Kylee threw the spider-silk rope to him. In one motion, he swung it up, beneath the eagle's tail, catching both its legs just as it lifted off the ground. Its legs snapped together as the noose pulled taut around its ankles. The momentum of the eagle's forward lunge at Shara toppled it beak-first to the dirt.

Brysen swung the loop he'd made at the opposite end of the rope to Nyall, who arrived, breathless but just in time, and whipped it down over the eagle's body. With the bird's next thrash, the power of its own bound legs pulled the knot tight and pinioned its wings to its side. It flopped like a river trout stranded on the banks. Its dark eyes were gripped by the same animal panic Brysen had felt only moments before.

While the ghost eagle panted, Brysen looked to the night sky, tried to see where Shara had flown, but found nothing— not the stars blotted out in the shape of a small and wounded hawk, nor the rustle of a bush where she might've taken shelter. In vain, he whistled once, but he knew she'd flown for safety much farther than he could call her.

"REEEEE!" the trapped eagle cried.

Come back when it's safe, my friend, Brysen thought in the direction Shara had flown. *Please come back to me.*

She'll never come back to you, he also thought, but the voice, he knew, was not his own, not really. *She'll leave you, and she'll die alone in the wilderness.*

The eagle flopped and flailed, but every move it made only tightened the rope more. Brysen bent down in front of it. It snapped at him, but he squatted just out of reach. He'd caught a much smaller eagle this way before: with one rope that tangled and twisted until it was beyond any hope of escape. This time, however, he'd actually meant to do it. This time, he'd planned it. This time, he wouldn't burn.

He placed his hand on the ghost eagle's heaving chest, his fingers brown with Jowyn's dried blood. On his palm, he felt the rapid, terrified heartbeat beneath the eagle's soft black feathers. It felt no different from that of a trapped pigeon or sparrow or hawk. The bird looked at him with char-black eyes, radiating hunger and hate and fear. All of which were essentially the same. He felt Kylee place her hand between his shoulder blades.

"You know nothing," he said aloud. With the eagle in front of him, his friends by his side, and his sister's hand resting on his back, he smiled.

The eagle shrieked again.

32

FOR SUCH A MASSIVE BIRD, THE GHOST EAGLE WAS SURPRISINGLY light, trussed and tied to Brysen's back with its wings folded and its legs tucked up beneath it. Nyall, being so much taller, would've had a much easier time carrying the big raptor, but Brysen wanted to do it himself. The bird was his burden and his trophy and his bargaining chip all in one. No one else could carry it for him. "REEEEE!" it screeched as they helped him hoist it onto his back.

He carried it like a pack, with the eagle's head facing away from him so it couldn't turn and slam its beak through his skull. It wriggled and writhed, but was too tightly wrapped to do Brysen any harm. It could only stare out behind him, forced to watch the nighttime sky and the moonlit peaks shrink away during its descent as a captive.

"REEEEE!" it shrieked again.

They'll never let me have this victory, he thought, and felt his chest tighten. Already, the eagle was in his head again. The panic must have shown on his face, because Jowyn rushed to tie a piece of his scarf around the raptor's beak, shutting its mouth and stopping its screeching, and with *that*, its troubling whispers in the mind fell silent.

"It's not magic," Jowyn said. "If it can't speak, it can't speak."

Brysen was grateful, but some of the damage was already done. He couldn't stop looking around for Shara, hoping to find her waiting on, circling above or flitting from boulder to boulder as she followed them down the mountain. There were an infinite number of ways to look up, he figured, and not all of them were hopeful. The sky brought rain as sure as it brought sunshine, and not everything that went up was promised to come back down. *Who am I*, he wondered, *without her?*

Brysen had bandaged Jowyn's leg with the rest of his scarf, although the bleeding had stopped long ago. Even his own shoulder wound had begun to heal. Kylee and Nyall carried whatever supplies they could scrounge from the half-buried campsites of less fortunate expeditions into the Nameless Gap. They found firecakes for long-burning fires; they found dried fruits and nuts still safe for eating; they found a shovel and some picks that would've made digging those blinds a lot easier had they decided to scrounge *before* trapping the eagle. They found an unsheathed blade or two—blades that had done nothing to protect the trappers who'd drawn them.

Brysen wondered if some of the supplies had belonged to his father, but nothing looked familiar. Maybe Kylee had avoided those on purpose. Surely some pieces of him had been left behind the night he died.

They decided to take a different route down the mountain than the one they'd taken up, in order to keep their distance from the blood birches. They'd lose time, but if they ran into the Owl Mothers again, they might not return to the Villages at all. Brysen didn't know how much longer he had before Goryn Tamir tired of waiting, but he couldn't make the journey much faster. The new route would force them to cross Reychs Icefall, a huge slope of collapsing glacier, with thin paths and switchbacks of solid ice winding their way between endless gorges. They'd lose a full day traversing it, but

better to go slow than fall to their deaths. Climbing was a
great teacher of patience.

"No one would ever know about our glory if we vanished up
here," Brysen said, holding an old trapper's rope steady as
Jowyn slid his way over a narrow ice bridge. After a day's gru-
eling journey, they were crossing the longest gorge in the
Reychs Icefalls.

Jowyn had sacrificed his scarf, but he didn't look cold. Brysen watched his lithe movements and thought about his tattoos. Was there someone back in the Six Villages good enough
to add this journey to Jowyn's body? Surely he'd want it there.
Brysen felt another pang of guilt over Jowyn's exile. Now
he was returning to the place he'd long ago fled, again on
Brysen's behalf. The least Brysen could do for Jowyn was find
a decent body artist. Nyck would probably know one. Nyck
knew everybody.

"And Dymian would suffer if you didn't return," Jowyn said
as Brysen took his hand and pulled him up over the crest of an
icy ridge.

"Right," he said, flushing. "Obviously." He'd been so caught
up in the near-impossible victory, the capture of the greatest

prize of their civilization—and in staring at the mysterious boy from his past who'd made it all possible—that he'd forgotten for a moment *why* he'd caught the eagle strapped to his back in the first place.

The eagle on his back shuddered in its bonds, and for a moment Brysen could've sworn it was laughing.

Of course, eagles didn't laugh, not even ghost eagles. That was just the wind passing through its feathers. All the same, he had Jowyn tighten the fabric around its beak the first time they stopped to rest.

Kylee offered to carry the bird for a while, but Brysen refused. In truth, his back was hurting and the awkward way the huge eagle forced him to hike was making his legs sore, but he didn't like the way Kylee looked at it with such unrelenting intensity. She was studying it like she studied a new climbing route, something deadly she could conquer. And before he heaved it onto his back again, he saw the eagle looking back at her the same way.

That night, they camped inside a cave, hooding the ghost eagle beneath a blanket and keeping their fire low lest anyone was following them. The firecake burned blue and steady and they didn't need to tend it like a wood fire. They wouldn't have found wood up here anyway, Kylee had pointed out, a subtle dig at Brysen's lack of planning, but one with which he couldn't argue. *Luck favors the bold*, he thought, and liked considering himself one of the lucky.

After they ate some of the fruit-and-nut mixture Kylee doled out, Brysen took the first watch and sat at the cave entrance, staring at the high slopes and crags on the mountain range. Every now and then, he'd glance to the others, make sure they were sleeping, and then hold out his fist and whistle.

Shara didn't come.

Two mornings later, they reached a narrow stream alongside a goat path that ran into the Necklace. By that afternoon, the air was warm and they'd reached the cliff over the battle pits of the Broken Jess. As he'd hoped, the market was still underway. A few tents had packed up, but most people were trying to squeeze every last bronze from the market days— uncertain if they'd have another one next season. Others had probably stuck around just to hear if the ghost eagle had killed them all.

"I say we march through the street with the eagle in open view," Brysen suggested. "Show them who we are and what we've done. Let them know we're not to be trifled with."

" 'Trifled with'?" Nyall shook his head. "Kinda grandiose, no?"

"I've got a ghost eagle taller than I am bundled like firewood on my back," Brysen said. "I'm allowed to be grandiose."

"We need to have some element of surprise," Kylee said. "Don't give Goryn a chance to scheme anything."

"You okay?" Brysen asked Jowyn. His eyes were wild as lightning skies, taking in the bustle of the Villages, the clatter of the market, the clusters of round houses with hearths smoking, the squawking from the mews, and the shouts and laughter of civilization.

"I never thought I'd see this place again," he said, a hint of regret in his voice. He looked back at Brysen. "But I'm fine."

"Maybe we should go home first?" Brysen suggested. "Check in on Ma. Let Jowyn stay there."

"I want to come," Jowyn said.

"What if Goryn recognizes you?"

"He won't."

"And it actually helps us if he does," Kylee added. "Throw him off balance. It's the best way to make sure he doesn't pull anything."

"Maybe I should go alone then, to check on Dymian?"

Brysen suggested, hoping he didn't sound frightened of seeing Goryn Tamir or too eager to get away. He just wanted a moment with Dymian, a moment alone to show what he had done . . . what he had done for them.

"The longer we wait, the more risk there is of someone taking the eagle from us," said Kylee. "We have to do this now. And look who it is." She pointed down to the battle pits below the cliff, where a thin crowd had gathered for a fight. Nyck was wrangling the battlers, and there, in a leg splint by the edge of the crowd, was Dymian, chestnut hair pulled back behind his ears, brightly colored falcon on his glove. He was smiling, laughing, carefree as ever.

Looking at him, Brysen remembered how Dymian could make a day flash by like lightning and a night turn on and on forever. He remembered the heat of their skin when they touched and the ice in his veins when Dymian pulled away. His throat went dry and he reached for a pinch of hunter's leaf, which, of course, he didn't have. He chewed his lip instead.

Two of Goryn Tamir's "attendants" were in the yard, watching Dymian like he was quarry. The carefree attitude was an act; Dymian wasn't the type to let them see him cower, but he wasn't half as brave as he acted. Brysen remembered him in the tent that day, how shaken he'd been, how frightened. But thanks to Brysen, he wouldn't have to be frightened anymore.

"Let's get down there," he said. "Let's make this exchange."

He pushed himself up, made his way toward the steep path down into the yard, but Kylee got in his way, stepping right in front of him. "Wait," she said. "We can't."

"And we can't just sit up here all day, either," Brysen told her. He'd made the original deal with Goryn. It was up to him to close it out now.

"No, I mean, we can't give Goryn the eagle."

"What are you talking about?"

"The Owl Mothers made a deal with the kyrgs," Kylee said. "They made a deal for me and the eagle, so they can defend Uztar. And Yves Tamir wanted it, too, didn't want her brother getting ahold of it."

"Yeah . . . and we took care of *both* of them," said Brysen. "We won."

"But if Goryn's not after the ghost eagle for a kyrg or for his own family," Kylee said, "then who is he after it for? What'll he do once he has it?"

Brysen cocked his head at her. Had she not been there on this whole quest with him? Had she not known the point of it, the point of saving Dymian, who was down below them right now, trying to act like he didn't have an executioner's blade hanging over his neck? This was the plan. This had always been the plan!

He tried to push past Kylee, but she blocked him again.

"Let's just think this through," Nyall suggested.

"No more thinking," Brysen said. "This is over. I said I'd catch the ghost eagle to save Dymian, and I did."

"*We* caught the ghost eagle," Kylee corrected him, which made him clench his jaw.

"Let me just check the cloth around its beak," Nyall offered meekly.

"It hasn't slipped," Brysen said. "My sister's just trying to control me, like she always does. It's not magic. And it won't work this time."

"You can't do this." She stepped back into his path when he tried to go around. "It's too dangerous."

"I know what I'm doing," Brysen told her. "I'm not some dumb, lovesick songbird. This is my destiny. I'm bound to this eagle, and what I do with it is what's meant to be done."

"You're *bound* to it?" Kylee cocked her head.

"Be careful, Brysen," Jowyn warned. "No one is bound to the ghost eagle."

"Stay out of this, please!" Brysen answered him. He met his sister's stare. *Time for the truth*, he figured. "Kylee, I am bound to this eagle, because it saved my life. I was there when it got Da. I was hiding in the bushes and nearly got caught. That's how I got Da's knife. He was going to cut me open with it. But before he could, the ghost eagle took him." He looked over at Jowyn. "You're right," he said. "When you save a life, you're bound to it. That night, I became bound to the ghost eagle."

Kylee's lip trembled. He should have told her sooner, should have told her a long time ago that he'd snuck into the mountains after their father and seen him killed. But he'd never quite found the way to admit it, to admit that the thing every Six Villager was raised to fear was the thing that had set him free—set them both free. That a part of him loved the ghost eagle because of it.

So it surprised Brysen when a tear traced a slow line down her cheek and she shook her head. "It wasn't the ghost eagle that saved you that night, Brysen. It was *me*. I did it. I was there. I killed our father for you."

FEATHER AND ASH

TEARS OF GRATITUDE MEANT AS MUCH TO ANON AS CRIES OF PAIN.
Less, even.

The tears of his victims he could understand, but those who wept, grateful for their liberation from the sky cultists of Uztar, simply baffled him. Why should they weep to him in gratitude when they should have been apologizing? They could have taken steps toward their own liberation at any time, but only now, in tears amidst the flaming ruins of their camps, did they make a show of their long-buried hopes.

In short, Anon hated those who had refused to help themselves more than he hated the enemies he slaughtered. As the

Kartami kite warriors stormed across the desert and the grasslands, wiping out any trace of Uztar on their way to the foothills and the heart of false civilization, he found himself reluctantly in control of an ever-growing population. He had no desire to rule; his service was to the dust itself, a return to the mountains and a clearing of the sky. He hadn't the time or the desire to devise taxation plans or to enforce water and grazing rights, to settle disputes or regulate the provision of festivals.

To solve the latter problem, he made it clear that true believers would have no festivals of any sort, not until the last stone was toppled from the Sky Castle's tower and the blasphemers had been wiped from dirt and air alike.

Then, and only then, would there be a festival for the ages.

It was a convincing proclamation, although he really couldn't have cared less if some run-down goat herder wanted to fête his son's wedding to another run-down goat herder. Why should he involve himself in the people's marriages? Neither his faith nor his power demanded it, but such was the way of the world. The daily desires of the foolish flock would always weigh on a triumphant conqueror. This was an inescapable symptom of success. The grander the salvation you offered, the pettier the salvation people sought from you.

He finally appointed regents to stay behind and rule any

territory under Kartami control as they saw fit. His regent pairs objected—they wanted to continue on with him to lay siege to the heart of Uztari power—but he urged them to be patient. Their true enemies would not fall as easily as a bunch of hunting parties and scattered grassland settlements.

Uztar had armies of falconers prepared to fight back against the rolling kites; they had spies who'd reported on Kartami vulnerabilities; and, most ominously, they had their own hunting parties in the mountains, pursuing the ghost eagle. If they captured it, manned it, and cast it against Anon's forces, it could put an end to them.

He had to move with intelligence now. He did not mean to aim straight for the seat of their empire with his first thrust of attack. Instead of its showy crown, he had his eyes fixed firmly on what he considered the vulnerable roots of Uztar: the Six Villages.

That was the center of their cult, and any chance they had at manning a ghost eagle would come from there. Their best trappers and trainers were born and raised there, and if they were wiped out, not only would the end of that cursed place be a blessing, but it would expose the fragility of Uztari tradition. Without the Six Villages, the people would begin to forget their old ways, and in time, those who lived would become obedient and faithful servants.

"Cut out the roots, and the branches die," Anon told his chiefs when they gathered that night beneath the shelter of all their kites. "The Council of Forty have had their eyes fixed on the sky so long, they've forgotten how life grows from the soil. That forgetting will be their death."

"But what if they capture the ghost eagle?" Visek asked, unafraid to show his fears.

Anon had his own doubts about his plan's success. It had long odds to begin with, and the complexity of the task was compounded by the fact that his twin trappers were terribly young and completely ignorant of whom they served.

The twins had, on the other hand, the same advantage the Kartami forces had in battle, the advantage of fighting in pairs: The young falconers had gone into the mountains for love. Love, Anon knew, made the impossible possible, made the un-imaginable into reality, and could drive even the gentlest soul to the heights of brutality. Love was a merciless master, and none who'd heard its song could resist it.

"As the Uztari like to say, two feet hold a branch more firmly than one," Anon told Visek.

"But will Goryn Tamir do his part?" Visek asked. "What's to stop him from keeping the ghost eagle himself?"

Anon patted the boy's cheek. The first whisper of a beard was beginning to grow, but his youth belied his ferocity.

Anon had seen him fight harder than a dozen older men and women. "A ghost eagle will not be kept . . . by anyone. Not by Goryn Tamir, and not by me, either."

"You won't keep it if you get it?" Visek frowned.

"I have other plans for it."

From the corner of his eye, Anon saw Aylex the hawk master feeding his bird from the fist, but the look on his face was one of listening. He'd been their captive too long, grown too comfortable. When they first took him, he would not have dared feed the falcon in front of Anon. And now he dared to eavesdrop?

Perhaps he'd outlived his usefulness.

"If the brother and sister fail, or if Goryn Tamir tries to withhold the prize, he will not be spared when the Six Villages inevitably fall. He knows this."

"You intend to spare him if he complies?" Launa asked, full of contempt. "One who profits off birds battling each other for sport?"

"I promised that he alone would rule the Six Villages, and I will keep my promise." Anon smiled at the thought. Goryn Tamir imagined himself a rising eagle, but Anon would make a vulture of him, a carrion bird picking at the dead. All that would remain of the Six Villages when Anon was through was feather and ash. Let Goryn Tamir rule his wasteland. He assumed the world would be as it always was, the cast of men and women in power changing, but the laws of ruler and ruled remaining.

The comfortable imagined themselves comfortable forever. Only the exiled could truly conceive a different world from their own, and only the merciless could create one.

"Aylex," Anon said quietly. "What do you think of Goryn Tamir?"

The hawk master responded to his own name, although he should not have been able to hear it. He realized his mistake instantly, and his complexion went ashen.

"Sorry, ser, were you addressing me?" He played like he hadn't heard anything, but Anon beckoned him over. The hawk master hooded his falcon and shuffled to Anon, head bowed.

"You call your bird Titi, yes?" Anon asked. The hawk master hesitated. Anon cocked his head, waited. At last, Aylex nodded, wise enough to remember Anon's command that he never *speak* the name again. "Do you think it enjoys being your pet?"

"Ser." Aylex bowed his head deeper. "She is not my pet but a partner with different abilities than mine. She is free to fly away at any time."

"Unlike you."

"Yes, unlike me."

"But it returns to you, even in your current captivity," Anon observed. "Why do you think that is?"

Aylex didn't answer. He had been beaten before for speaking of the falconer's art as anything other than a disgusting perversion of nature, and he'd learned the lesson well, his lips as sealed as if they'd been sewn shut.

"You may answer," Anon said.

"She returns because she—I mean, *it*—is accustomed to returning," he said, as neutral a statement as he could make.

"It has a habit, you might say?"

Aylex nodded.

"But you love this bird. Don't deny it. I have seen it in your eyes. You love it, but it cannot feel the same about you."

Aylex nodded again.

Anon pulled a knife from his belt and presented it, hilt first, to the hawk master. Visek and Launa watched, their faces as blank as the bird's hood.

"Take it," Anon ordered, and Aylex obeyed. "You love your hawk, and it does not love you. So you must make a choice that spurned lovers often make: Your life, or *hers*?"

Aylex was puzzled.

Anon rubbed his chin. "Your time with us is over. You have served well, and so I will free one of you. Slit your bird's throat and hold it until it expires, and you may go. Or slit your own, and it will have no one to whom it has a habit of returning. It will fly free, wild again. Your choice."

Aylex's eyes widened. He looked at the blade, at the bird, and back at Anon. His hand shook.

"Choose."

He raised the blade, turned it in the moonlight. Edged it toward his hooded falcon's neck. Then he lunged for Anon.

The hawk master was not a warrior, and Anon dodged easily, spun the blade, and sliced across the side of Aylex's neck, severing the pulsing artery and dropping the falconer to the dirt.

His bird felt the fall and flapped free of the fist but, still hooded and tethered, was helpless and slow. Anon caught it by the foot and pulled it down in front of its gasping master.

"That was not one of your options," said Anon. "Now you both are forfeit."

As the falconer's blood pooled at his feet, Anon snapped the lovely falcon's neck, removed its hood, and tossed its body onto the falconer's chest.

"You'll be past pain soon," Anon told him. "And this falcon is past disgrace. Rejoice that you will not see the fall of Uztar. You could have suffered far worse than this."

Aylex's mouth moved, his voice a whisper. Anon had to kneel down to hear his final words. "You will fail," he choked out. "You slaughter . . . travelers and herders . . . but . . . the armies of Uztar . . . will crush you . . ."

Anon smiled at him, patted his head. "Believe what you must," he said.

As the falconer died with his dead bird on his chest, Anon rose again. He looked across the grasslands to the foothills of the mountains and the dark purple peaks beyond. He marveled at the wonder of the new world he was making, how so much of it turned on a few young people, the love they felt for one another, and the power they had without knowing why.

He closed his eyes and wished them success, even a measure of happiness, before he pulled the sky down around them.

KYLEE

SHADOWS

33

ALL THOSE SEASONS AGO WHEN THEIR FATHER LEFT, IT WAS THE START of the ice-wind, when the rivers first freeze. The ground in the Villages made a satisfying crunch underfoot. It was a good time for the birds to rest, a good time for people to prepare for the cold months ahead by stocking fuel and food, mending their mews, and secreting away pleasant surprises for each other so that there'd be moments of light in the dark, indoor days. These "cold kindnesses" made a small house feel bigger and were as vital to surviving Six Villages ice-winds as firecakes were for burning. They were a tradition Kylee loved.

Even their mother got into the spirit of cold kindnesses

when the time came. She surprised them with a song or a story and a rich meal. Kylee had hidden some candied ginger she planned to give Brysen after the first snow fell and a new hood with a pretty plume for Shara, and she'd found the colorful beads he'd hidden for her along with a piece of candied ginger, though she wondered if he would be able to make the candy last until it was time to share. In spite of his intentions, Brysen didn't have much self-control when something sweet was involved. The beads were nice, though. Altari desert glass. Never mind that she'd never shown any interest in beadwork before and wouldn't know what to do with them; it was more about the gesture. What she really hoped for were new boots for climbing, and she'd dropped so many hints that there wasn't a soul in the Villages who didn't know.

She didn't have her hopes up that the boots would appear, expensive as they were, but her old ones were fine for most seasons, anyway, and she wouldn't let unfulfilled desire ruin her morning climbs.

On one morning early in the season, Kylee was on a route called the Hunter's Tooth, a narrow cut in a smooth rock face that was easy for solo climbing without a rope—as long as you didn't mind navigating a few outcroppings by hanging upside down. It was one of the more fun climbs and would soon be impossibly covered in snow. This was her last chance to see how fast she could do it before the ice-wind came.

She was dangling two-handed from one of the outcroppings that jutted out over the Necklace, searching for a foothold, when she glanced toward home and saw Brysen high up the northern slope above their house, climbing, but not like she was. Not for fun. His gray hair made him easy to spot, and oddly, he didn't have Shara with him. He did, however, have a large pack with ropes and blankets, like he was going on an expedition. It was too big for him. What was he doing trekking into the Upper Jaw when the ice-wind season was starting?

Kylee's heart quivered when she thought he might have finally done it, finally decided to run away without her—and he hadn't even told her.

But then she remembered that their father had gone into the mountains that same way. She and Brysen thought that was the greatest cold kindness present they'd ever received. Their father had gone to trap the ghost eagle—in spite of their mother's objections—and he'd be gone for no one knew how long. They could all breathe easier with him out of the way. Brysen's latest bruises would heal. The most recent one his father had given him across his jaw had started to brown and purple like rotten fruit.

A few days earlier, Brysen had overfed a brown-winged rat

catcher. Because it'd eaten well already, the hawk wouldn't hunt when their father had taken it out to show a client, and it had cost both a sale and the humiliation of being a dealer who couldn't manage a working bird's weight. He'd made Brysen eat in the mews with the birds that night and eat what they ate: raw chicks and rotten seeds.

"You're so generous with the bird's feed, maybe you should eat it yourself!" he'd thundered. When Brysen had tried to sneak into the house to grab some fresh bread, he got a swift punch in the jaw and was sent back to the mews.

Their mother snuck him bread anyway. She had Kylee deliver it.

"He hates me," Brysen had said.

"Who cares?" she'd told him. "He hates everyone."

"Not you."

Kylee had snorted. How could she explain that their father hated her worse, hated her so much that he hurt Brysen to spite her? But she and Brysen hadn't really spoken the same language since the day she'd refused to run away with him. "Maybe he won't come back from the mountain," she'd said. "He'll never catch the ghost eagle on his own."

"How do you know that?"

"Because no one ever has," Kylee had said, and Brysen had reacted strangely.

He didn't agree with her, but he also didn't argue. Instead, he'd straightened up and rubbed his jaw, and a twinkle had appeared in his eye.

She thought he'd been fantasizing about a life without their monstrous father, but she now realized what he'd really been thinking: He thought he was going to help. He was following their father up the mountain to show how *useful* he could be, like he could impress their father so much that Yzzat wouldn't hate him anymore. Kylee already knew at that age that love wasn't something you could earn. It was a gift some people gave and some people hoarded and some people ruined rather than share.

Their father was a ruiner.

Kylee didn't even have to convince herself to help Brysen. She immediately descended the Hunter's Tooth, threw what she needed into a roll, tied it up with a strap, and headed out. Their mother was down in the Villages bartering for ice-wind supplies. When she came home to find the house empty and her children gone, she'd be upset, but Kylee figured that all would be forgiven when they got back safely. If she didn't follow Brysen now, she was pretty sure he wouldn't come back at all.

Still, she left a note. Her mother knew where she'd gone and why. In all the seasons that followed, they never spoke of that note.

She climbed after Brysen for days, rationing her dried meats and handfuls of nuts so that she'd have enough for the way back down, too. Brysen had climbed fast despite the difficulty of the Cardinal's Crest, but he was clumsy and left an easy path to follow. His campsites were a mess, and Kylee was worried, by the size of his meager campfires, that he wasn't eating enough. He surely hadn't packed dried food, and she found almost no bones, which meant he either wasn't hunting, or he wasn't catching anything. Either way, he wouldn't make it much longer on an empty stomach.

It was late at night on the fourth day when she saw him. He was on a ridge just above the Nameless Gap, and she watched him descend. Forced to follow, she climbed up the hard side of the Demon's Beak with the wind slashing at her back, but at least she had a clear view down.

Brysen was scrunched in the scraggly brush along the slope, poorly concealed. She scanned the area for their father but couldn't make him out. He was, no doubt, invisible in a hunting blind somewhere.

She looked to the high crags above, all the way toward the highest peak. How many ghost eagles lived up there, no one could say, but at least one brought back its quarry to a nest in the Nameless Gap. You could sometimes hear the eagle's shrieks all the way down in the villages. Kylee had read fragments of Ymal's *Guide*, along with the tales of Valyry and the Stych sisters, so she knew that juvenile eagles hunted lower in the mountains where there was more variety of prey and less competition from others of their kind. It was their father's foolishness to think a juvenile would be a safer target for his hunt.

Of course Da would go after a young eagle, Kylee thought. *He'd never risk the harder climb or the fairer fight against a full-fledged adult.*

Looking down into the Gap, Kylee saw an injured corral hawk not far below Brysen's shrub. Kylee studied its ankles, followed the line to a lump of stone and snow. That must be her father, waiting.

She shuddered at the memory of his quick hands flashing out in rage to cuff Brysen on the ear, to slap him on the cheek, to knock him into the dirt. Were those vicious hands quick enough to catch the ghost eagle?

Suddenly, their father stood from his hiding spot, and Kylee's breath caught in her throat. He was looking straight up at Brysen's shrub, and he'd drawn his knife, crouched into fighting stance. He'd seen Brysen. He was about to strike.

Kylee could picture what might come next as clear as living it: Brysen lifted by the hair, their father enraged, driving the knife into Brysen's gut, tossing him facedown beside the corral hawk, laughing. Brysen's bleeding body would be- come fresher bait for the ghost eagle, and their father would return to the village victorious. A hero who'd lost his son in the hunt but gained fame and fortune in return.

And Kylee and their mother would be rich. Their father would grow gentle with wealth and treat Kylee with all the kindness she'd lacked before. She'd have no reason to hold back her skill, and she would one day be celebrated as a great falconer. Her mother would embrace Uztari faith, and their family would find harmony. All that held them back was Bry- sen. All she had to do to be free of him was . . . nothing.

These were not her thoughts. She didn't recognize them at all.

Their father was about to lunge with his black-talon blade just as Kylee had imagined, but she felt that terrific heat inside her, the shuddering flame that burned blue-hot within her lungs.

That was hers. The burning urge to shout belonged to her, and she knew well the pain of holding it back. She'd held it back for Brysen's sake for so long. Now, for his sake, she let it out. She opened her mouth and let the strange sound escape her lips, no louder than a whisper.

She couldn't remember the word she'd said, but the mo- ment her father slashed forward for Brysen, a shadow dropped from the sky above and dove with the silent speed of a tear-drop falling. The ghost eagle snatched their father from the ground and carried him away, aloft, alone.

She watched him go. Watched Brysen step from his hiding place to look up at their father's disappearing silhouette. The man screamed as Brysen picked up their father's blade and freed the corral hawk with it. The bird cocked its head at him, shook out its feathers, and took off in the opposite direction, up and over the mountain. Brysen watched it go, then looked around. Kylee flattened herself against a nearby boulder.

And then Brysen, thinking himself alone, sat in the dirt and wept. Kylee could hear his sobs, but she also saw the flash of his white teeth and it looked to her as if, through his tears, he was laughing.

34

NOW, ON THE CLIFF ABOVE THE BROKEN JESS, BRYSEN STOOD IN FRONT of Kylee with the ghost eagle tied to his back, and he was not laughing.

"You" was all he said.

"Me," she replied.

He nodded and looked around, eyes glassy and distant. Jowyn and Nyall had frozen in place, and both looked like they wished they could fly away right then, a dove and a raven side by side. It wasn't clear Brysen could even see them. He might as well have been back on the mountain, watching their father get carried off. He was rethinking everything he thought he knew about that night.

Then he grabbed the rope that tied the large black eagle to his back and swung it around, dropping the bird roughly on the ground in front him. He fell into a squat over it and rubbed his face with his hands. He studied the bird for a long time in silence, his pale blue eyes locked on its abysmal black stare.

She feared it had gotten into his head even with its beak tied shut, but then he looked up at her. "I lost two birds on this journey," he said. "And both were all I've ever wanted."

"I'm sorry, Bry." Kylee moved toward him, knelt by his side, rubbed his back. His lips trembled and she so badly wanted to make it okay. Ever since they were small, just being in the world was often a wound for Brysen. She had never meant to make it worse, but a breeze can't blow through a tree without shaking leaves. She'd saved his life; she hadn't meant to hurt him by doing it.

"It's yours." He didn't look at Kylee, just down at the big eagle, its chest rising and falling with every rapid breath. "It's always been yours . . . but . . ." Now he turned to her, now he looked at her. "Please don't let them take Dymian from me, too . . ."

She took his hand, searched herself for the right words to

reassure him. She'd done everything for Brysen, spent every day since their father died trying to protect him—but could she do this? Could she turn over this kind of power to a monster like Goryn Tamir? "I can't," she told Brysen. "This is bigger than us."

"If we give it to him, he'll probably never master it. It might even kill him," Brysen pleaded. "But if we don't give it to him, he'll definitely kill Dymian. We have to turn it over, Ky."

Kylee squeezed Brysen's fingers. She felt for him and was tempted to agree. In the absurd algebra of Brysen's broken heart, saving one boy was worth risking the world . . . but that wasn't a chance she could take.

"I can't just let Goryn Tamir have the eagle," she said. "We don't know what he'll do if he—"

"If!" Brysen pulled his hand away so fast, it was like he'd been burned. "I won't trade Dymian's life away on *if*." He looked at Kylee now like he'd looked at her the day he'd asked her to run away and she'd said no. This time, however, he didn't give in quietly.

"Up here!" he yelled at the top of his lungs. "Goryn Tamir! I'm up here, and I have your prize!"

He reached for the eagle's ropes, but Kylee knocked him back, threw herself over the bird's prone body. She could feel its rapid breath against her; its whole body was shaking. Brysen popped to his feet and drew his black-talon blade.

Kylee didn't have to look down to know that every head in the yard of the Broken Jess had snapped up to the top of the cliff, over the ancient painted mural. Whatever happened next would happen for all to see.

35

VYVIAN REACHED THE TOP OF THE CLIFF FIRST. HER EYES WENT FROM Kylee to Brysen to the heap of black feathers tied up below her.

"Kylee . . . you *did* it!" She smiled. "You really did it!"

Kylee didn't take her eyes off her brother. His face had turned hard, his jaw was set, and the black blade was pointed her way.

"*I* did it!" he yelled.

"Brysen, calm down," Nyall tried to soothe him. "You don't want to do this. It's just that thing messing with your mind."

"No," Jowyn said. "This is him. This is Brysen's choosing, his choice to make."

Her brother looked between the boys and Kylee. The knife shook in his hands and then he turned, startled, just as Goryn Tamir himself arrived, white-and-silver gyrfalcon on his fist and three burly attendants on his heels. Two of them held Dymian up between them, while the third, Yasha, held her six-talon whip ready.

Goryn pulled Vyvian back and dropped one of his pouches of bronze into her hand. "I *am* grateful you sold my sister the wrong route up the mountain. Thanks for that. Now get out of here." Vyvian mouthed an apology at Kylee, although for what Kylee wasn't sure. Her friend had done exactly as Kylee had expected her to do. Consistency was a virtue Kylee valued, and Vyvian, as duplicitous as she could be, never pretended to be anything other than what she was: a spy for hire. As she left, she glanced back at Kylee once more, signaling something with her eyes, but Kylee didn't know what and didn't have the mental space to figure it out at the moment. She had more pressing concerns.

Goryn directed his attention to Brysen. "Well done, little nestling. Very well done."

"Let Dymian go," Brysen said. "And the eagle's yours."

"Brysen, don't," Kylee pleaded.

"Your sister had a change of heart?" Goryn raised an eyebrow. "Seems like I should negotiate with her then, huh?"

Kylee ignored him, spoke only to her brother. "Imagine what Goryn will do. His own sister doesn't want him to have it. The kyrgs are trying to stop him. *No one* will be safe."

Goryn clucked his tongue. "Oh, Kylee, child, no one is safe now. The Kartami are coming. The kyrgs can't stop them. Uztar *will* fall. But thanks to me, the Six Villages will be spared. Things will go on here like they always have. With one small exception. I will be in charge."

"You already are," Kylee said.

"My mother and sisters have different ideas," Goryn replied. "The Kartami, however, see my value. And I see theirs. It's a mutually beneficial arrangement, and one that shouldn't concern you terribly . . . if you cooperate right now."

Kylee shook her head.

"Please, Kylee," Dymian called to her. "Don't let them kill me. I know we haven't always gotten along, but I care for your family. I care for your brother just as much as you do. *Please.*"

"I, for one, am moved to tears. Look at the good faith I'm showing," Goryn said. He nodded at his attendants to let Dymian go. "Bring me the eagle, and you're free. All debts forgiven." The scruffy hawk master hobbled over immediately. He didn't go to Brysen, however; he went to Kylee and bent painfully down in front of her.

"Please," he said, reaching out, placing a hand on the eagle's black feathers. "Let Goryn take it."

"Dymian . . ." She looked at him and frowned. "I can't."

And with one quick motion, she broke the knot that kept the ghost eagle's wings bound. Her brother could make a tangle of anything, but every knot he'd ever tied had flaws.

In a burst of black, the eagle launched from underneath her and into the air, knocking Kylee and Dymian off their feet.

"Scuzzard!" Dymian yelled, and in a flash he'd slapped a backhand across her face, cracking his knuckles on her cheek.

The ghost eagle flew silently overhead in a wide circle, but it didn't flee, nor did it screech. Kylee had left its beak tied shut. In the yard of the Broken Jess below, everyone screamed and scrambled for cover. Even Goryn and his attendants ducked. Goryn's beautiful, silvery, snow-white gyrfalcon shrieked and tried to flee his wrist, where it was leashed. In a panic, it clawed madly at its master's face, and his attendants scrambled to save him while still keeping themselves under what paltry cover there was atop the cliff.

"Call it back!" Dymian raised his fist over Kylee. "Call it back now!"

"Dymian, don't!" Brysen ran over, dove to Dymian, and wrapped his arms around him. "Look! You're free! Let's go! Let's go together now!"

Dymian turned his head to Brysen and met his eyes, put a hand on the back of his neck, and pulled him close. For an instant Kylee thought they'd kiss and embrace and everything would be forgiven—and together, they would all break free.

Instead, Dymian spun Brysen around and snatched the black-talon blade from his hand, pressing it against his neck in exactly the same move the long-hauler had caught Brysen with in the battle pit.

"Call it back now!" Dymian barked at Kylee. "Or I slit his throat."

"Dy?" Brysen whimpered, the shock knocking the wind from him.

"Sorry, Brysen," Dymian said. "But we need that eagle."

"*We?*" Brysen tried to squirm free of Dymian's grip, but the same arms he used to wake up in now held him tight as talons. "You and—?"

"I'm sorry," Dymian repeated. "But if your sister will just do this one thing, I promise I won't hurt you."

"You're working with Goryn?" Brysen asked.

Brysen didn't sound like himself. He sounded like an injured animal. It filled Kylee with rage. It filled her with a burning inside, the first stirrings of a word forming, but she fought it back. She knew that a slip of Dymian's blade was all it would take to steal her brother away, and she couldn't risk it.

"Goryn's going to get me my titles back," Dymian explained, like it was the clearest thing, like surely Brysen would forgive the lies and the threats once he knew the reason for them. "All my family property will pass to me once the Kartami wipes them out. I know it hurts, Brysen, but you don't understand what it's like to be disinherited. I can't live like this anymore: in the Villages, in debt, practically a peasant. It'll be okay once it's over, though. You can come live on my estate. Look after my hawks. *I'll* be able to pay *you* from now on."

"But," Brysen whined, "we were going to travel together . . . just us . . . sharing everything . . ."

Dymian looked up, a wary eye on the circling eagle, whose wide black wings cast a swirling afternoon shadow over all of them. "We had fun together, Bry," he said gently, "but I'm meant for wealth and power, not rolling around in the dirt with a kid from the Villages. I know you understand that. That's what I've always liked about you. You've never pretended to be more than you are."

Kylee saw the moment Brysen's fragile heart broke. She saw it pass across his face like the eagle's shadow. He looked from Dymian to her and back again, and his lips turned down. He closed his eyes and the wind ruffled his gray hair. He might've collapsed right then.

But then his eyes opened, and they were hard as ice. His

jaw set like stone. Love and hate weren't that different, and one could become the other with amazing ease. Brysen wasn't broken. He wouldn't break.

And when he looked at her, he was her brother again.

"I've always been more than you think I am," he snarled at Dymian. As the eagle's shadow crossed over them again, and with Dymian's attention divided, Brysen stomped his foot, rolled sideways and forward so that the blade sliced his chin but not his throat, and broke away. He charged and tackled Dymian around the waist, knocking him back toward the edge of the cliff, driving a knee into the side of his broken leg. "I would've died for you!" he yelled.

"You still can!" Dymian yelled back, punching Brysen in the side. They tore at each other and were on their feet again, grappling. Dymian had lost the blade, but he was stronger than Brysen, was using Brysen's body as support to stay standing. He had Brysen in a headlock and was dragging him in hopping steps to the cliff's edge.

"I'll throw him over!" Dymian yelled. "Call the eagle!"

Nyall and Jowyn both rushed from cover to help Brysen, and Kylee ran with them. But the ghost eagle dropped between them, spreading its wings wide, blocking Dymian and Brysen from view. The whole blue sky beyond was blotted out by its black feathers.

"Beautiful," Goryn whispered from where he was crouched and cowering behind his attendants.

"Call it off!" Dymian screamed, panic rising in his voice.

"I didn't call it in the first place," Kylee said, and felt something odd stir in her, a kind of elation at the terror in Dymian's voice.

Among all the animals of the world, humans have the strangest appetites. A falcon's cruelty stretches only as far as its hunger demands. There is no hatred there—just need. Only people can thrill at another's suffering.

Kylee smiled. She thought about her brother and Dymian, remembered the days they'd laugh at some joke from which she was excluded, the way the secret of their laughter had puffed her brother up, because he hadn't seen the hollowness inside Dymian.

She remembered the tears Brysen had cried when Dymian ran off for days at a time to hunt with Nyck or Vyvian or passing wealthy strangers. Dymian seemed to choose anyone and everyone *but* Brysen. She recalled how he'd return, all gifts and sweetness, and Brysen would become docile again. Dymian was a hawk master, and he'd managed her brother like he managed hawks: keeping him just barely fed, hungry enough so that he'd always come back for more.

At that moment, the ghost eagle swiveled its massive head

toward her. The only evidence of a face in its deep-black feathers was the malevolent glint off its black eyes and the bright strip of white, feathered fabric that clamped its beak shut.

Then the eagle shuddered, and she watched the fabric fall. For a fleeting moment, the ghost eagle's eyes looked ice-melt blue.

"REEEEE!" it cried, and the burning words swelled inside her. If she spoke the truth of what she felt right now, the eagle's wrath would be terrible. Dymian, Goryn, his attendants—all of them would be ripped to shreds. She could unleash hell.

But she could never control it.

Kylee hesitated. Brysen's and Dymian's feet were at the cliff's edge. Nyall and Jowyn stood next to her, trying to inch their way forward, but they'd never get past the eagle, never be able to save Brysen. The eagle looked at all three of them like it was daring them to act, like it wanted Kylee to call out the death within her.

She tried not to speak, and from behind the eagle, still locked in Dymian's grip, Brysen spoke.

"I know you," he said.

Was he talking to Dymian or the ghost eagle? The giant bird's head whipped back around to him. It took a step forward, pushed the pair back so that Dymian's heels hung over the cliff's edge.

"I know you," Brysen said again, and new scenes flashed through Kylee's mind.

There was the ash tree in the yard, her brother's fingers woven in between her own, their stories weaving, too.

That's the kingdom of Brrrr, he was saying, *where it's always frozen.*

And here are the hot springs of Ahhh, she responded, *where the warm water bubbles from below the world.*

Bubbles from a giant's farts! Brysen added, giggling, and she was giggling, and then they heard the *click click* of their father's approach through the yard.

Click click. Click click.

She'd held his hand tighter, and he'd held hers, tried not to look scared, tried to show her he wasn't scared, whatever happened, as long as they had each other. She hadn't been able to help him then. She'd longed to help him then.

"I know you," Brysen told the eagle, but he *wasn't* telling the eagle. He was telling Kylee. The words were for her. These thoughts were her thoughts.

"Do it!" Brysen yelled, and the eagle lunged at them. Brysen leaned back as Dymian tried to shove him forward, then dive out of the way. But Brysen clutched his clothing, held tight, didn't let go.

They went over the cliff together.

"No!" Nyall yelled as the ghost eagle dove after them.

Kylee yelled, too. "*Vaas!*"

It was a simple word in the Hollow Tongue, with a simple meaning, one she knew without knowing how or why she knew it: "us." She yelled it and she meant it as truly as she could: "us." Her brother and her, the ash tree, the fire in the mews, the six-talon whip, the stink of hunter's leaf and overcooked stew. His first kiss. Her first free-climb. Every skinned knee and broken heart. The mourners' crows and the cold kindnesses. The truth of both of them. All of it.

And the ghost eagle obeyed.

36

FROM THE YARD BELOW, THE CROWD SCREAMED. KYLEE RUSHED TO
the edge of the cliff, peered down past the painted mural, and
saw one broken body bent and twisted at the bottom of a battle
pit. And she looked up against the pale blue sky and saw in
silhouette a wide-winged shadow circling and the shadow of
the boy it held. It swept wide over the Six Villages, Brysen's
hands holding its ankles, its talons gripping his shoulders. It
arced around and glided down, straight for the cliff, straight
for her. Then the ghost eagle set Brysen on the ground, bruised
and disheveled but whole and alive, at her feet.

The eagle looked in the direction of Goryn Tamir and his

attendants, who were cowering behind a too-small stone. Goryn's white gyrfalcon panicked, screeching and flapping and clawing at his face, trying to escape its tether. In one quick move, Goryn pulled the bird from his face and snapped its fragile neck.

Kylee remembered a fragment of Ymal the Cask-Breaker's *Guide to the Sighting and Capture of the Ghost Eagle*: . . . *take care of your own birds, for the ghost eagle sees the respect you show all her avian sisters and counts offenses against them double.*

The ghost eagle charged at them, and the three attendants screamed, running for the slope, while Goryn, crying out, dove flat into the dirt. The eagle, however, didn't strike. Instead, it launched over his head and flew up, flapping its mighty wings to catch a wind and glide, circling so high, they couldn't see it anymore.

"REEEEE!" Its screech told them it hadn't gone away, only above.

Brysen looked up at his sister from the ground, tears in his eyes. "I *flew*," he said.

"I know," she said, half crying with him, half laughing with relief. "You dirt-biter, how did you know the eagle would catch you?"

"I didn't," he said, his blue eyes the pale of a still lake with just a glimmer of mischief—the kind of half-planned mischief that always led him to trouble. "But I knew you would."

He hugged her for a long time, and she helped him up before Nyall broke the silence.

"So . . . what do we do about him?" he asked, pointing to Goryn, who was still cowering on the ground. He tried to pull himself to his feet when he saw them all looking at him and realized that he was now alone. His face was scratched and bloody, and he'd wet himself.

"I did what I thought I had to do to save the Villages," he told them. "The Kartami are coming, and if you think you can stop them . . ." He shook his head. "And Brysen . . . Brysen . . . Dymian was a loser; everyone knew it. You are better off without him."

Kylee agreed with Goryn on this one point but let Brysen answer. It wasn't her place to tell him what to feel or how to grieve.

"Are you asking for forgiveness?" Brysen scoffed. "Are you *begging* for it?"

The man dropped to his knees, held his hands across his chest in the winged salute, and begged.

"It's up to you." Brysen turned to Jowyn. "He's *your* brother."

At that, Goryn's head snapped toward Jowyn, his forehead crinkling. He studied the strange pale boy with the illustrated skin. Goryn shook his head. "It's not you. Jo didn't look like . . ."

"It's me, Gor," Jowyn said. "I lived. I grew."

Realization dawned. Goryn saw through the changes wrought by the sap, and time, and sorrow. He recognized his family. Jowyn nodded. It was then that Kylee saw the boy was clutching a rock.

"No one would blame you if you wanted to bash his head in," Brysen said. "Although I thought you'd sworn off violence."

"Can't take a life if you can't give one," Jowyn quoted the Owl Mothers' mantra. "But I gave you yours." He lifted the rock up, arm muscles flexed. "I've earned the right to take his."

"Jo . . . ," Goryn muttered. "Jo . . . Jo . . . Jo . . ."

"But that's not who you are," Brysen offered gently, stepping up beside Jowyn, placing a hand on his wrist.

Jowyn looked at him. "I'm not sure who I am down here."

"Well, there's time to find out," Brysen suggested.

"Just hold on there, owl boy. If you don't break his head open, there's a reward in it." Vyvian pulled herself up over the last ledge to the top of the cliff, sweating and dusty. "From my actual employer." Vyvian now had two pouches of bronze on her belt, the one with the Tamir emblem and another that bore a kyrg's seal.

Kylee narrowed her eyes at her friend, then looked to the yard of the Broken Jess below and saw a retinue of soldiers filing in. When she turned back to Vyvian, Yval Birgund, defense counselor for the Sky Castle, was hauling himself up over the ledge onto the cliff top, with six soldiers huffing up in single file behind him. The last to pull herself up, but the least winded of all of them, was Üku, the Owl Mother.

The defense counselor looked into the deep-blue sky, shielding his eyes as he scanned for the ghost eagle's shadow.

"It's still here." Üku said. She had no owl with her, but her eyes watched Kylee, not the sky. "Waiting on," she added.

"You're *not* welcome here," Kylee told her, wondering if she could call the eagle back and send Yval's people scattering like she had Goryn's.

"You've intrigued it, Kylee," Üku said. "That's more than most can manage. But don't think for a moment that you've earned its obedience or tamed it in any way. Yet, in spite of what you did on the mountain, I remain willing to teach you what I can."

"You have my answer," Kylee said.

"Yes." Üku nodded as she frowned. "And it cost us dearly. We hoped you'd reconsider."

At that, Yval's soldiers turned and hauled one last person up from the drop-off behind a shrub. Her ankles and wrists were tied, to make climbing on her own impossible, but Kylee and her brother both tensed when they saw who it was: their mother, bound and gagged and a bit scraped up from being dragged up the rocky cliff.

"Apologies for the rough treatment," Yval Birgund offered, "but her ranting grew tedious."

"Let her go," Kylee snapped at him. With the slightest tilt of his head, his expression changed, reminding her that he was a high kyrg of Uztar, and she was a village girl whose usefulness was the only thing keeping her and everyone she loved alive. "Ser," she added, saluting across her chest.

"She is lucky I didn't cut her head off," he replied. "When we arrived, her prayers sounded a lot like Kartami oaths."

"She's just committed to the old religion," Brysen said. "She wouldn't ever *do* anything about it."

"Your loyalty to your family is very admirable," Yval told them both. "I wonder how far it extends?"

"Don't hurt her," Kylee said. "She's harmless." Their mother was trouble and troubled, but she was the only mother Kylee and Brysen had.

Yval sucked his teeth. "It hardly matters what I do to her. She is in danger, as are your brother, your boyfriend"—from the corner of her eye, Kylee could have sworn she saw Nyall smirk—"and everyone else you've ever known. The Kartami are making for the Six Villages. It will not take them long. Our Council has been slow to see the threat and organize a response. We would like you to be a part of that response now. Come with us, train at the Sky Castle to lead a new battalion unlike anything our enemies have ever seen, and you and your mother and your brother and your village will all be protected."

"And when I refuse?" Kylee asked.

One of Yval's retinue set down a rug and a sack. He looked up at Brysen for an instant with pure scorn before he began removing the sack's contents and placing each item delicately in a row on the rug.

Skulls.

One by one, he removed the gleaming skulls of hawks and falcons and set them in a row. Kylee's mother groaned. The sight of a sack of bird's skulls must have been deeply offensive to her. The dead birds had elicited a larger response than the sight of her own children in the battered and bloody state they were surely in. In a way, just like Vyvian with her spying, Kylee's mother stayed true to herself and her faith. No surprises in that woman, however much Kylee sometimes wished there were.

"The Kartami will empty the sky," Yval warned. "That's the goal they claim, but they do not limit themselves to the sky alone."

The servant began removing larger skulls from the sack. *Human* skulls. He placed them in a line, five of them, and then ten. He ran out of room on the rug and began to stack them in a pyramid. Fifteen now and they kept coming.

"The Kartami attacked a hunting convoy taking a leisurely route to the market," Yval explained. "They spared no one, not even one of our kyrgs." Twenty-five skulls. Thirty. "They did not even spare his son." Then a small human skull—a child's. "By the time our cohort arrived, vultures had picked the bones clean."

She could feel Nyall tense at her side. Brysen, she noticed, had not let go of Jowyn's wrist.

"They will continue their massacres until we stop them," Yval said. "And your reluctance to kill will not spare you."

"REEEEE!" the eagle screeched from its invisible height, and everyone flinched.

Either they will kill you, or the ghost eagle will, Kylee thought. She couldn't imagine the creature obeying her, couldn't imagine willingly calling it to her side or sending it out to tear her enemies apart. She *could* very easily imagine its talons turning on her the moment she lost control.

I can't do this, she wanted to say, and though she knew the eagle was in her head, the thought felt no less true.

But the grim faces arrayed behind the pile of skulls were looking to her with hope. They were serious women and men, set on their mission, but they were all afraid. She looked at Vyvian, her sometimes friend, and she, too, looked frightened. In the village below, the battle boys were huddled in the doorway of the Broken Jess. Others had fled the yard to hide in their market tents or take shelter in their homes.

They were as afraid of the ghost eagle as she was, and they didn't understand what Kylee could do or how she could do it—she didn't, either—but, nonetheless, they were looking to her for help.

She wanted to say no. She was good at "no." She'd spent her whole life saying no, trying to protect her brother, pushing away Nyall, rolling her eyes at Vyvian's latest affair or Nyck's latest outrageous hijinks. She didn't want to leave this place, her home. She loved the way the cooking fires smelled and how the foothills turned pink at sunset. How she could walk out her door, click along the stone path, and soon be free-climbing up a vertical rock, looking out over the flowing Necklace to the grasslands and the desert.

She didn't want to leave.

"Time is short, and it's many days' travel to the Sky Castle," Yval said. "We must go."

"I don't know if I can do this," Kylee said, and she expected Yval to argue, but it was Brysen who responded from behind her.

"You can," he told her. "And we need you to. *I* need you to."

37

BRYSEN TOOK HER HAND. "LIKE YOU SAID, IT'S YOUR FATE THAT'S BOUND to the ghost eagle's, not mine."

"I don't believe in fate," she said.

"Well, I do," he told her. "And maybe mine isn't to be some great hero. Maybe mine is to kick your butt until *you* are."

She shook her head.

"Look, Ky," he continued. "You followed me into the mountains to protect me. *Twice*. This is no different. Every skull in that pile was a person who needed protection. They weren't lucky enough to have you looking out for them, but I was. I think I should share my luck. I think you should do this. I think you can save everyone."

"I'll make this easy," Yval grunted, interrupting them. He ordered an exchange. Their ma, still bound and gagged, was shoved toward them as a cluster of soldiers surrounded Goryn Tamir. They pulled a hood over his head and bound his arms to his sides like a captive hawk before hauling him up. "Kylee will come with us now."

Two of Yval's soldiers moved to grab Kylee just as roughly, but Brysen stepped to her side.

"*He* stays," Üku commanded, pointing a strong finger at her brother. "Kylee must learn to control her words without him."

"I won't leave my family," Kylee barked. "Now back off, or I'll call down the eagle."

"If you knew how, you would have already," Yval said, although he cast a nervous look at Üku. She nodded slightly; he was right. She didn't have that kind of control.

"I won't go without my brother." She looked over at her mother, sighed. "Or her," she added.

"No," Üku replied.

"Be reasonable," Yval said, but not to Kylee.

"Reasonable?" Üku grunted, and then shoved one of the soldiers toward Brysen. "Attack him," she ordered.

"Stop it," said Kylee.

"Do it," said Üku. The soldier looked at Yval, who nodded his permission.

"Don't," said Kylee, as Brysen braced himself for another fight and the soldier moved toward him.

"Stop!" Kylee ordered.

"REEEE!" the ghost eagle shrieked in the sky. Kylee hadn't spoken, hadn't even begun to form a thought or a word to command the eagle, but at its shriek, the soldier froze, his face confused. He shook his head, started to back away.

"No," he said. "No no no no no no . . ." And then, he tripped.

The soldier fell from the cliff's edge, screaming, to his death before Yval could help him. The defense counselor's shoulders sagged as he stared down into the pits.

He cares about his soldiers, Kylee thought. *That's good to know.*

"I didn't tell it to do that," she said.

"The eagle knows what her brother means to her," Üku said. "As long as they are together, she—and therefore it—will be tethered to their passions. It won't be safe."

"Wars are never safe," Yval pointed out.

"It won't be effective," Üku said.

"It won't be effective if she refuses to come," Yval replied. "You're telling me you can't train someone who cares about her family? Sorry excuse for what you call wisdom among the Owl Mothers."

"What we call wisdom is the only hope *you* have for survival, so if I were you, I would not question my methods or their requirements!"

"I question whoever I want under my command."

"I am *not* under your command, Kyrg Yval Birgund, and you should remember that."

As Üku and the kyrg argued, Brysen turned to Kylee. "I think you should go without me," he said. "Learn what your words can do."

"What?" Kylee balked. "No."

"You saw what just happened," he said. "Maybe the owl mother is right. Maybe I'm . . ." He looked away from her. "Maybe I'm in your way."

"You're not," she said. "I've only ever done what I can do for you. I need you with me for this."

"But maybe you shouldn't," he said. "Maybe it's time to figure it out on your own."

"But what about you?" Her voice cracked; her throat was dry as desert wind.

"At least I'll be somewhere Shara can find me." Brysen shrugged, but she could see that his heart was breaking all over again. He was telling her to go, but he didn't want her to go. How could she leave him now, when he'd lost everything that he thought was dear to him? How could he ask her to?

"Do it," he said. "I'll be fine."

He was a liar, but he was also right.

Kylee still didn't know how to speak the Hollow Tongue, not well enough to fight off an army, not well enough to protect the Six Villages. Not well enough to bend these kyrgs and tyrants to her will.

But she could learn.

And once she'd learned, no Tamir or kyrg or Owl Mother or Kartami kite warrior would be able to order her around. She could protect the ones she loved and destroy anyone who threatened them. She would be the one with power, and it would be hers alone to wield. A woman who'd mastered a ghost eagle would be revered. She could command armies and decide the fate of dynasties. She could crush a rebellion or ignite one. If she wanted, she could rule.

Whether these were her thoughts or the ghost eagle's, she didn't care. The beak and talon cut for their reasons, the rabbit runs for its own. The kyrgs in the Sky Castle didn't need to understand why she would go with them, but once she had, she would be the one to decide her own destiny.

She would return to Brysen, and she would return with power. Enough for both of them.

She nodded and Brysen smiled through his tears.

"You'll be doomed!" their ma cursed, finally having worked

her way out of her gag. "No human should have congress with a raptor like the ghost eagle, and you have too much of your father in you to succeed. It will find a way to destroy you, like it does everyone. Its loyalty's to the sky, and if you try to pull it down, it'll punish you."

"What do you know about punishment?" Kylee barked back at her. "You looked away whenever it came into our house. Never once protected Brysen from it. Why try now? Or are you trying to protect the eagle, not your own children?"

"You're too much like your father," she repeated, her eyes red-rimmed and furious.

"I am not," Kylee said.

"The violence you've unleashed says different," their ma sneered. "You've shed more blood than he ever did."

"Shut up," said Kylee.

"You'll become him. You'll relish the pain of those who can't stand up to you, and the more power you think you have, the more like him you'll be. You'll never escape his shadow. You will become—"

"Shut up!" Brysen silenced her with a raised fist in front of her face, his other hand grabbing her neck. She froze, shocked, and he did, too. Though his fist was raised, he looked more afraid than she did, and his hand quivered in the air. All he'd ever known of love was wounds, and no one could've blamed him for punching her, but some other part of him, the tender part that no violence could touch, reached up in him and stayed his hand. All things were bound to their opposites. The hawk didn't always win against the mouse, and brutality didn't always conquer gentleness. It was rarely celebrated, but sometimes gentleness won. Sometimes predators flew away hungry.

Brysen let go of their ma's neck. He lowered his fist. His face softened and he spoke in almost a whisper. "You don't get to talk to Kylee like that," he told her. "You never get to speak to her like that again."

Their mother tried to form words, but her mouth just hung open. All she'd ever known of love was wounding, too. Brysen had managed to surprise her. He'd surprised himself.

"Bry?" Kylee said.

"I'm fine," he replied, still staring at his shocked mother with a kind of serene anger. "I think she and I are going to be just fine."

Their mother looked down at the earth and murmured her prayers. Brysen's sky-blue eyes were clear as a cloudless day.

"Whoever comes, whoever stays, the time to go is now," Yval commanded. He ordered his troops to move, and his servants motioned for Kylee to join them.

"I'll come with you, Ky," Nyall volunteered. "Someone's gotta watch your back while you're saving our skins. And besides, I've always wanted to see the Sky Castle."

"It's a den of assassins and thieves," Vyvian interjected. "They'll eat you alive."

"Or maybe they'll fall head over heels for an honest guy." He let loose a dimpled grin, and Üku grunted.

"Objections?" Yval Birgund asked.

"Not to him," Üku said. "He's harmless."

Nyall bit his tongue. He wasn't volunteering to come along because he wanted to see the Sky Castle, but Kylee was glad to have a friend coming with her anyway. It was selfish to leave Brysen without his best friend, but the honest truth was that she was scared and didn't want to leave alone. Besides, she knew that Nyall could be far from harmless. It never hurt to have a battle boy at your side.

Brysen nodded at her that he was okay, that he'd be fine. She really hoped he was right.

Brysen and Nyall saluted each other across their chests, which was the closest they'd get to a tearful parting, although she caught Nyall giving Brysen a mischievous look, glancing toward Jowyn. Brysen shook his head but let his eyes linger on the phantom white Tamir boy a moment longer.

Maybe he'll be fine here after all. Kylee tried to let her heart believe it. She embraced her brother then. With their hearts close and heads together, Brysen whispered a warning: "Be careful . . . and not just with the eagle." He looked at the defense counselor and at Üku, rubbed the crusted scab on his wrist. "They're tyrants."

Kylee felt her throat tighten. Her mouth tasted suddenly of sawdust. She'd never imagined that she'd be the one to leave the Villages, certainly not without him. Brysen had been ready to fly off since the moment he could walk, while she had wanted nothing more than a safe place to call home.

"You be careful, too," she warned Brysen. She tapped him on the breastbone, over his heart. "You've got your own tyrant to guard against."

He laughed and looked at her through damp eyes. She had so much that she wanted to tell him: warnings and advice and apologies and questions.

"REEEEE!" came a shriek from the sky. This time, when everyone else flinched, Kylee and Brysen stood completely still, like there was no one else in the world.

"You've got the eagle's attention," he said. "Think it'll really follow you all the way to the Sky Castle?"

"Part of me hopes not," she said. "So I'm sure it will."

"Make me a promise?" Brysen asked her. "No matter what happens, just come back to me."

"I will," she told him. "Until I do, you stay safe. Don't do anything reckless."

"I'll stay safe," he promised her, leaving off the last part, because who was he without a little recklessness? But the heart of this promise, they both knew, was unbreakable. There was an invisible tether that bound them to each other. Each of them was the falcon, each the falconer.

She turned and joined the departing soldiers, picking their way single file down the narrow path from the cliff top until they were marching with the rest of the battalion through the yard of the Broken Jess. She looked back over her shoulder as they left, saw her brother standing on the ledge just above the painted mural of the falcons locked in battle. Across his chest, he made the winged salute. She returned the gesture and then the line turned down the road through the market.

They had a hard march ahead that would lead her beyond all she'd ever known, and Kylee had no idea what she could expect to find when it ended. The wind of the world was wild, and it mocked human expectations. But it wasn't the wind that carried you. It was the flex of the wing and the spread of the feathers. It was up to you how far to fly and how to come home again.

ACKNOWLEDGMENTS

THE MOST EGREGIOUS LIE A NOVEL TELLS IS THE AUTHOR'S NAME appearing alone on the cover. This book would not exist without the hard work, intelligence, energy, and generosity of a flock of professionals, artists, friends, and family lending their considerable gifts to the world I created.

First among equals, editor Grace Kendall encouraged this project from the start, fought for it, and then shoved me out of the nest—hard—to make the manuscript soar. I promise, most anything that works in this story is due to her intense and bighearted editorial interrogation, while anything that falls flat is entirely mine. Thanks for the unflagging assistance of Nicholas Henderson, who helped get this manuscript into shape and on time, while the eagle-eyed copy editing of Kayla Overbey brought order to the chaos of this world and clarified my thinking immeasurably. Seriously. We should all be so lucky to have a copy editor with her skills. Meanwhile, designer Elizabeth H. Clark's gorgeous cover makes me look way cooler than any author deserves.

The rest of the team at FSG/Macmillan Children's Books— the publishers and publicists, production staff, school and library marketing and conference planning teams, and the sales reps and warehouse crew—all work long hours with little fanfare to help readers connect with the right book at the right time, and I'm grateful for their efforts on behalf of mine.

I never would have been able to maintain this career without the advice and support of my agent for over a decade of publishing now, Robert Guinsler. He's held together far more than my contracts, and I'm grateful to have a friend and ally in him. Also, he kept me from being eaten by a hawk in rural Pennsylvania, which is above and beyond an agent's job description.

To create a plausible falconry tale, I had the expert advice

of Master Falconer Mike Dupuy, who took the time to intro-
duce me to some wonderful birds of prey and to answer my
endless questions about everything from hawk food to hawk
furniture. I also got advice (and a field trip!) from bookseller
Emily Hall, who now owns Main Street Books in St. Charles,
Missouri, but used to work at the World Bird Sanctuary. If
you ever need an independent bookseller who knows raptors,
she is your go-to resource and I'm glad to know her.

Thank you to some writers who still surprise me whenever
they answer my emails and who gave me key manuscript
advice and support when I needed it: Brendan Reichs, Marie
Lu, Veronica Roth, Kendare Blake, Fran Wilde, Mackenzi
Lee, Dhonielle Clayton, Katherine Locke, and Adam Silvera.
For more vast and varied reasons than I can name, I'm grateful.
Also their books are wonderful.

I'm also grateful to the teachers, librarians, and booksell-
ers who've supported me more than I deserve and more than
I can thank them for. They are too numerous to list here, a fact
which is a delight and an honor to me.

I want to thank my parents, on whom none of the parents
in this book are based, whose kindness to me and faith in me
have made most of the good things in my life possible.

Lastly, thanks to my husband, Tim, the best thing in my

life. (Maybe the second best by the time this comes out . . .) Ironically, he hates birds. I'd be nowhere without him and can't imagine a better friend or partner to fly with on this wild wind. As our flock gets bigger, I'm so grateful he's my wing-man and that I'm his. Always.